THE
REDEMPTION
of *Emma Devine*

a
pine bluff
novel

NANCEE CAIN

Serrated Edge Publishing

Serrated Edge Publishing
PO Box 969
Jasper, AL 35502
www.nanceecain.com

First published October 2017

This is a work of fiction. Names, characters, businesses, places, events and
incidents are either the products of the author's imagination or used in a
fictitious manner. Any resemblance to actual persons, living or dead, or actual
events is purely coincidental

ISBN: 978-0-9976139-4-0

10 9 8 7 6 5 4 3 2 1

Editor: Jessica Royer Ocken
Line Editor: Coreen Montagna
Cover Design by Shannon Lumetta
Cover Photographer: Chantell Reid
Cover Model: Taylor Kendal
Interior Book Design by Coreen Montagna

Printed in the United States of America

To Kelley .J and Michel R.
Thank you for always having my back!

Part
one

Chapter One

David Patterson watched the kid's trembling fingers reach out and pull back empty-handed not once, not twice, but three times. He held his breath, praying the kid wouldn't do it. Then the jar disappeared under the dingy gray hoodie.

Sometimes you don't get what you pray for.

"Put it back!" David used the voice that made his class sit up and take notice. Though he couldn't see the kid's face to recognize him, David bet he was about the same age as the high school students he taught.

The boy jumped and yelped as the peanut butter fell out of his jacket.

David stood with his hands on his hips. "Thou shalt not steal. It's the eighth commandment. Ever hear of it?"

Head ducked and face hidden, the teen flipped him off and ran, slamming the door to the convenience store so hard the bell clanked against the glass.

David shook his head and reshelved the peanut butter. *Kids.* It was probably some stupid dare. He hoped the boy hadn't been hungry…He looked toward the door, but the kid was long gone now. He took his groceries to the counter and paid, but didn't mention the incident to the cashier. Nothing had been stolen, and the kid had seemed too nervous to be a hardened criminal. Plus, it was Christmas Eve. Peace and goodwill toward all, even would-be petty thieves.

Sleet now mixed with the drizzle of rain—as close to a white Christmas as they ever got in Alabama—making it miserable outside. David pulled his collar up and sprinted to his car. He should've listened to the weather and left church sooner. Two blocks away from the store, he spotted the young shoplifter plodding along. Hands stuffed in his pockets, head down, the boy's backpack bounced with each slow, measured step. He shivered and rubbed his arms. David doubted his oversized jacket provided much protection against the icy rain and slowed beside him, lowering the passenger window.

"Hey, kid, need a ride?"

Once again, the boy flipped him off without a glance and kept walking. The rain slanted harder against the windshield, ice pelting the glass. No one should be out in this kind of weather, especially a kid. David pulled over. As he stepped from the car, the teen took off running. Determined to get more than a bird-flip, David ran after him. Within a few moments, he'd easily caught up to the boy, and he grabbed him by the arm.

"Hey! Come on, I'm not going to hurt you. I just want to help. Where do you live? Let me call your parents to come get you. It's too cold and too late for you to be out in this kind of weather."

"Lemme go, goddammit," the kid snarled, refusing to look up as the bitter wind howled.

"Nice. That's commandment number three. Are you going for a record?" David could feel the boy shaking, which made his tough act less convincing.

"If you don't let go, I'll add murder to the list," the boy hissed.

David rolled his eyes and laughed, keeping a hand on the kid's shoulder as they walked back toward the car. "Nice. I'm terrified. Get in."

The boy paused for a moment, as if weighing his options.

"Look, I'm a teacher at Pine Bluff High School. Do you want to use my phone to call someone, instead?" He opened his wallet and handed the young man his identification.

Keeping his head down, the kid looked it over. Without a word, he handed it back and got in the car, slamming the door.

David slid into the driver's seat and started the car. "Buckle your seatbelt and tell me where to take you."

"Hell. And fuck you." Angry hazel eyes finally met his, and David raised his eyebrows. The teen wasn't a boy at all. She was a filthy, trash-talking girl with a split, swollen lip and black eye.

Emma buckled her seatbelt, too tired and hungry to put up much of a fight. She could do this. She'd done it before. Maybe this was a fuckin' Christmas miracle. This might be the answer to her so-called prayer—earn a little money, maybe beg for some food and score a few bucks. At least he wasn't a fat troll. And the car was warm. He was tall—well over six feet—with wavy brown hair and eyes the color of dark chocolate. Built like an athlete, he spoke like a preacher with his talk about the damn commandments she'd broken. *If he only knew*…Unsure what to make of him, she decided he seemed harmless. Besides, she had a knife if his innocent look proved deceptive. She'd almost pulled it on him back on the sidewalk, but dizziness had dulled her reaction time.

The man stared at her for a moment.

"Look, I'm sorry I got a little rough—"

She snorted. *He considers that rough?* She found his scrutiny unnerving and picked at her cuticle, pretending to ignore him, while keeping her guard up.

With a shake of his head, he rolled up her window and asked, "Where to? I know it's warmer in hell, but I bet the food sucks."

If she wasn't so tired, she'd laugh at his poor attempt at a joke. She pointed down the street, and he pulled out at a snail's pace. Emma rolled her eyes. *I should've known Mr. Goody Two-Shoes would drive the fuckin' speed limit.* The steady swipe of the windshield wipers and the heat made her drowsy. She tried unsuccessfully to stifle a yawn.

"So why were you stealing? A dare? The thrill of it? Gang activity?" His soft voice wrapped around her like a comfortable quilt, the tone surprisingly nonjudgmental. "Are you hungry?"

Feeling impudent, she shrugged and stared out the window.

"Do you have a name?"

He's persistent. I'll give him that. To break the uncomfortable silence, she relented. "Emma."

"Nice to meet you, Emma. I'm David."

After that they drove in silence, except when she told him where to turn.

His name is David. Emma swallowed the lump in her throat as she remembered another David, with laughing blue eyes. God sure had a sick sense of humor.

"That's my car." She pointed to the dilapidated piece of junk parked on the side of the road. It wasn't much, but it was home, so to speak.

"I see. Does it run?" His brow furrowed.

"No gas. Look, you can just pull over behind me. I don't see anyone around."

Before she could offer her services, he'd made a U-turn.

"You could have mentioned that earlier," he muttered.

"You didn't ask. Isn't that illegal?" she asked snidely.

"Yes. Where are your parents?"

She shot him a bemused look. *Dumbass.* "Just how old do you think I am?"

He glanced at her with those soulful, chocolate brown eyes and shrugged. "Sixteen?"

Emma snorted. "I'm twenty-one. I don't need parents, a savior, or a fuckin' knight in shining armor."

David glanced over at her, his face skeptical and sad. For a second, she almost regretted being such a bitch.

"No one is an island. Everyone needs someone, Emma. You don't look twenty-one, and I'd appreciate it if you'd curb your language."

"I know I don't *look* twenty-one." She sighed and shifted in her seat. Looking underage was part of her appeal. Scott had often shilled her as a schoolgirl; he got more money from the pervs. They pulled up to the now-darkened convenience store. "It's closed; you can just take me back to my car. I'll be fine. Or if it's out of your way, I'll walk."

David sighed, tapping his thumbs on the steering wheel. "I can't leave you in your car. I'll take you to the motel. There's only one in town, but I can't imagine they're booked. I'll pay for it."

Of course you will. Typical. Men are interested in one thing only. "No. I can't go back there." Despite her best effort, panic laced her voice. *Oh, hell no.* Scott had already beaten the hell out of her and stolen all her money. The commotion he'd instigated had caused someone to call the cops, and she'd been lucky to escape out the bathroom window instead of being arrested. She'd suffered beatings in the past, but this one had been unexpected. And brutal.

That was two days ago. Since then she'd hung out in her piece of crap car, trying unsuccessfully to find a job or a john in this small town—until hunger had forced her to try to steal something to eat. *Stupid holidays.*

"Why not?"

"I skipped out without paying my bill." She lied without a qualm.

David blew out a breath and clenched the steering wheel. "Fine. You can come home with me and call someone to come get you."

She snickered. "Yeah, right. Okay."

Did he think she was dumb? She knew what was in store for her. He must think what they were about to do would be less sleazy if they did it at home instead of a car. They drove in silence, and she grew mildly alarmed as the town faded farther into the distance. *What if he's a serial killer? Oh shit...* Finally, he pulled down a long driveway and past a darkened house.

"Mrs. Jordan lives there, but she's visiting her family for the holidays. I'm here in the apartment over the garage."

Emma peered out the window, feeling like Little Red Riding Hood, alone in the dark woods. There were no lights, no sign of anyone nearby. She prayed she hadn't just made the biggest mistake of her life.

The young woman sat hunched over his kitchen table, chewing on her bottom lip, while he put the groceries away. Frozen pizza wasn't exactly his meal of choice for Christmas Eve dinner, but like an idiot, he'd been too busy with holiday church activities to buy groceries. Not that the church ladies hadn't plied him with home-baked goodies, which came with a price: promises of introductions to their daughters and granddaughters who would be home for the holidays.

Clutching the dirty canvas backpack to her chest like a shield, the sullen girl watched his every move from underneath her long, dark lashes. Her foul mouth wasn't the only thing in need of soap. Her matted brown hair needed a good washing, and her jeans and that ridiculously oversized jacket were filthy. She appeared to be slender, but it was hard to tell. The top of her head barely reached his shoulder, which is why he'd thought her to be a teenager.

Flushed cheeks offset her pale face, and dark purple smudges under her eyes attested to her weariness and accented the black eye. He wondered who'd hit her. Violence of any kind was abhorrent to him, but especially toward women. Old-fashioned and chauvinistic as it might sound, he believed women should be protected and cherished.

Wary hazel eyes tracked him around the kitchen. They were her prettiest feature, despite being disturbingly pain-filled. They appeared to shift in color from green to topaz, depending on her mood. An upturned little nose with a smattering of freckles and a decidedly stubborn chin completed the picture. *Why is she bruised, alone, and out of gas on Christmas Eve?*

She surreptitiously eyed the pizza, biting her lower lip.

She's hungry. He tried to think of a way to offer her something to eat without hurting her tough-girl pride.

"I don't know about you, but I'm starving, I and can't eat this pizza by myself. Want to share it with me before you call someone to come get you?"

She eyed him a moment before giving a small, hesitant nod.

"Thanks. I hate leftovers. I also have a ton of cakes and cookies I can't eat. You can have all of them, if you want. And please take them with you when you leave."

"Why can't you eat them?"

"I'm diabetic. It sucks to be me at the holidays." He smiled as she fidgeted in the chair. He pushed a plate of goodies toward her.

She reached to grab one, but pulled back and stuck her hand in her pocket.

"I, uh, need to use the bathroom." As an afterthought, she added, "Please, sir." She picked up the backpack.

"Sure. It's just off the living area, and no need to say sir. Leave the backpack; I promise not to steal anything." He didn't want her sneaking out the bathroom window and breaking her neck.

With a huff of annoyance, she dropped the backpack to the floor and darted toward the bathroom while he set the table. When she returned, her hands and face had been scrubbed, and she'd attempted to make some order of her hair, knotting it into a loose bun, secured with a pencil, of all things.

"Can I help or anything?"

"May," he corrected automatically, as if she were one of his students. "No, there really isn't anything to do but wait on the pizza. Why don't you go ahead and call your family?"

She snorted. "I don't have any family. But don't worry, I'll eat and leave."

"Where will you go? Can you call a friend?" *No family? She has no one?*

A nonchalant shrug met his worried look. "My car. I've got quilts. It won't be the first time I've slept there and probably not the last."

"You're homeless?" He pulled out his glucometer as he contemplated the sad girl before him.

"Pretty much, yeah."

"Emma, who hurt you?"

She jumped at the sound of the glucometer's click. "I, uh, tripped. I'm clumsy as shit." Her eyes shifted to the floor.

He sighed at the glucometer reading, disappointed in his lack of control. He knew better, but had still eaten one of Mrs. Jordan's chocolate chip cookies earlier. Some days he was stronger than others.

"Okay, well, regardless, you can't sleep in your car, especially not on Christmas Eve." He unbuttoned his shirt, bunching his stomach for the insulin injection.

"Holy shit. You have to stick yourself in the stomach?" Eyes wide, she worried her bottom lip again as she watched him.

"Yep, but I rotate the sites. Arms, thighs, stomach." He disposed of the pen and buttoned his shirt. "I could get a pump, but this works, and I'm used to it."

"You look like you work out a lot."

David felt heat rise in his cheeks. *Is she flirting now?* He turned away from her scrutiny and tucked in his shirt.

"Yes. Exercise is a must with type 1 diabetes."

The timer on the oven dinged. Hiding his discomfort, he busied himself with the hot pizza, cutting it in large slices. He opened the refrigerator and handed her a can of soda.

"All I have is diet, sorry."

Her pink tongue licked her full bottom lip as he placed the pizza on the table. "Do you have any milk?" she asked, staring at the floor.

"Sure, a brand-new carton. Help yourself." He served her two pieces of pizza, wondering how long it had been since she'd eaten.

Emma poured her milk and sank into the chair with a soft grimace. He figured her eye and busted lip weren't the only places bruised. Grabbing a slice of pizza, she took a bite. David reached for her hand and bowed his head, hiding his smile when she dropped the pizza as if burned.

"Sorry," she mumbled.

"It's okay. God won't strike you dead. I promise." David peeked at her and smiled before closing his eyes and offering a quick blessing. He released her cold hand and took a bite of pizza.

Emma devoured her first slice before he'd taken three bites.

"So why are you alone?"

"Why are you?" she asked around a full mouth, glaring at him.

He chuckled. "Good stall tactic—answer a question with a question. My folks live down in south Alabama and have grandchildren to spoil on Christmas. My obligations were here for the holidays."

Shoving the pizza toward her, he offered her another slice. She had all but inhaled the first two. With a red face, she accepted another piece. It pained him to know she was that hungry. He poured her another glass of milk, which she chugged like a frat boy with a beer.

"You like living in this hick town?" She licked her finger, making sure she got every crumb and dab of sauce on her plate.

"I've only been here a few months, but yes. It's quiet. Are you from around here?"

"Hell, no. Just passing through." Closing her eyes, she chewed her third slice like it was a gourmet feast to be savored.

"When did you last eat?"

Emma shrugged. "I dunno. What's it matter to you?"

"There's no need to be defensive. I'm not the enemy."

"You're male, aren't you?"

Her contemptuous laugh gave him pause. *What a terrible way to view the world.* He put down his pizza, no longer hungry.

Grimacing, she rose from the chair, grabbed her backpack, and placed her dishes in the sink. For a moment, she stood with her back to him, her shoulders slumped, head low. She took a deep breath and straightened her shoulders before turning around, holding her backpack in front of her.

"Have you had enough to eat?" he asked.

"Yeah, I'm fine. I might take a cookie for later, if you don't mind." She paused as if conflicted. "So...I, um, I think I'll shove off now. Thanks for the meal. Just point me the way back to my car." She yawned and rubbed the eye that wasn't black. Exhaustion rolled off her like the thick fog on the lake.

He reached for her hand, and she kept her head down, but didn't pull away. She reminded him of the fragile, wounded bird he'd nursed back to health when he was a kid. It had taken patience and a tolerance for being pecked until he earned its trust.

"Emma, I'm not letting you sleep in your car. You can stay here tonight." He spoke before thinking about how inappropriate the situation would look if they were caught. Immediately he justified: where else could she go on Christmas Eve? The only people he knew well enough to ask for help were out of town for the holiday. At least tomorrow was Christmas. Folks would be busy with their families, and likely no one would even know Emma was even here. He didn't need anyone in this small town finding out a woman had stayed overnight at his home. No matter how innocent, gossip would have him in a flagrant affair.

"Stay here? Uh, no thanks." She glared as if he were the Devil himself.

"Look, it's Christmas Eve. How will Santa find you if you're in your car? No chimney."

"Santa hasn't visited me since I was six. I haven't exactly been a good girl." She gave him a wry smile and yawned again. "Besides, you don't have a chimney either."

"I doubt you've been that bad. Look, stay here tonight, and we'll figure something out in the morning. Then you can be on your way. Okay?"

Emma looked away for a full minute, her throat bobbing. Her face flushed as her teeth worked her bottom lip. "Yeah, sure, whatever." Her shoulders sagged.

David walked into his bedroom and came out with a pair of gray sweatpants and a college sweatshirt. "These will probably swallow you whole, but take off the clothes you're wearing, and I'll wash them for you. I need to run a load anyway. Come with me."

Her face bunched up, and for a brief second, she looked as if she might cry. Then her face grew impassive, almost resigned, before she nodded and followed him to the bathroom. He handed her a towel and a new toothbrush and showed her where the deodorant, shampoo, and toothpaste were kept. Without looking at him, she unzipped her hoodie, starting to undress.

Shocked, David averted his eyes and hurried out of the bathroom, closing the door behind him, puzzled and disturbed by her lack of modesty.

Emma bit her swollen lip to keep from crying and sucked in a ragged breath. She should have known he was too good to be true. After the meal, she'd thought maybe she could leave without going through with it...*Idiot*. When would she learn nothing in life was free except misery? Oh well, back to her plan. She'd offer just enough to get the money she needed for gas. At least she'd gotten a meal and a warm place to stay for the night. And he wasn't gross—far from it. Maybe that's what made it so hard. He was handsome and seemed like such a nice guy. Something about him even reminded her of Ken, whose real name was, coincidentally, David. She shoved the thought away, too depressed to think about him.

The warm shower beckoned, and she stepped in, humming with pleasure as the water cascaded over her tired, bruised body. Closing her eyes for a moment, she hoped the heat would ease the persistent ache in her lower back. She scrubbed her hair and body twice, though nothing would ever cleanse her of the filth and shame she held inside.

Easing out of the shower, she gingerly dried her body, wincing a few times. David had been right; the sweatpants were way too big.

But by pulling the drawstring tight and rolling the legs up, she could walk without tripping. The immense sweatshirt hung to her knees.

Emma brushed her teeth and combed her hair, securing it in a bun with the pencil she'd found earlier. She spent as little time as possible looking at her reflection in the mirror. It had been a long time since she'd liked what she saw.

Taking a deep breath to steady her nerves, she covered her eyes and gave herself a mental pep talk. Every damn time this happened, she hoped it would be the last.

She didn't want to live like this anymore. Someday she'd be different. Someday she might even like herself. But for now, it was time once again to pay her debt.

With luck, it would be plain vanilla and over in minutes. She was limited in what she could do right now. She wrinkled her nose and sighed at the memory of his surprisingly cut abs. Dammit, he was in good shape. With her luck, he'd be a marathon man. All she wanted was to get off her swollen feet and go to sleep.

Holding her head high, she walked back to the living area with her dirty clothes. It was a cozy room with an overstuffed brown sofa and blue recliner, and a large television mounted on the wall to her left. Multicolored lights twinkled on a small Christmas tree. It reminded her of the last Christmas she'd spent with Ken and Angel. They'd all been so damn happy this time last year. She'd been free…

Shoving the thought aside, she waited, unsure what to do. David stood with his back to her, staring out the window. When he turned around, his eyes softened, and he gave her a warm smile.

She didn't trust his offer of food and a place to sleep.

She didn't trust the home-like ambience of her surroundings.

She didn't trust his smile.

She didn't trust him.

Her heart told her to run, but her body overruled. She was too damn tired and hurting. *Put your big-girl panties on — or rather, take them off — and deal.*

He took her clothes and started the washer. Emma sank onto the couch, grabbing the embroidered throw pillow. She wrapped her arms around it, protecting her battered stomach. She stared at the lights on the Christmas tree, trying not to brood over what was to happen next. *Just get it over with; then you can rest. If you do a good job, maybe you won't get smacked around.*

David returned and sat beside her, smiling. She dug her nails into her palms to keep from snapping like a rabid dog.

"You look exhausted. Ready for bed?" he asked.

Her breath hissed through her clenched teeth as she pulled her gaze up to meet his. "Okay, let's skip the niceties and just get this the fuck over with. Your choice, oral or regular, but it will have to be doggie style. No kinky shit, and you have to wear a condom. If you don't have one, I've got ya covered."

Chapter TWO

"Excuse me?" David's mouth dropped open. He was a teacher, so not much surprised him, but surely he hadn't heard her correctly. Maybe his insulin hadn't kicked in yet, and his mind was fuzzy. He shut his mouth and rubbed his brow.

Emma cocked her head to the side. "You heard me. Now let's just do it and be done, okay? I'm beyond tired. Want to tell me which commandment this is we're about to break? The one about adultery? If you want me to pretend to be madly in love with you and that you're the best lover *ever*..." She air-quoted the word *ever* and rolled her eyes. "I can do it. No extra charge."

David attempted to stifle an embarrassed, confused smile. "It wouldn't technically be breaking a commandment," he blurted. "I'm not married."

"Whatever." She graced him with another eye roll, drumming her fingers.

He pinched the bridge of his nose and sighed. "Emma, I'm not going to have sex with you."

She shrugged. "Fine. Not really my top priority either. I told you, you have a choice. I can blow you." Sliding off the couch, she knelt in front of him. Her hands reached for his belt, but he stopped her by cupping her cheek in his hand, and forcing her to look up at him. His other arm lay protectively across his lap. "*Emma. No. Just go to bed.*"

Her lip quivered, and her breathing hitched as she stared at his chest. "I-I said no kinky shit. P-Please, don't hurt me."

Her pupils had dilated so large it was difficult to see her irises.

David dropped his hand and reeled as if he'd been struck. She sat back on her heels, staring at the floor again. He sprang to his feet and paced, rubbing the back of his neck.

"What has happened to you? I don't want anything from you — certainly not sex. I just want you to go to bed, to sleep. *Alone.* You can sleep in the bedroom, and I'll take the couch."

She refused to look at him, her arms wrapped around her chest.

"Oh my God. Do you know Scott? Is this a test? Please don't tell him…" Fat tears spilled down her face.

He let out a ragged breath and stared at the pitiful girl. "Scott? Is he your boyfriend? Is he the one who hurt you? We can go to the police—"

She shook her head, crying harder. "No! No police."

David sighed. *What am I supposed to do?* "Okay. I don't understand, but we'll talk about it in the morning. I think you're just tired and overwrought. Come with me." It took a few seconds, but she finally placed her trembling hand in his. Helping her up, he guided her to the bedroom and switched on the light. He grabbed some clothes from a drawer and pointed at his double bed, covered by an old quilt. He didn't have a headboard, and the furniture was mismatched, but the room was clean, if somewhat cluttered with books.

"You'll sleep there. Just move the stuff off the bed. Good night." He turned to walk out, but paused at the doorway. "Not that you'll need to, but if it makes you feel safer, you can lock this door." Closing it behind him, it didn't surprise him one bit when he heard the lock click.

After locking herself in, Emma stood with her back to the door, frozen in place. *What's his angle?* The not-knowing was worse than the knowing. Maybe he was a weirdo — one of those who just wanted to watch. She shivered. The watchers were creeps. She'd rather put up with sweaty grunts and thrusts. Nervous energy took over, pushing her to wander around the bedroom, taking in her surroundings. It was surprisingly neat for a guy. There weren't even any dirty clothes on the floor.

He liked to read, judging by the books scattered everywhere—by the bed, on the small folding table that served as a nightstand, and all over the dresser. He seemed to have a wide variety of tastes, too. She could see bestselling novels, history books, and even theological texts. A Bible lay open on the bed with a legal pad and a pair of glasses. She sat down and glanced at the notes.

Holy shit. It looks like a sermon. Is David a preacher, too? It was rare, but she'd known girls who had ministers as johns.

Yet David seemed genuinely non-sleazy and respectful. Her cheeks flushed with embarrassment, and she wondered what he must think of her. The refrain of her life whispered viciously in her conscience, shaming her further. *Whore, slut, tramp, prostitute, trash...* She grabbed a pillow and quilt off the bed and went to offer an apology. The water was running in the bathroom, so she left them on the couch and retrieved her backpack. Scribbling a quick apology on his legal pad, she left it on the couch next to his pillow. She hated being such a coward, but she was relieved not to have to face him. After a quick nap, she told herself, she'd sneak out before he woke up. Or make a dash for it if he did wake.

With limbs that felt like lead and her back aching like a mother-fucker, she unzipped the backpack and retrieved her old, worn teddy bear. Hugging it to her chest, she snuggled down in the comfortable bed. Though having him was stupid and childish, Teddy provided comfort. Despite the aches and pains of her battered body, she closed her heavy eyes. David's pillow smelled like him. Nice and clean. Too bad dreams never come true, not for dirty girls like her.

David awoke with a start. He wasn't sure what had woken him, but he doubted he'd slept more than an hour. He'd lain awake, staring at the ceiling, trying to come up with a plan to help the poor girl in his bed. Her beautiful, sad eyes haunted him. Rubbing the heel of his hand into his eyes, he sat up, yawning and stretching, working out the kinks from years of high school and college football. Hearing muffled sobs, he frowned and turned his attention to the slit of light under the closed bathroom door. His heart pounded as he approached and knocked.

"Emma?"

The door cracked open, and she looked up at him, tears streaking down her pale, pinched face.

"It's too early," she cried, bending over, her hair shielding her face.

"Yes, it's only around three in the morning. Did you have a bad dream?"

She shook her head no. Grabbing his hand, she begged, "*Please! Please take me to the hospital. It isn't time, but I'm bleeding, and there are huge clots.*" She doubled over, clutching her belly.

His eyes widened at the sight of the gray sweatpants stained with blood below her small, rounded stomach. What was wrong with him? Why hadn't he noticed she was pregnant? True, her clothes were baggy. And, as a male high school teacher, he always made it a point to pay attention to female faces, not bodies, but missing this? Downright stupidity.

"Okay, hang on, Emma."

He ran and yanked his red plaid shirt off the back of the couch, shrugging into it without bothering to button it. It took him a full minute to find his shoes, and he slipped them on the wrong feet. Hopping around like a crazed man, he finally got them right. He pulled on a jacket and grabbed a coat for her, placing it around her shoulders.

"You'll be okay. Don't worry," he told her, sounding much calmer than he felt.

"Wait, I'll need my backpack."

"I'll go warm the car; you get what you need." Grabbing his car keys and wallet, he raced down the steps two at a time to start his car, slipping once on a slick spot. *Should I call an ambulance? Does she have anyone to call?* Running back up the flight of stairs, he wished he didn't live in Mrs. Jordan's garage apartment with its five million steps. How would Emma get down all those stairs? He met her at the front door where she stood holding the bathroom trashcan, her backpack swinging from one trembling arm.

"I feel sick," she whimpered, her eyes filled with pain and fear.

"I've got you, Em." He swooped her into his arms, carefully carrying her down the stairs to the car.

"You okay?" he asked, pulling out of the drive and flipping on the flashers.

She nodded, wiping away her tears, her color ghostly pale by the lights from the dashboard. "There's no traffic. Do you really need the flashers?"

"Of course. Every male driver over the age of sixteen dreams of driving above the speed limit with the flashers on." He grinned and winked at her, hitting the gas pedal a little harder, driving at least thirty-five miles over the speed limit until he hit a patch of ice, which forced him to slow down. Luckily, she was right. There was little traffic on the road, and the rain had stopped. "How far along are you?"

"I dunno, seven, eight months." Her lower lip quivered, and she threw up in the trashcan. "Oh God, that's gross. I'm sorry."

"You're fine. You can't help it. Have you had any prenatal care?"

Grimacing, she shook her head and doubled over in pain. She panted like a dog on a hot day.

"Look, I don't even know your full name."

"Emmanuelle. Emmanuelle Summer Devine." She rolled her eyes. "Don't laugh. I was destined to be a pole dancer or a porn star."

"Well, it's unusual; I'll grant you that." He kind of liked her unusual name, but Emma fit her better.

He pulled into the ER in record time. Despite her protests, David carried her into the emergency room, yelling for help. As a nurse whisked her off behind closed doors, he gave what little information he had to the woman at the front desk. He dug through Emma's backpack, finding an old teddy bear and her pathetically empty wallet. A torn, barely legible copy of her birth certificate was her only form of ID. He gave them his address and phone number, not knowing what else to put. After he'd filled in the blanks that he could on Emma's paperwork, another nurse led him to her room in labor and delivery.

The monitors, tubes and IVs, and busy personnel unnerved him. He shoved his hands in his pockets as he struggled to get a better glimpse of Emma. A nurse in blue scrubs checked her blood pressure and hurried out of the room. Another nurse stood at the bedside, blocking his view. He cleared his throat, and she glanced back at him with sharp look before an impassive mask of professionalism settled on her face.

Charting her findings in a computer, she asked in a clipped voice, "Your name? Are you the father?"

He had the strangest feeling she was angry with him.

"David Patterson. What?" He took off his jacket and realized with embarrassment that his shirt was still unbuttoned. He began buttoning it, fumbling in his haste. "Is she going to be okay? Is the baby okay?"

The nurse finished her charting and moved the computer to the wall.

His eyes widened when he finally saw Emma.

Her face was an alarming, pasty color, and her nostrils flared with each shallow breath. The hospital gown shoved up under her breasts left her pregnant belly exposed, along with the bruises that stained it purple down one side. David frowned. She didn't look as far along as she'd said—no wonder her clothes had concealed her pregnancy. Maybe she'd miscalculated? Sickened by the sight of her bruised stomach, he looked away. *Who hurt her? What kind of man beats a pregnant woman?* He took a deep breath and prayed for strength to help Emma get through this.

"The doctor will be in to speak with you, but Emma must sign consent for you to be in here. Do you want him in here and to have access to information about you and your baby?"

Emma gazed at him with wide eyes and nodded. A tear slipped down her cheek.

The nurse sighed and glared at David. "Okay. I'll be right back with the form." She stepped out, leaving the door open.

"I'm sorry, David."

"No, no. Everything will be okay." He took her hand and gave her a comforting smile. "Is it a boy or a girl?"

"I don't know." She turned her face from him and stared at the wall. "This is my fault. I didn't want this baby. What kind of mother would I be? I'm a prostitute."

"Don't say that; it isn't true. This isn't your fault."

Tears coursed down her face. "I didn't want the baby, but I don't want it to die. I'm scared."

"Have faith, Emma. You're in good hands here." He gently squeezed her icy fingers and looked up when the nurse came in with papers for Emma to sign. The doctor followed.

"I'm Dr. Jones," he said in greeting. "Well, young lady, let's see what we have here. How long have the cramps, bleeding, and nausea been going on?" He studied the ultrasound.

An older man with gray hair, he exuded an aura of calm reassurance and experience, which David found comforting.

"Since last night, but the bleeding started this morning. I went to the bathroom, and it felt almost like a pop or something. Then blood and clots just gushed out—" Her voice broke off, and she grimaced as the monitor jumped with her contraction. David traced the blue veins on top of her thin hand with his thumb and listened.

"Basically, the placenta has ripped away from your uterus, probably from the—" he glanced at David with a questioning look "—*fall* you took. We're running out of options. I'm going to ask this young man here to step outside for a bit while I do an exam and talk to you."

David nodded and stepped out, unable to speak. He felt shaky and nauseous from his plummeting blood sugar, the sight of Emma's bloody clothes, and the horrific bruises on her belly. In the waiting area, he found a vending machine with orange juice and drank it, feeling better as his hypoglycemia abated. Alone, his nervousness increased as time seemed to stand still, and there was no word on Emma. He paced back and forth, praying for her and her baby.

"Mr. Patterson?" The nurse with the blue scrubs stood at the doorway.

"Yes?"

"Come with me." He followed, almost having to trot to keep up with her. "Emma's having complications, and they're going to do an emergency C-section. The baby's in distress, and this is the best option for both of them."

"Okay." He didn't know what else to say or to do. "They'll be okay, right?"

"We'll do everything we can to make sure both are fine. Emma wants you in there. She said you're her support person."

David stopped dead in his tracks. "Me?" The nurse turned and raised an eyebrow at him. "Right. I mean, yes. Yes, I am." In the delivery room, the nurse assisted him into a paper gown, hat, mask, and booties. They provided him a stool to sit on near Emma's head as they prepped her for the cesarean.

Tears streaked down her face, and she grabbed his hand, squeezing it tight. "Is the baby going to die?" she asked in a hoarse voice.

He smiled at her. "Absolutely not. Have faith. Everything will be okay."

"Am I going to die? I don't want to go to hell. Please pray for my baby...and me."

"You're not going to die, and you're not going to hell. Just breathe, Emma. You can do this, honey." The anesthetist put an oxygen mask on Emma's face and began talking, explaining to them what the doctor was doing. David gripped her hand and squeezed it. Embarrassed by the thought of seeing Emma give birth, and feeling a little faint at the sight of blood, he stayed by her head, declining the offer to watch the birth. He prayed harder than he'd ever prayed in his life. The operation was over much sooner than he'd expected and was also a lot bloodier.

"It's a girl," the doctor announced.

Emma nodded but didn't seem to comprehend. Her glassy eyes stared at the ceiling.

David kissed and squeezed her hand with excitement, watching the nurses work with the tiny infant.

"She's so little," he said, awestruck. His grin faded when Emma didn't respond. He watched as the nurse hung a bag of blood. Turning, he looked over to where several nurses and a doctor worked with the purple, silent baby. His heart gave a painful lurch.

"Hang in there," he whispered into her ear.

He silently prayed for the child. In the background, he could hear the medical staff discussing the Emma's blood loss. Tears blurred his vision. He couldn't distinguish between their concerns for the baby and those for Emma. Two nurses and a doctor remained huddled over the incubator, and fear knotted his stomach. The breath he'd been holding released with a whoosh when the baby finally let out a tiny howl of protest.

Spinning back to Emma, he grinned and kissed her cold, lifeless hand. "You did it, Em! You're a mama, and she's beautiful."

Emma still didn't respond. All color had leached from her face.

"Sir, why don't you go with the baby to the neonatal intensive care unit as we finish here," the nurse said with quiet authority, placing a firm hand on his shoulder and motioning him to move out of the way.

He nodded, but frowned as the staff scurried around Emma, raising the foot of her bed higher than her head, saying words like *hemorrhage, tachycardia,* and *hypotension.* For all he knew they were speaking Greek, except he'd probably understand Greek better.

"What about Emma? Is she going to be okay? You can't let anything happen to her! Her baby needs her." Anxiety raised the volume on his voice. He didn't want to leave her; she was all alone. "Emma…"

"Sir, she's lost a lot of blood. We're doing everything we can, but we need you to leave. Please, go to the nursery, and you can see your baby."

His heart pounded and his gut clenched as he backed away, almost tripping on his own feet. Nurses and doctors swarmed around Emma, preventing him from seeing her. She didn't respond to any of their questions. He didn't want to leave, but the nurse in blue scrubs escorted him from the room. She assured him they would take care of her.

When he arrived at the neonatal intensive care unit, another nurse helped him dress in a new paper gown, hat, and booties and led him to the tiny baby girl. The nametag on her incubator read "Devine, Baby Girl." A heart monitor beeped at an alarming rate and tubes and wires went everywhere. She looked like a tiny wizened gnome in her little pink hat, and when she cried, it sounded like a kitten mewling. The nurse checking her vital signs smiled at David.

"She's three pounds, ten ounces and twelve inches long. Does she have a name?"

"I don't know. This was unexpected," David murmured. He kept his hands behind his back as he mentally counted ten fingers and ten toes.

"You can touch her," the nurse offered, smiling.

David hesitantly stroked her little hand. The baby grasped his index finger, and it was as powerful and humbling as the moment he'd dedicated his life to serving God. His heart expanded and filled with an outpouring of wonderment and love.

"She's so beautiful," he whispered. "Will she be okay?" His voice choked with overwhelming emotion.

"She may have problems with eating. We'll also be keeping a close watch on her heart rate and breathing. Later, she may develop a little jaundice, but she should be fine."

"She's perfect." He leaned in and kissed her hand, marveling at the tiniest fingernails he'd ever seen. Unable to stop grinning, he took several pictures with his phone and thanked the nurse when she snapped one of him with the baby. Then he left to check on Emma.

Chapter
Three

Emma struggled to sit up, guarding her tender stomach and trying not to get tangled in the line tethering her to a beeping IV machine. Two pink camellias in a Styrofoam cup sat on her bedside table.

To her further surprise, David sat in the corner of the room, his head thrown back, snoring softly. He wore the same clothes as when he'd brought her to the hospital. She had no idea how long she'd been here.

A nurse walked in to hang another bag of fluid and cut off the beeping noise that had awakened her. She smiled over at David. "Poor Dad, he's exhausted. How do you feel? If you need something for pain, punch the IV button. You can't overdose; it's regulated."

"Thanks. I've felt better, but I'm okay." She paused. *Wait—did that nurse just call David "Dad"?*

The nurse breezed out, and David stretched and yawned loudly, giving her a sleepy smile. The disturbing thought crossed her mind that he looked sexy as hell with tousled hair and beard stubble. Shaking her head, she determined it must be the after-effects of the dope they'd given her.

"Hey! How do you feel? And Merry Christmas." He stood and his back popped. "Old bones from playing football." He reached over to push her hair out of her face.

"How's the baby?" A knot of fear clogged her throat.

"She's a fighter like her mama, but definitely not a heavyweight at three pounds, ten ounces." David smiled. "She's beautiful and perfect, with ten tiny fingers and toes."

Emma exhaled. "You actually counted her fingers and toes?"

"You betcha. Want to go see her?"

She looked away. "I don't know." Her heart felt torn. She wanted to see and hold her. But she doubted she had the strength to do so and still do what was best for the baby. "Where did the flowers come from?"

"I guess you could say I broke commandment number eight," he admitted with a shrug. "They were in front of the hospital. It's Christmas. Nothing's open today, so I couldn't buy you flowers."

"You shouldn't have done that. I don't want you going to hell, and I don't deserve them. What time is it anyway?"

"Almost midnight. You've mostly slept since they returned you to your room." He rubbed her cheek with the back of his fingers. "I'm not going to hell, and neither are you. And you do deserve flowers; you just gave birth to a beautiful baby girl. On Christmas."

She rolled her eyes, trying to conceal how much his kind words and support affected her. "Even an alley cat can give birth. It's no biggie."

"Are you hungry? Or in pain?"

"No. I'm fine. You don't need to stay. I'm sorry to have been such a problem."

He chuckled. "Not the quiet, boring Christmas I expected, for sure. But how better to celebrate than witnessing the miracle of birth?"

Emma snorted. "This wasn't exactly a virgin birth, David."

"Come see her," he coaxed. "What's her name?"

Emma's lip trembled, despite her best effort to keep her emotions in check. "I don't know. I can't keep her."

David stood and reached for something on the table behind her. Heat flushed her cheeks when he handed her the old, worn teddy bear.

He took her arms and wrapped them around her well-loved bear. Sitting on the side of the bed, facing her, he held her hands, his warm eyes filled with sorrow.

Something's wrong. She shivered, and tears sprang to her eyes. *Please don't let anything be wrong with my baby...*

"Emma." He looked down at her hands, giving them a light squeeze, before returning his eyes to hers. "There were complications after the birth." His brow furrowed as he seemed to struggle with his words.

"You said she was okay!" Her heart leaped into her throat, and a desperate, primal need to see her baby rose to the surface. She struggled to swing her legs over the side of the bed, but David blocked her way.

"The baby's fine, Emma. She's fine…But you had a lot of bleeding after the delivery. They tried to stop it, but they couldn't." He looked down, and she hugged her teddy bear tighter. "They had to do a hysterectomy," he choked out. "I'm so sorry."

She couldn't breathe.

She couldn't move.

She wasn't even sure she'd heard him correctly through the roaring sound in her head.

"I want to see my baby. Take me to my baby!"

David started to help her sit on the side of the bed, but she pulled away and began rocking back and forth. "No, wait. I can't do this. If I see her, I won't be able to give her up."

With a deep, guttural sob, she crumpled in his arms. Life was so damn unfair.

She wasn't positive, but after a moment it felt like he kissed the top of her head as he stroked her back.

"Come see her. She's beautiful. Don't give her up."

"I'm a prostitute. What kind of life is that for a kid?" she cried, choking on her breath.

"Shhh, I'm not listening to that. Today is about new beginnings. Your daughter needs you." David smoothed her hair out of her face. "Come see your daughter."

After several torturous minutes, her breathing steadied, and she stopped crying. She didn't want to leave the comfort of David's arms. How long had it been since anyone had held her without expecting something in exchange? She bit back the urge to draw him closer when he pulled away.

"Ready?" he asked, giving her hand a gentle squeeze. "You can do this, honey. You're strong."

"Sorry. Hormones," she mumbled, wiping her tears and snotty nose.

He rang for the nurse. Together, they helped her into a wheelchair, and she grimaced with pain, surprised by her weakness and uncontrollable shaking.

"That's left over from the anesthesia. You'll be okay," the nurse reassured her.

David tucked a blanket around her and wheeled her to the neonatal intensive care unit. Another nurse helped them into paper gowns, and David guided her to the incubator. It was relatively quiet with only two other babies there.

With David's help, she stood next to her daughter's incubator. The nurse assisted by keeping her medical equipment and lines straight. Emma bit her lip to keep from crying as she gazed at Devine, Baby Girl. Eyes closed, the baby stirred, shaking her small fist.

David chuckled. "Look at that. Maybe you should name her Scarlett."

Afraid to move and unable to breathe, Emma stared at her newborn daughter. The lump lodged in her throat prevented her from speaking. Monitors beeped rhythmically, and Emma tried to make sense of all the different lines and electrodes hooked up to the fragile-looking infant.

More tears tracked down her cheeks. She kept her arms wrapped around her chest and stared at her daughter, unable to look away.

"Breathe, Em," David murmured, placing an arm across her shoulders.

Emma sagged against him and took a deep breath, letting it out with a whoosh. Using his thumb, he wiped her silent tears.

The nurse patted her back and smiled. "Merry Christmas, Emma. What a wonderful way to celebrate with a baby daughter. She's doing remarkably well. All of the monitors are scary, but they're just to make sure she's okay." Professional and even, the nurse's voice soothed some of her anxiety.

With reluctance, she looked away from the tiny newborn. "She's really g-going to be all r-right?"

The nurse nodded. "She's having a few problems eating due to her poor suck reflex, but she'll get there. Would you like to try breastfeeding? It's time for her to eat, and your milk will provide her everything she needs to get healthier."

Emma looked back at the little red face of the baby, who yawned and attempted to stretch. When she opened her eyes and let out a tiny, fretful wail, Emma instinctively reached out and stroked her cheek. The infant turned her face toward her finger.

"Shhhh, don't cry. Please, don't cry. I'm so sorry." Her shaking returned as she struggled to keep herself together.

David helped her to a rocking chair and assisted her as she sat. Everything seemed to hurt as she sank into the chair. The nurse placed the wrapped baby with all her tubes and monitors into her arms. David snapped a picture with his phone.

She looked up and rolled her eyes. "Stop it. I'm pretty sure I look like shit." Emma held the baby gingerly, afraid of hurting her. "Crap, I didn't mean to say *shit*. I don't know what to do." She sighed, embarrassed to have said a cuss word in front of the baby. And this seemingly honorable man.

David patted her shoulder. "You can do this. Be brave."

"Let me help get you started," the nurse said. She untied Emma's gown.

David's face turned six shades of crimson. "I, uh, I've got to eat something. I'll be back in a few minutes."

She watched him rush out of the nursery, suppressing an idiotic impulse to call him back.

"Her daddy seems to be crazy about her."

"Who? Oh, um…he's just a…"

What would she call David? Savior? Friend? The thought vanished when the baby's tiny mouth latched on to her breast. Dumbfounded, Emma stared into the baby's eyes, unable to speak.

The heart she thought no longer existed commenced to breaking, piece by painful piece. And her resolve to stay detached imploded, filling her gut where her uterus had once resided. Unchecked tears poured down her face. Then the monitors beeped, and panicked, Emma looked to the nurse for help.

"It's okay. She just has to learn to breathe and eat at the same time," the nurse assured her. "It'll take her a while to get the hang of it. We'll have you pump your milk and keep trying, but we may have to supplement her with a bottle. We had to tube feed her the first two feedings, but she's doing better. You're doing fine." She smiled and patted her shoulder.

Emma nodded, feeling stupid and inadequate.

Twenty minutes later, she looked up when David snuck back into the room with an easy grin on his scruffy face.

He couldn't keep his eyes off the baby. "How's everything going?"

"I suck at this," Emma confessed, still trying to coax a burp from her the way the nurse had shown her.

"I think that's her role," David pointed out.

"They had to feed her with that tube thingie." She cradled the newborn in her arms, memorizing every detail of her sweet face.

"Have you decided on a name?" David knelt in front of her, making silly faces at the baby and chuckling when she latched on to his finger with her tiny fist.

"I don't know." She looked at him. "If she'd been a boy, I'd name her David. I don't know what to name her. Certainly not something horrid like my mother did to me."

"Really?" David tapped his chin with his finger as if in deep thought. "So I guess that means Luscious Aphrodite Devine is out of the question?"

Emma giggled. "Totally out." She struggled to stand while holding the baby, but pain made it difficult.

David took the infant and stared into her face for a moment before carefully placing her in the incubator. He smiled, and his dark eyes shone. Emma's heart flip-flopped. She couldn't help but smile when he leaned over and gave the baby a kiss on the forehead. The look of pure joy and adoration on his face matched the sudden lightness in her heart.

She looked at him thoughtfully. "David, what's your full name?"

"David Michael Patterson. Why?"

"Kensington Michaela, that's her name."

"Really?" He grinned. "Wow, I'm honored. Thanks."

Emma nodded and looked away. She wished she'd met David years ago, before her life went to hell in a hand basket. "Kensington was the name of…a friend."

"Are you sure? That's an awfully big name for such a little peanut." His smile faded to a worried frown when he looked at her. "You're shaking again and pale. Let me take you back to your room."

"Yes, please. I'm exhausted."

As she left the nursery, Emma willed herself not to look back at Kensington. She knew her name would likely change once she was adopted, but for now, it honored two very important men. The physical pain from her daughter's birth was nothing compared to that of her breaking heart.

Chapter
Four

David dragged himself up his front steps, his heart hammering. After checking his glucose level, he made himself a ham sandwich and inhaled it. Temptation took hold, and he ate a chocolate chip cookie before guiltily packing up the rest to take to Emma later.

Dazed by the events of the past thirty-six hours, he collapsed on his couch and closed his eyes. No wonder it was called "the miracle of birth." Championship football games, graduating college, and even completing his master's degree early—nothing compared to witnessing Emma's bravery giving birth to Kensington.

He hoped she would stay in touch and send him pictures of the girl as she grew up. Better yet, maybe he could convince her to settle in the area. He could help her find a job or go back to school. And even after he received his acceptance letter and went to seminary, Atlanta wasn't that far away. He'd be able to visit during breaks from school, and Mrs. Jordan would surely let him stay as a guest for a quick visit.

Ugh, school. It was imperative that he complete his application for seminary and scholarships in the next week so he could be considered for fall admission. His letters of recommendation, transcript, and resume sat on the table ready to go, but he still needed to submit an autobiographical statement, a plan of study, and a sample of his academic writing. Too tired to even think, he decided to put it off until tomorrow.

Forcing himself to get up and get busy, he stripped the bed, throwing the sheets and mattress cover away. There was no way he could explain to Mrs. Jordan how they'd become so bloodstained. Nope, he'd just buy her a new set. An hour later, he had the apartment straightened, and after a quick shower, he collapsed, exhausted, into the freshly made bed.

A pounding at the front door woke him up. Opening his bleary eyes, he glared at the clock. It seemed like he'd just gotten to sleep. Grumbling under his breath, he staggered to the front door. His best friend—and ex-girlfriend—Jennifer barreled into his home.

"Merry late Christmas!" She threw herself into his arms. Caught unaware, he winced when his head cracked against the doorframe. Her violet-blue eyes sparkled as she laughed. "Sorry!"

Scrubbing his face with his hand, he yawned and with one arm, hugged her back. With a weary nod, he acknowledged her husband, who stood behind her, glaring. He and Dylan mostly tolerated one another for Jennifer's sake.

"Merry Christmas. Come in, I'll start some coffee." He motioned them into his tiny kitchen.

"I can't believe you weren't up. We waited until ten. Here." She shoved a wrapped gift into his hand. "I know we said no gifts, but this is funny. Why, David, I do believe this is the first time I've ever seen you in your pajamas." She made a purring noise and wiggled her eyebrows.

He rolled his eyes. "Stop. Please don't make Dylan grouchy this early in the morning. I'm not awake enough to win a fight." He yawned as he looked around for a shirt to put on with his navy pajama pants. Putting the gift down, he grabbed a clean sweatshirt out of the dryer and shrugged into it. "I'm surprised you made it up the steps there, little mama."

"Are you saying I'm fat?" Jennifer laughed and patted her obvious baby bump. "I didn't. Dylan carried me. He's such a Neanderthal, even after two years of marriage. Open your gift!"

"Got a muscle relaxant?" Dylan quipped, faking a strained back as he blew a strand of his shaggy hair from his eyes. He drew out a chair and put a hand on Jennifer's shoulder, urging her to sit.

"Oh hush, it would serve you right if you did throw your back out. I'm pregnant, not incapacitated."

David chuckled. "How long before you move into the new house? I went over with Mrs. Jordan, and she gave me a tour. The recording studio in the basement is amazing."

He opened the gift and laughed. It was a black T-shirt with a fake white clerical collar painted on it. Across the chest were the words: Father To Be.

"Thank you. But, um, *Father?* I'm Methodist."

"It was Dylan's idea. Once a Catholic, always a Catholic."

Dylan kissed the top of Jennifer's head and rubbed her neck. "I thought it was funny as hell, since you're applying to seminary. As for the house, we hope to be in just after New Year's. I've got to get Jen settled so she can start nesting."

David smirked at Dylan's possessive stance. Best friends with Jennifer growing up, David had loved her long before she ever met Dylan. He'd envisioned marrying her and having a family, but his dreams were railroaded when she accepted the job as Dylan's private duty nurse. She'd fallen head over heels in love with the musician and married him two years ago.

As graciously as possible, David had stepped aside, and he and Jennifer had eventually managed to rebuild a solid friendship. She'd been instrumental in getting him the teaching job here in town, not to mention his housing.

"Hey, Jennifer, do you mind?" David held up his glucometer and insulin pen. If he didn't have to stick himself, it was better, and Jennifer was a nurse, after all.

"Not at all." She stuck him with finesse and awaited the results.

"I have another favor to ask." David flinched when Jennifer looked at his glucose reading, shook her head, and narrowed her eyes. *Here comes the lecture.*

"What have you been eating?"

"Vending machine stuff and one of Mrs. Jordan's chocolate chip cookies," he mumbled, flipping on the coffee machine.

"David! You know you can't do that. Use some common sense." Jennifer picked up his insulin pen. "Where do you want it?"

"Supposed to be my thigh, but with Dylan here, I better take it in the arm." David smirked at the annoyance that crossed Dylan's face.

Jennifer gave him his insulin with a little more force than he thought necessary, probably as payback for the high reading.

He poured them all a cup of coffee. "Anyone hungry? I need to eat."

"No, thanks. We ate breakfast with my brother's family before coming home. What's the favor?" Dylan asked.

David heated a pan and cracked two eggs into it. "I need to get some gas and take it to a car stranded on the side of the road about fourteen miles from here. Would you mind giving me a ride?" David hated asking Dylan for anything, but he was here and available.

"Whose car is broken down?" Jennifer asked, rubbing her tummy.

David smiled when her stomach visibly moved.

"Ouch, did that hurt? Is that kid gonna be field-goal kicker?" he teased.

Dylan laughed. "Maybe a soccer player."

"No, it doesn't hurt. But good grief, I wish she'd calm down. With all her tap dancing on my bladder, I have to pee every five minutes. I'm ready for this kid to turn around. I'll be right back." Jennifer excused herself.

David sat down with his breakfast across from Dylan. "Jennifer looks better than ever. She's going to be a great mom." He paused and added, "I think you'll be a great dad, too."

Dylan didn't say anything for a moment, but his blue eyes crinkled with pleasure. "Thank you. I hope so. I didn't exactly have the best role model. I figure if I do everything the opposite of my old man, I'll do all right and not fuck the kid up too badly."

David laughed and nodded. "Look, I need to ask Jennifer for some help. But I want to make sure you're okay with it first…You know…because…" David wiped his mouth with his napkin.

Jennifer wandered back into the kitchen area and sank into her chair.

"Go on, what kind of help?" Dylan asked, taking out a piece of candy. His battle with smoking continued.

"The car out of gas belongs to a girl named Emma. I brought her here on Christmas Eve to crash for the night."

"Whoa, dude. *You* let a single woman stay here?" Dylan leaned forward, an interested gleam in his eye. "Hey, I mean, not that I see anything wrong with that, but let me give you some advice. You're a single, male teacher in a small town. You need to be discreet, ya know what I mean?"

David huffed. "It wasn't anything like *that*. She didn't have anywhere else to go; it was Christmas Eve. And not that it's any of your business, but she slept in the bedroom, and I sacked out on the couch."

"Figures." Dylan smirked. He winced, rubbing the arm Jennifer had smacked.

"Where is she now?" Jennifer asked.

"Well, she's in the hospital. She was pregnant, and the placenta ripped or something. Anyway, she had an emergency C-section and—"

The color drained from Dylan's face, and he grasped Jennifer's hand.

"No, no, don't worry. She's fine," David assured them.

Jennifer patted Dylan's hand. "Things happen. I'm healthy as a horse with no complications. Relax, Dylan." She turned back to David. "Girl or boy?"

David grinned, still under the spell of witnessing Kensington's miraculous birth. "A beautiful little girl, named Kensington Michaela Devine. She weighs three pounds and ten ounces, and she's twelve inches long."

"Aw, is her middle name for you?"

David nodded and grinned, unable to contain his excitement. "Yes! I was there for her birth. It was an emergency, so I became Emma's support person because she didn't have anyone else."

"What kind of help do you need?" Dylan asked. Some of the color had returned to his face, but he still held Jennifer's hand.

"Emma's homeless and had no prenatal care. The baby was born early, and she doesn't have anything for her. They'll be in the hospital for a few days, but I'm lost on what to get for them, aside from diapers."

"Is she breastfeeding?"

"Um, she's trying. Kensington isn't quite catching on, but the nurse said she would get better." He shifted in his seat and changed the subject. "She's really cute and so tiny. Did you know babies have *fingernails?*"

Jennifer laughed. "*Really?* Imagine that. I must've slept through that lesson in nursing school. You're quite taken with her. What about the mom?" She pinched his cheek.

"She has fingernails, too," he replied, swatting her hand away. "Emma? Come on, stop it. I only met her two days ago. I thought she was a boy at first."

Dylan snorted and laughed. "Either you've had your nose too long in the books, or you need your eyes checked. How can you mistake a pregnant woman for a boy?"

"She had on an old hoodie, and she's petite like Jennifer. I caught her trying to steal a jar of peanut butter because she was hungry." He closed his eyes and rubbed them, wishing he could remove the picture of her battered body from his head. "Someone did something horrible to her. She has a black eye; her lip is split and swollen. There were bruises everywhere, even on her stomach, which may be why the baby was early. They…" He paused to compose himself. "She's only twenty-one and started hemorrhaging. Kensington is the only baby she'll ever have. They had to do a hysterectomy."

"Oh, David, I'm so sorry." Jennifer patted his hand.

Dylan clasped him on the shoulder. "Take Jen shopping. She'll be in heaven having another baby to buy for. It'll be our gift."

David smiled tiredly, relieved to have at least one problem solved. "Thank you. I've got a little saved, but with seminary looming in the fall, every penny is stretched four ways to Sunday. I'll pay you back—"

"No. You will not. Like I said, this is a gift. Let's go get some gas." Dylan stood, and for the first time since they met, David felt true warmth for the man.

Emma made her way down the hall to check on Kensington. After six long days in the hospital, she'd been discharged, but Kensington wouldn't be released until she gained some weight. Emma stopped to catch her breath. *Breastfeeding.* No surprise, she was a colossal failure at it. Her entire life had been one disaster and disappointment after another. The only thing she seemed to be good at wasn't exactly something to be proud of.

She suited up with the paper gown, and the nurse handed her Kensington. Although it wasn't time for her to eat, Emma wanted to hold her before leaving. A tear slid down her face as she rocked her baby. She angrily wiped it away, blaming it on hormones, never having been a crier until this last week. She sighed, her heart heavy with the burden she carried, and the knowledge that her actions would impact so many.

When she'd first found out she was pregnant, she'd been ecstatic. A few weeks later, her hopes and dreams had died in a roadside bomb overseas. After Ken's death, she'd been numb and in denial. Their best friend, Angel, had fallen apart and relapsed to heroin use, leaving her alone and scared. She'd considered an abortion, but couldn't bring herself to do it. This baby had been conceived carelessly, but she'd loved Ken.

Having no money and no skills, she'd decided she had no choice but to return to Scott, foolishly thinking he cared about her. What a joke. She was nothing but a commodity to him. And once her pregnancy had started to show, she was useless. When she found out he'd arranged an abortion, she'd run away with Angel's help. But three days before Christmas, Scott had found her. He'd taken the little money she had and beat the hell out of her before she'd escaped in the commotion...

Emma clutched the sleeping baby to her breast and rocked, wondering if one could die from a broken heart. "I love you more than you will ever know or understand," she whispered.

A hand stroked her hair. "Emma? You okay?"

David knelt in front of her. She dashed at her tears, embarrassed. He wiped off one she'd missed with his thumb and kissed Kensington on the forehead.

"I didn't hear you come in." She looked away, terrified he'd somehow discern her secret. She didn't want her dark, evil soul to tarnish him. He was good, kind, and loving—everything she wasn't. She couldn't bear the thought of watching the light leave his eyes.

"Aw, honey. Don't cry. We'll be back in a few hours for her feeding." He rubbed her arm, thankfully misunderstanding her emotional state.

She tried to speak, but the words wouldn't come. Emma looked up at him and cradled his cheek with her hand. She couldn't tell him what she'd done. She could only pray he'd forgive her. Dropping her hand, she gazed back down at her daughter.

"I-I never knew a person could love another s-so much," she stammered.

"What's not to love?" David teased, stroking Kensington's soft hand. He looked back at her, concern pulling his brows together.

Emma knew he worried about her. Earlier she'd overheard him and the nurse talking about postpartum depression. Her discharge paperwork included a prescription for a mild antidepressant. It would remain unfilled. She knew the reason for her depression and emotional state.

Emma gave Kensington a kiss and attempted a smile when David snapped another picture. The day after Kensington's birth, he'd thoughtfully brought her some makeup to cover her fading black eye. He'd already taken dozens of pictures and had them printed for her. She looked horrid in all of them. The nurse offered to take their picture together with Kensington. David made a silly face, Emma rolled her eyes, and Kensington scrunched her face with a raucous cry. He proclaimed the terrible picture his favorite and laughed when she fussed about how horrid it was.

David placed Kensington back in the incubator, and Emma watched him kiss the infant's tiny hand. Still sore, she winced a little as she stood. David immediately put his hands on her lower back and shoulder to help. She tried to brush him away, but he ignored her protests with a kiss to her forehead.

The gesture surprised her, and she froze, unsure how to react. David pulled away, not meeting her eyes as he stuffed his hands in his pockets, and shifted his gaze to Kensington.

Giving her daughter one last kiss, she whispered, "Goodbye, my love."

In the hall, she broke down, a sobbing mess. David held her, rubbing her back until her weeping receded to sniffles. Then she felt his entire body stiffen, and an almost imperceptible huff of breath escaped his lips.

"Hi, Mr. Patterson. What are you doing here? I have an issue with my grade and want to talk to you about it."

Emma pulled away from David and wiped her eyes. Heat infused her cheeks under the intense stare of a teenaged girl and an older woman, who appeared to be the girl's mother. The curious look on the teen's face was nothing compared to the contemptuous look on the other's.

"Hello, Carrie. The grade posted was not a first offer. It's the one you earned. Good afternoon, Mrs. Meadows." David's voice sounded formal as he pulled Emma toward the exit, ending the conversation.

She followed him immediately, eager to help him out of this awkward situation. She knew she wasn't the type of girl nice men appeared with in public.

"Who was that?" she asked.

"One of my students and her mother. Lydia Meadows works at the local grocery and is one of the nosiest women in town." He ran a hand through his hair.

"I forgot you were a teacher."

"For now…I'm applying to seminary."

"What do you teach?"

"American history."

"Oh. Wow. Four score and all that stuff, huh?"

"Yes, indeed. And I'm cruel. They have to memorize it." He rubbed the back of his neck. Emma already knew it was his tell when nervous or upset.

"So, you don't preach at all?"

"No, not yet. That's my dream. Right now, I teach a Sunday school class. Why?"

"Just curious." Emma's heart flipped, and she broke out in a cold sweat. Did this make it better or worse? Taking a deep breath, she shoved the thoughts to the back of her mind.

What was done was done.

David turned into the driveway, but stopped in front of the cozy, white frame house instead of his garage apartment. Emma's piece-of-shit car was parked by the garage, and relief filled her troubled mind. One problem solved…

The front door opened, and an older woman wearing black pants and a red sweater stepped out, drying her hands on a dishtowel tucked in her waistband. She smiled widely and waved, hurrying toward the car before Emma had a chance to collect her thoughts.

"Hello, hello, Emma! I'm Eloise Jordan, and I'm so glad you're home. David has shown me the pictures of your beautiful baby. Such a little doll. I adore babies. I have two grandchildren, and Dylan and

Jennifer's new baby will be here soon. I'm going to be like a grandma to her, too. I plan to spoil her rotten and make her daddy pay for his raisin'." Mrs. Jordan chattered nonstop as she escorted Emma into her home. David followed, carrying her backpack and a stuffed pink rabbit he'd had in his car.

"Th-Thank you. It's nice to meet you." She looked around, wondering why they were here. She could smell freshly baked bread as they passed the kitchen. The living room was full of antiques, but warm and inviting, much like the owner. In the corner stood an old spinning wheel, and framed pictures adorned the mantle and bookcases.

David walked past her, carrying her belongings up the stairs. Anxiety slithered through her, but before she could say anything, Mrs. Jordan smiled, motioning for her to follow. Trudging behind them, she stopped at door and gripped the doorjamb, fighting the overwhelming urge to run. David and Mrs. Jordan stood with expectant smiles on their faces. A beautiful quilt covered the brass bed, and beside it stood an antique cradle with a huge pink bow. Pink bunnies decorated the white cradle bedding. David placed the stuffed pink rabbit in the baby bed and stuck his hands in his pocket, rocking on his heels. Everything was so damn *pink*. She wanted to vomit.

Emma stood motionless, scanning the room. "I don't understand." Baby diapers, baby toiletries, and tiny pink outfits were arranged on the oak dresser.

It was too much. She didn't want this. She didn't deserve this.

"Emma, you can't stay with me," David explained. "I'm single and a teacher. But Mrs. Jordan has graciously opened her home to you and Kensington until you can get on your feet."

Mrs. Jordan nodded. "I'm so excited! Two new babies! Jennifer and Dylan live next door through the woods. Your children will be so close in age. She's due in a couple of months. Maybe they'll grow up to be best friends. Wouldn't that be nice?" She beamed at Emma and straightened the cradle bedding.

"Jennifer and Dylan?" Unable to process any of this, Emma's eyes darted back and forth between David and Mrs. Jordan.

"I grew up with Jennifer. She's married to Dylan McAthie, and they helped with all of this." David motioned around the room. "Jennifer can't wait to meet you. Like Mrs. Jordan said, her baby's due in February. I hope you like all of it, the bunnies and stuff—"

"Wait, *the* Dylan McAthie?" He'd been the lead guitarist for her favorite band of all time—he lived next door? Emma slipped into the room and sank into the rocking chair. *Is this a dream?* This couldn't be real; in a moment, she'd wake up in the back of her car, cold and hungry. She pinched herself. *Not dreaming.* Biting her lower lip, she wrapped her arms around her chest and began to rock back and forth. This was too surreal.

"Yep, that would be him, but don't fawn all over him. His ego's big enough as it is," David teased.

Mrs. Jordan laughed, but her smile faded as an uncomfortable silence took over. Emma looked around the room, attempting to absorb the sudden change in her living situation.

"Don't you like it, dear?" Mrs. Jordan wrung her hands.

"No, I mean, yes. It's just that, I can't accept this. It's too much." She didn't want to be beholden to anyone. Nothing was free, and she'd be damned if she'd pay the price.

David motioned for Mrs. Jordan to leave, and she disappeared into the hallway. Shutting the bedroom door, he squatted in front of her chair. She stared at his hands holding hers and resisted the urge to bury her face in them. It was as if they grounded her somehow, and a part of her never wanted them to let go.

"Em, look at me."

With reluctance, she looked up. His eyes softened, and he gave her hands a squeeze. Her cold, dying heart stuttered to life, and a jolt of need for what this sweet man had to offer zipped straight to the pit of her stomach.

She snatched her hands away, terrified. Damn these hormonal emotions. This couldn't happen. David was a teacher and wanted to be a *minister*. What could she offer him? She was a prostitute. The most decent job she'd ever had was as a pole dancer, still not worthy of this man.

"These things are a gift. Buying them made Jennifer and Dylan happy, just as it's made Mrs. Jordan happy to open her home to you and Kensington. As hard as you may find it, sometimes it's best to just accept the gift and not overanalyze the motive behind it. You may not believe me, but you and Kensington deserve nothing but the best."

David was the nicest person she'd ever met. He represented everything good about humankind, full of hope and compassion, but he was naïve. She hoped he'd never witness the ugly world she lived in. The real world. Emma shook her head.

"I'm *not* overanalyzing. I truly don't deserve all this…kindness. I'm not a *good* person, David. I'm a—"

David placed a finger over her lips and shook his head, his gaze unwavering. "Stop. Don't say it. Don't think it." He stood and pulled her into his arms, holding her tight and stroking her hair. "Emma, Emma, Emma. I don't know what circumstances made you do the things you did. But I wish you would believe me. You *do* deserve all of this. Just trust me."

Emma pulled away, turning her back on him, and stared out the window.

Oh, how she wanted to believe it.

And how sad it was going to be when David realized she was the one speaking the truth.

Chapter Five

Hesitating for a moment, Emma clenched her fist and took a deep breath. When her nerves steadied, she entered the screened porch and knocked on the front door. After sneaking away from Mrs. Jordan's, she'd crossed through the woods to the modest cottage. Next to it stood a large new home still under construction, overlooking the lake. The sound of hammering and men laughing and calling out to one another permeated the air. Emma rocked back and forth on her heels and waited.

The front door opened, and she caught her breath when the man once voted "Sexiest Musician Alive" stood in front of her. The pictures in the media didn't lie. He ran a hand through his sandy brown hair and looked at her with gorgeous blue eyes. He was a god, no doubt about it—even with a sucker stuck in his mouth.

"Hello."

Emma opened and closed her mouth three times before she croaked out a greeting in return. "Hi."

Dylan McAthie smiled and motioned her into the cozy house. "I take it you're Emma. Jen's at the store, but come on in." He offered her a seat at the kitchen table as he crunched the candy. Throwing the stick in the garbage, he poured a cup of coffee and offered her one, which she declined. Gratefully, she sank into the kitchen chair before she collapsed. Nervousness, combined with the walk through the woods barely a week after Kensington's birth, had left her weaker than she'd anticipated.

"Happy New Year's Eve." Dylan saluted her with his cup of coffee.

"Oh, right. Thanks, uh, back at ya." She sat on her hands and glanced around the kitchen, bouncing one leg with nervous energy. The kitchen was like something from forty years ago. Not at all what she'd expected for a famous musician. "I wanted to thank you and your wife for all the baby shit—um, sorry, I...er, mean stuff."

"You're welcome. Jen had fun buying all the shit. I mean stuff."

He winked at her, and Emma nearly fainted.

Dylan McAthie winked at me!

"She can only buy so much for our baby, so the shopping trip helped get it out of her system."

"B-But I can't accept it. It's too much."

"I see." He peered at her with a mixture of curiosity and assessment.

She shifted in her seat, squirming under his scrutiny. According to David, he was a happily married man. She wouldn't risk insulting him with her first thought on how she could pay him back.

"Look, I don't have any money right now, but I *will* pay you back, for everything. It will just have to be a little at a time." The words tumbled out, and she stared at the sugar bowl on the table.

"It was a gift, Emma—"

"Please," she interrupted, lifting her chin. "Please let me pay you back. Just write down how much I owe you, and I'll make sure you get your money."

"I don't need the money." His eyes narrowed as he tapped the table with his thumb.

Damn all these well-meaning people! "I know you don't need the fuckin' money," she ground out through her teeth. "But *I need to do this*." She made herself look him in the face, determined to get her point across.

Dylan ran a finger around his coffee mug several times before nodding. "All right." He emptied an envelope on the table, wrote a figure on the back of it, and handed it to her.

Emma gasped. The amount was more than she'd imagined. *He doesn't need the money. David said it was a gift. He said it was a gift. Take it. No. I'm doing this for Kensington. For me.*

Standing, she straightened her shoulders. "Thank you. Thank you very much, Mr. McAthie." She shook his hand before fleeing his house.

"Come on in, it's open." David looked up from the computer when Emma entered. He stood and motioned for her to sit. Her hand clutched her stomach, and her color matched her gray hoodie. He wondered how in the world she kept from tripping in those baggy jeans, especially coming up all those stairs. Would it be inappropriate to buy her a new outfit? One that fit?

"Hey, Em. Just give me a few minutes, and I'll run you to the hospital for Kensington's feeding. You shouldn't have struggled up the stairs. I told you I'd pick you up at Mrs. Jordan's."

Emma crumpled on the couch, and he sat next to her. Picking up his laptop, he hit save on his plan of study.

"No hurry. I'm trying to get stronger." She peered over his shoulder. "What are you working on? Lesson plans for school next week?"

"No, stuff for seminary. How did you sleep last night?"

She shrugged and looked everywhere but at him. "Okay. The room's beautiful, and Mrs. Jordan is really nice. I just feel…I dunno, like a burden."

The overwhelming hopelessness that surrounded her frustrated and saddened him.

"What makes you happy, Emma?" he blurted. *Is she ever happy? Does she ever laugh? Could I make her happy, if she'd give me a chance?*

"You and Kensington." She stared at the floor and blushed, looking uncharacteristically soft and vulnerable.

David smiled, liking this rare glimpse of what he felt in his heart must be the true Emma.

"I-I meant the baby, I guess." Looking despondent, she shoved a strand of hair behind her ear and folded her arms against her chest. "I dunno." And instantly, the hardened Emma was back.

David put the computer on the coffee table. Her startled confession had made him inexplicably happy. Her face flushed a brighter red, and she shifted away from him. She was an attractive girl, even though she didn't smile nearly enough.

"You and Kensington make me happy, too. I can't imagine my life without both of you in it. I just wish you'd relax. Come on, I haven't bitten anyone since I was four, and that was my sister, Carole. I want to be your friend." He gave her hair a teasing pull, just like he used to do to Carole.

But if he were being honest, he'd had far from brotherly thoughts about Emma.

The thought of nibbling on her neck was quite appealing.

Emma turned, startled by the gentle tug on her hair and unsure how to act. No one had teased her in a long time. Who was she kidding? Prior to Kensington's birth, no one since Ken had even touched her unless they paid for it. Or took it…

She found herself staring at David's lips. They were perfect—not too thin, not too full, and always smiling, like now. She liked the scruff on his face and wondered what it would feel like against her neck. And he smelled good, too—a soft aftershave that wasn't too overpowering and clean laundry detergent. Not cheap men's cologne, body odor, and sweat. Not stale beer and rotten teeth. Not what she was used to.

Without thinking, Emma reached over and cupped his cheek. She ran her thumb across his bottom lip. He sat still, watching her face. His pupils dilated, and his breathing hitched. Leaning forward, she closed her eyes and brought her lips to his. Marveling at their warmth, she was pleasantly surprised when David shifted, drawing her closer. She didn't kiss many men. They usually weren't interested in the niceties of foreplay.

His hand raked through her hair as his lips parted and moved against hers. She deepened the kiss, and her tongue darted in his mouth, exploring, running along his teeth. When she moved her hands to his neck, running her fingers through his dark waves, a jolt of longing snaked down her body into the pit of her stomach.

She couldn't remember the last time she'd felt something for a man. The only other man she'd ever cared for had died a world away, more than seven months ago…David moved his lips to trail kisses across her jaw. He murmured her name softly in her ear, his warm breath and beard tickling her neck.

Emma pulled away, her world spinning like a bad acid trip. She covered her hot cheeks, shocked. That kiss had moved her more than she cared to admit. Even her toes had curled.

"Wow. You don't kiss like a preacher." *Was that really my voice—all breathy and soft?*

"Kissed many, have you?" His dark eyes crinkled with amusement.

"Not that I'm aware of, but you never know. Kissed many hookers?"

"Not that I'm aware of." His grin widened, and he laughed. "Probably not."

Moving in for another kiss, she jumped back and looked down at her wet T-shirt. Her breasts were leaking. Mortified, her cheeks now burned with embarrassment.

"Dammit. I don't know what to do with these things." She circled her chest. "I've never had boobs, much less boobs that hurt all the time and leak."

She slapped a hand over her mouth when she realized what she'd said out loud. *Please, if there is a God, will you open the Earth and swallow me now?*

Red-faced, David handed her a flannel shirt from a clean pile of laundry on the coffee table. "I, uh, guess it's time we head over to see Kensington. I don't want you to explode like a water balloon."

One corner of her mouth lifted, and she started to giggle. David bit his lip and looked away, but his shoulders shook. In a moment, they were both laughing, holding on to each other for support as they gasped for breath. She couldn't remember the last time she had truly laughed, which seemed so odd.

How she wished she could be this carefree girl who giggled. But this girl was an illusion.

David fiddled with a glass, moving it closer to the sparkling grape juice. Sighing, he snuck a piece of cheese from the fruit and cheese platter before resuming his pacing. *Is she ditching me?*

After her leaking incident today, Emma had been distant and distracted. At Kensington's last feeding, she'd sobbed to the point that the baby had cried too, sensing her mama's distress. He didn't understand what was upsetting her. The baby was improving and gaining weight. Worried about her, he'd spontaneously invited her to celebrate New Year's Eve with him.

Okay, it wasn't just worry that had prompted the invite. There was something about her that intrigued him. She was different from any girl he'd ever known. And not just in the experience department. He sensed she was much more fragile than she let on, under her tough exterior. A problem solver, he wanted to peel away those layers and discover the real Emma. He felt drawn to her, which was crazy. They were so different, and the last relationship he'd been in was with Jennifer...She'd ended up dumping him.

Emma was nothing like Jennifer, and yet there was an innate sweetness about her.

He also longed to hear her laugh again, the way she had earlier today. She'd seemed carefree and relaxed in that moment, and he liked her that way. *A lot.* And God help him, he couldn't quit thinking about that kiss...

With a glance at his watch, his hope faltered. It was almost midnight. He rubbed the back of his neck. *She must be too tired.* Or the kiss hadn't rocked her world the way it had his. Ready to call it a night, he paused, hearing a timid knock. Grinning, he threw open the door. Emma stood shivering in her old gray hoodie, her arms crossed in front of her chest.

"Come in and get warm. We need to buy you a decent coat."

"I'm fine." She stepped in and shoved the hood back, releasing her long, wavy hair. He wanted to bury his hands in it and kiss her, but she moved away, circling the room several times like a caged tiger. Stopping in front of the coffee table, Emma picked up the bottle of sparkling grape juice and smirked. "The hard stuff, huh? Party animal."

"You can't drink and breastfeed. I'm being a considerate host." He poured a glass of the juice and handed it to her, glad his hand remained steady. Opting for bottled water, he tapped her glass. "Happy New Year. I'm grateful you and Kensington are in my life."

She cringed.

Wonderful. Not exactly the reaction he'd hoped for. He popped a slice of apple in his mouth and frowned. "Are you okay? Please, sit."

Emma refused to meet his gaze as she perched on the edge of the couch. Warily, she watched him from under her long, dark lashes.

He sat beside her, nervous as a teenager on his first date. What was wrong with him? Maybe he needed to channel Dylan and his jerk-like bravado. *Nah, I'd come across as ridiculous…*

"I'm okay, just really tired."

Her unsettled, turbulent eyes dominated her wan face. Immediately, she dropped her gaze back to the floor. But the depth of pain he'd seen there made him flinch. Silence reigned for a moment while she bounced her leg, her hands stuffed in the pockets of that atrocious hoodie.

Clearing her throat, she took a deep breath. "I can't begin to thank you for everything you've done and tell you how glad I am you're in Kensington's life…"

He placed a hand on her knee to still her bouncing. She jumped up, slamming her glass so hard grape juice sloshed out. "I think I need to go."

Desperate, David stood and grabbed her hand. "No, wait. You just got here. You'll miss the fireworks. We can walk down to the dock and see them. It's almost midnight…Please, don't go."

Her amazing eyes reflected her quicksilver emotions as they switched from topaz to green, and she chewed on her bottom lip. Seeing her waver, he walked her toward the front door and grabbed one of his coats hanging on the rack. He helped her into it before shrugging into his own.

"Come on, let's go watch the fireworks. Mrs. J says they're amazing." He pulled her through the door.

Emma held back for a moment, but a shy smile lit her face, and she nodded. "I've never seen fireworks in person, just on television."

Is that a tiny hint of excitement in her voice? He smiled to himself, pleased that she didn't let go of his hand as they stepped into the frigid night air.

"According to Mrs. Jordan, the people who live across the lake throw a spectacular party with fireworks twice a year: on New Year's Eve and the Fourth of July."

He steered her down the path, using the flashlight on his keyring to light the way. Laughter and music drifted from across the lake, mixing with the sound of the crunching leaves beneath their feet. He couldn't have planned it any better, for as they stepped onto the boat dock, colorful fireworks burst above them like glittery confetti, giving the inky sky a magical look.

Emma stood frozen, her mouth open and eyes wide. "Oh my God!" she whispered.

David didn't watch the fireworks. Stunning as they were, nothing compared to Emma's expressive face as she stared in wonder. He smiled when she pointed, *oohing* and *ahhing*. For a few moments, her eyes remained unguarded, void of the deep-seated sorrow that seemed to linger there.

When the finale lit up the sky, Emma clapped, her surprised gasps billowing into the cold night air. To his delighted surprise, she threw her arms around him.

"Thank you, David. Thank you so much for everything."

David lowered his mouth to hers. Her lips parted, and he hungrily explored, savoring her sweetness. Holding her soft, warm body next to his ignited a different kind of fireworks on the cold dock, and he pulled her closer. Her soft moan had him growling in the back of his throat as he deepened the kiss. Much too soon, she tore away from him and stepped back, her arms once again wrapped around her chest in a guarded stance. Bright, wide eyes stared at him as her chest heaved with choppy, vaporous breaths. He couldn't be sure in the dim light, but her eyes appeared to sparkle with unshed tears.

"I'm sorry," he lied. He was not a bit sorry, just unsure of what else to say.

"No, David. I'm sorry—*for everything.* I've got to go." She gave him a quick kiss on the lips, and he felt the tears on her face before she ran toward Mrs. Jordan's.

"Wait, don't go…"

She continued to run from him, and he heard her strangled sobs. *Stupid.* He'd upset her and needed to apologize.

"Emma, I'm sorry!"

"Leave me the hell alone. I have to go." She yelled without turning around.

David trudged behind her, berating himself for being such an ass. He'd apologize to her tomorrow when they'd both had time to calm down. Watching to make sure she got into the house safely, he sighed when she slammed the door without looking back.

Discouraged, he rubbed the back of his neck. Emma Devine had to be the most frustrating, fascinating girl he'd ever encountered. He turned and walked up the steps to his apartment, wondering why the slamming of that door gave him such an ominous feeling of finality.

Chapter
Six

The next morning, Emma was gone. David sat in Mrs. Jordan's kitchen, holding the tear-stained letter, not quite believing she'd left. Surely this was a nightmare. There was no way she could do this to him. To Kensington.

Dear David,

I know you love my baby. That's why I'm giving her to you. I know you won't understand why I've done this, but she deserves better in life than me. Like you, she's everything that is good in this ~~fucked~~ bad world. It was never my plan to keep her, but I can't give her to strangers. I told the nurse you were her father when she filled out Kensington's birth certificate. This way maybe you won't have the legal ~~shit~~ stuff to go thru to keep her. Please tell her I love her.

I'm sorry,

Emma

What was he to do? Kids under the age of fourteen terrified him—that's why he taught high school. For heaven's sake, he worked full time. How could he care for a baby? Would the school board even let him keep his job? What about his plans to attend seminary? How would he afford a child?

Overwhelmed and paralyzed with fear, David put his head down on the table and tried to collect his scattered thoughts.

Jennifer rubbed his back in soothing circles while Mrs. Jordan cried into her dishtowel.

"How could she leave her baby? What kind of woman abandons her baby?" Jennifer spat, her voice rising. "She's a horrible person. I'd like to give her a piece of my mind. Kensington needs her."

"That poor lost girl, no wonder she looked so unhappy. She must've known she was going to leave. Dylan, can you do anything to bring her back?" Mrs. Jordan asked with a sniffle. "You have tons of people who work for you. They could investigate and find her."

"I suppose so. But what good would it do? She obviously didn't want to be here. What kind of mother would she be if she did come back? Emma's right; Kensington's better off without her," Dylan said.

The room remained eerily silent, except for the sound of Mrs. Jordan's sniffles. Tension hung thick as they waited for him to do something, say something about the unthinkable changes about to occur in his life. David kept his head down on his arms and silently prayed.

Decision made, he sat up and rubbed his face with both hands.

"What are you going to do?" Jennifer whispered.

"I'm going to see Kensington." He sighed, straightening his shoulders. "My daughter needs me."

David walked around the apartment, trying to console the screaming baby. *Colic*. Without a doubt, it was the vilest word in the dictionary.

He hadn't realized how easy he'd had it when Kensington was still in the hospital, gaining weight and suntanning to cure her jaundice. After a painful confrontation with his family—in which he offered vague answers and listened to countless lectures—his mother had come to help when he brought Kensington home. She'd stayed two miserable weeks, and he'd been happy to see her go, tired of the disappointed look in her eyes. Thankfully, Mrs. J now babysat while he was at work, and Jennifer had helped until Angela was born.

But now, alone with his daughter, the past week had proved to be even more of a challenge than he'd anticipated, especially with an infant who cried nonstop for hours at a time. At least daily he conjured the scenario of admitting defeat and asking the hospital if he could return her—not that he really would, he loved Kensington. But nothing he did seemed to soothe her, and he was at his wit's end.

Earlier this evening, convinced Kensington was dying—or at the very least dehydrated—he'd placed a frantic call to the doctor's office. Two hours later, the doctor on call had phoned and assured him the baby was fine and this would pass. *Easy for her to say, she wasn't the one dealing with the ear-piercing screams.*

"Hush, sweetheart, shhhh," he cooed, rubbing his daughter's back.

Tired and irritable after six nights of sleep deprivation, he was frustrated and near tears himself. He continued to pace, patting her back, mumbling useless reassurances and prayers. All his doubts and worries magnified a hundred-fold during these crying fits. He wasn't cut out to be a father. Whatever had possessed him to think he could do this?

Desperate, he dug out his phone and dialed the woman he truly dreaded talking to. But in desperate times, a man had to do what a man had to do. Relief flooded through him when she picked up on the first ring, her voice thick with sleep.

"David? What's the matter?"

"I can't do this. She won't stop *crying*. I take back everything I said. Come back. *Please?*"

His mother chuckled. "You do realize I'm five hours away, don't you?"

"I don't care; just come get her. I can't do this, Mom."

"She's fed, burped, and dry?"

"Yes, ma'am. She won't *stop*. Nothing pacifies her, and I'm so tired I can't even think straight, much less function. Yesterday, I fell asleep at my desk while the kids were taking a test. It's all the damn time, Mom. *She won't shut up.*"

"I doubt it's all the time; watch your language."

"Yes, ma'am." He sighed, placed the screaming child in her crib, and locked himself in the bathroom, feeling like a jerk for leaving his baby wailing. "Mrs. Jordan says she cries a little during the day, but is a good baby. I think she's lying. Or the kid is possessed. Maybe I should call a priest to exorcise her."

"We're Methodist, son."

He let out a desperate groan as the screaming took on an even higher pitch and raced from the bathroom. She had to be dying to scream like that. He picked her up once again, feeling helpless.

"I suck at being a dad," he muttered as he once again paced his apartment.

"Swaddle her tight, move her crib next to the dryer, and turn it on."

Do what? "Put her in the dryer?" It was difficult to hear over the high-pitched shrieks.

"No. Put Kensington *in the crib* and move it *next* to the dryer and turn the dryer on—to see if the rhythmic noise will help calm her down. Sometimes it works. I promise this phase will pass."

David sighed. *Why does everyone keep saying that?* "Okay, thanks, Mom. I'll try it. Love you. Sorry I called so late."

"I love you, too."

He hung up and checked Kensington's diaper. *At least now I can put a diaper on that won't fall off.* After swaddling her tight in the baby blanket the way the nurse had shown him, he placed her in the crib and moved it next to the dryer. What a waste of time, no way this would work.

Five minutes later, the only sound in the house was the turning tumble of the dryer. After so much screaming, the silence was unnerving. He snuck back in to make sure she was still breathing. Kensington scrunched her face in sleep and smiled. David did a fist pump of victory. Staggering to the couch, he collapsed into an instant, hard sleep.

A persistent ringing woke him up. *No! Don't wake Kensington!* Without opening his eyes, he fumbled and reached for the phone.

"Yeah," he mumbled, annoyed when no sound came from the other end of the line. *Stupid robo-calls.* Ready to slam the phone down, a muffled cry had him instantly awake.

"Emma?" he asked hoarsely, sitting up.

Another soft sob came through the line. He rubbed his eyes and glanced at his watch. It was two in the morning; he'd fallen asleep with the light on. Stumbling into the kitchen, he peeked at Kensington, who still slept soundly.

He hurried back to the living area. "Emma, where are you?" he asked.

"I-I'm so sorry," she whispered.

"Emma, come back…"

The line went dead.

Emma hung up and stared at the handful of pills she'd stolen from Angel. She had no idea what they were; she only prayed they would work. Something had to kill the pain inside of her—or kill her.

It didn't matter.

Nothing mattered.

She didn't matter.

Dragging her eyes away from the pills, she took a good, hard look in the mirror. And hated herself even more. *Sorry excuse for a woman, you don't deserve to live.* Deep purple circles surrounded her listless, dull eyes. Her face already had the pallor of a corpse, her sharply prominent cheekbones giving her a hard, pinched look. She turned away, disgusted. Angel had relapsed again and was getting aggravated with her depression. He kept telling her to "snap out of it." She'd officially become a burden to her best friend. Tired of living like this, she'd hatched her plan.

A pounding at the door startled her, and she dropped some of the pills. *Dammit!* She knelt, desperately retrieving them.

"Open up, Emma," Angel yelled through the door.

He sounded pissed; he must've realized she'd stolen his stash. As he kicked the door in, she shoved the pills in her mouth and gagged.

"Goddammit, Emma! You're not fuckin' doing this to me." His dilated eyes flashed with anger. He yanked her to her feet and squeezed her cheeks as he tried to open her mouth. When that didn't work, he forced her to her knees in front of the toilet. "You're not leaving me like this."

His grip on the back of her neck was unbreakable. She scratched, kicked, and struggled to escape, but he managed to stick his finger down her throat. She vomited, half in the toilet and half on the floor. Tears streamed down her face as he yanked her head back using her hair. Again, he slammed his finger down her throat, and again her stomach emptied. Bile stung the back of her throat. She gasped to breathe as tears of frustration streamed down her hot cheeks.

"Goddamn you." He let go and grasped his knees, hanging his head. His ragged breathing matched hers as they glared at one another, catching their breath. As she struggled to her feet, his glassy, bloodshot eyes tracked her movement. They were ice cold, lit by the demon of his addiction. She prayed he'd lose his shit enough to kill her. It was her last hope.

"I hate you," she screamed, trying to provoke him.

"I know. I hate you, too."

She slapped him hard across the face. He caught her wrist, and with her free hand she beat his bare chest, screaming every obscenity she'd ever heard. He withstood her assault, holding her. Spent, she shoved against him and collapsed into a sobbing mess on the vomit-slick floor of the cheap motel bathroom.

Angel sank down next to her and shook her shoulders. Sweat from his withdrawals trickled down his face. "How could you do this to me? I needed that fix. Taking this shit isn't going to solve your problems! Look at how it's fucked up my life. I'm a junkie, Emma. Do you want to end up like me?"

"No, I want to die," she shouted back.

"Fuck you. You don't get to die, you little coward. Goddammit, you need to fight this demon that's consuming you. This isn't the answer. This is a cop-out. Do you think Ken would be happy that you fuckin' committed suicide? Is that going to get you your little girl back? Is that going to make her proud of you if she ever finds out what happened? Fuck, no!

"If you ever try this again, I'll track down that kid of yours and tell her what you did. This is by far the stupidest stunt you've ever pulled."

A spike of fear buried itself in her chest. Moments ago she'd wanted Angel to kill her, but now she cringed, scared by his uncharacteristic anger and his fingers digging into her shoulders. Cowering, she covered her head. He grabbed her chin, forcing her to look at him. His face softened.

He brought his forehead to hers. "Fuck. Fuck, fuck, fuck! I didn't mean it. I wouldn't do that. I wouldn't hurt your baby; it's the damn withdrawals talking."

Dragging her into his lap, he rocked her, crying. "I'm sorry. I'm so sorry, Emma. I didn't mean to hurt you, but dammit, you scared the shit out of me. I'll save you. We can fix this."

"I hate you," she sobbed, clinging to his neck. *He doesn't understand. I'm not worth saving. I'm worthless.*

He held her tighter, rubbing her back. "No, you don't. You don't hate me. You hate yourself."

Emma wept, not denying it.

For it was the truth.

Part
two

Chapter
Seven

"**D**addy."

"What, Kensington?" David answered without opening his eyes. He should've known his plan to sleep in on the first day of summer vacation would never work with a four-year-old in the house.

"Are you awake?"

"No."

"*Daaddddy.* Yes, you are."

"No, I'm not." Snaking his arm out, he grabbed Kenzie by the waist and hauled her into bed. Nuzzling her neck, he gave her a good-morning kiss on her soft cheek.

"Ow, Daddy, biskers." She giggled and patted his scruffy jaw. When he opened his eyes, two hazel eyes met his, forehead to forehead, nose to nose.

"You're silly, Daddy."

"I'm silly? I'm not the one up at seven."

"Teddy woke me up." Kenzie waved the scruffy old brown bear in his face, the only remembrance of her mother, aside from a few pictures. The beloved bear was Kenzie's favorite stuffed animal.

"Did Teddy start coffee?"

"Nooo, he's a bear. Bears don't drink coffee." Kenzie rolled her eyes and scrambled off the bed. She waited, clutching Teddy to her chest.

At the sound of his daughter's exasperated huff, he hauled himself out of bed, stretching and yawning.

"Okay, okay. I'm up." Bleary-eyed, he stumbled to the kitchen and poured her a bowl of cereal, reluctantly agreeing that she could eat at the coffee table and watch cartoons. After a quick shower, he opted to skip shaving in celebration of the first day of vacation. Checking his glucose, he gave himself insulin and headed toward the kitchen for coffee and a piece of cheese toast.

Waylaid by his daughter's mess, he cleaned the coffee table. More cereal always ended up on the table and floor than in her belly. He finally sank on the couch to enjoy his first cup of caffeine and his toast. Kenzie curled in his lap, clutching Teddy, wiggling her bare, pink-polished toes as she sang along with the Disney cartoon. He clenched his teeth. *Honest to God, if I hear this theme song one more time, I'm going to need another shot of insulin.*

"So what are the plans for today, Kenzie McFrenzie?"

"Get a puppy? Puppies are cute."

He shook his head. "No puppy. I can barely keep up with you." This was her daily request. She'd even taken to slipping it into her nightly prayers.

"I'll take care of it!"

"Maybe if you ever learn to pick up your room, we'll discuss it."

She sighed. "Make cookies?" Her eyes lit up with hope.

"Okay." David prayed she'd always be this easy to please. He finished his coffee, despite his daughter's urging to hurry. From experience, he knew Patterson cookie-making was a messy process. To save on the cleanup, he allowed Kenzie to stay in her nightgown. He put on some music and cranked it up loud as they gathered the ingredients.

Kenzie sat on the kitchen table next to Teddy, clapping and squealing as he entertained her. He played air guitar with the wooden spoon, singing along with Def Leppard's "Pour Some Sugar on Me." Kenzie burst in on the chorus, and he laughed.

His mother would cringe at his song selection, but he could only take so much of the Disney stuff. Kenzie smeared cookie dough across her face, which then smeared on his shirt when he picked her up for a dance. Placing her back on the table, he pulled his sticky shirt over his head. With the music blaring and his shirt in front of his face, he didn't hear what she said.

"What, Kenz?" He tossed the shirt on the floor.

"Mama." She stopped spooning raw cookie dough into her mouth and pointed to the doorway.

He frowned. "Who?" Spinning around, he froze.

Standing in the doorway with Mrs. Jordan was the woman who'd walked out on Kenzie four and a half years ago. Slack-jawed, he stared as The Rolling Stones began to sing about being shattered.

Emma barely noticed David when she and Mrs. Jordan entered the kitchen that had belonged to Dylan and Jennifer McAthie the last time she was in it. Thirty minutes ago, she'd knocked on Mrs. Jordan's door. After the woman overcame her initial shock, she'd walked with her through the woods to the little house near the lake. Emma drank in the first view of her daughter like a woman dying of thirst. Even with cookie dough on her face, Kensington's beauty stole her breath.

"Mama." One simple word — barely audible above the loud music — and Emma's heavy heart burst with happiness.

My daughter knows me.

"Kensington," she whispered, choked by her emotions and shocked at her daughter's recognition.

Curious eyes the color of her own gazed at her from under a mop of Ken's curly hair. Reluctantly, Emma turned to face the man who had cared for her child as his own.

David hadn't changed much at all. Even unshaven with his hair uncombed, he remained devastatingly handsome. She bit her lip to keep from smiling at the bit of cookie dough tangled with a strand of hair that fell over his forehead. He also remained fit, with defined abs and just the right amount of brown hair on his chest and stomach. She wondered if he still had to inject insulin into those muscles.

He brushed past her, turning off the music, and the resulting silence magnified the tension in the room.

"I'll leave you three alone," Mrs. Jordan said quietly, closing the front door behind her.

David turned toward her, but remained silent, his arm wrapped protectively around Kensington. Emma felt her stomach twisting and turning.

"Hello, David." She clasped her hands behind her to hide their trembling.

David's lips pressed into a grim line as he removed the spoon from Kensington's hand and carried her to the sink. Sitting her on the counter, he washed her hands and face, drying them with a dishtowel.

"I-I know this is a shock. I should've called first…" Her voice trailed off, her mouth too dry to speak.

Still not saying a word, he stood at the sink, looking out the window, his arm around her daughter's waist. Kensington's legs swung back and forth as she peered at her with frank curiosity. David shifted his stance, blocking her view, and kissed the top of Kensington's head.

"Why are you here, Emma?" His voice sounded strained, and the muscles in his back bunched.

"Mama."

"I know who it is, Kenz," he snapped.

Startled, Kensington pulled away. Her feet stopped swinging.

"I'm sorry. I'm not mad at you." He hugged her tight.

Emma's heart slammed in her chest, and she gave him a moment to collect himself. Taking a deep breath for courage, she said, "I wanted to see my daughter." She was amazed she didn't stutter.

David whipped around. His eyes narrowed, and she swore she could hear his teeth grinding. "She's *my* daughter."

He picked Kensington up. "Let's go get you dressed, young lady."

He moved past Emma, careful to make sure neither he nor Kensington touched her, as if she were contagious.

Emma sighed. Friends and her therapist had warned her, begged her even, to make contact before this surprise visit. Why hadn't she listened to reason?

Because she'd been afraid he'd say *no*.

She took the tray of cookies out of the oven when the timer went off and put the last tray in. They were taking an inordinately long time. If it weren't for the noises from the back of the house, she would've wondered if they'd left. By the time David and Kensington returned to the kitchen, she had the last batch of cookies on the rack to cool.

Fully dressed in jeans, a faded pale blue T-shirt, and tennis shoes, David glared at her as Kenzie pranced in wearing pink shorts and a pink T-shirt with a panda on it. He'd combed her hair into two pigtails, complete with crooked pink bows. She looked adorable, and it took every ounce of restraint Emma possessed not grab her and shower her with kisses.

Kensington held David's hand, peeking from behind his leg. Every time she caught Emma looking at her, she hid her face. Emma held out a warm cookie to her.

"She doesn't need that right now. It'll ruin her appetite." David's rebuke was swift, his face a mask of fury.

Emma raised her eyebrows, confused. "Sorry, I didn't think—I mean, she was eating raw c-cookie dough only moments ago." She put the cookie back on the plate. The lump of regret forming in her throat made it difficult to speak.

"You don't have the *right* to decide what she can and can't eat."

He reminded her of a snake, coiled and ready to strike.

"I'm her mother," she retorted, but she stepped back. As soon as the words left her mouth, she regretted them. She wrung her hands, chewing her bottom lip.

He shook his head. "You were her mother four and a half years ago. *You walked out on her.* Now you're *nobody.*"

Emma flinched, but suppressed the urge to run. *Take it. You deserve it. It isn't like you're not used to being nobody, the girl with no name.*

David rubbed his brow, strain marring his face.

"Why are you mad, Daddy?"

David blew out a deep breath and straightened a bow in Kensington's hair. "I'm not mad." He hung his head. "I'm upset. I'm sorry, Emma. That was uncalled for."

The apology shredded her courage. She stared at the floor, concentrating on shutting off the pain. She could do this; she just had to slip into the part of herself that didn't feel…

A clock chimed from the living area, sounding like a death knell—the death of her ridiculous, ill-planned thought that she could return and made amends, that she could be part of her daughter's life. Emma kept her mouth shut, unsure how to respond. The awkward silence stretched as Emma and David both watched Kensington, and she watched the plate of cookies.

"Why? Why now?" he croaked, at last.

"Because I have no one else," she blurted. *Dammit.* The loneliness of her grief weighted her words and made her feel weak, both physically and mentally. She stood taller, gripping the back of a kitchen chair.

David pulled out a chair and sat, pulling Kensington into his lap. He wrapped his arms around her waist as if to protect her, or use her to shield his heart.

"Can I have a cookie?" Kensington asked.

"May I," David corrected, handing her one, seeming not to remember he'd said it would ruin her appetite a moment ago. He looked lost, shell-shocked. One hand remained fisted on the table.

Emma pulled a chair out and sank into it, feeling David's anguish. *Richard was right. This is harder than I thought.* She couldn't pull her gaze away from her beautiful daughter.

"May I have a puppy?" The sly grin Kensington cast toward David would've been funny if circumstances were different.

"No, not now!" He rubbed his forehead. "You didn't have anyone when you left, Emma. All you had was her, but that didn't stop you…"

With a jerking motion, he dashed at his eyes, and Emma looked away. It felt like a vacuum was depleting the air around them.

Fidgeting, Kensington turned and took David's face in her hands. "What's wrong, Daddy? Are you sad? A puppy would help."

"Nothing, Kenz. I'm not sad. And no puppy, so stop asking. No means no. I, uh, I need to talk to your—" he shot Emma an angry glare "—to Emma. Let's go next door and see if you can play with Angela, okay?" He stood with Kensington in his arms. "I'll be right back."

"You could leave her here." Emma swallowed nervously. "I mean, while you go call or ask…" her voice trailed off. His look of distrust nearly brought her to her knees.

"No, I'll take *my* daughter with me. I need to get her out of here for a few minutes."

"You don't think I'd run off with her, do you?" Emma asked, horrified.

He shrugged. "I don't know. I guess you'd be more likely to just run off and leave her by herself." He slammed the door so hard it knocked a picture crooked.

Emma let out a ragged breath. Despite her friends' warnings, nothing had prepared her for David's reception. The pain she'd borne for the last four and a half years seemed minor in comparison to his. This hadn't been her intent. She picked up her purse to leave, but paused, her hand on the doorknob.

"Mama," the little girl had said. *How did she know who I was?*

Had David mentioned her? And if so, why? Or was it innate knowledge? All her life, Emma had been the girl who didn't matter. Her father had left before she was born. Her mother had sold her for drugs. No one had ever fought for her or given a damn whether she came or went. Even Ken had abandoned her on some level, and she had perpetuated the generational cycle after Kensington's birth.

She didn't want her daughter to ever feel unloved or unwanted. She wanted to make amends as best she could, to prove to David—and to herself—that she had changed. She dropped her hand and walked back into the kitchen to wait. There was no way in hell she could leave now. *Be brave.* It was her daily mantra. There had to be a way she could make David understand she didn't mean to take Kensington from him, she just wanted to be in her life. Using her nervous energy, Emma cleaned the kitchen and prayed to any deity that might listen. She needed David to give her a chance.

Picking up the old, worn bear, she hugged it and wandered down the hall to get a glimpse of Kensington's room. Peeking in the first room, she knew it was David's. Neat, but with books piled everywhere—biographies, histories, true crime, and suspense. His Bible sat on the bedside table with his glasses on top of it, next to a picture of Kensington. Scribbled crayon drawings decorated his walls, revealing a man who loved his daughter.

Emma moved to the room across the hall and smiled when she stepped through the door labeled "Princess." A small, unmade bed with a pink bunny in it caught her attention first. It was the bunny David had bought right after Kensington's birth. Barbie dolls, puzzles, princess costumes, and books littered the hardwood floor. Someone had painted a castle in the clouds on one of the pale blue walls. Emma made the bed, then sat, holding her old bear as she looked around her daughter's room. On the bedside table was a fairy-tale book with a bookmark in it. She bet David read to her every night and felt a pang of jealousy as she pictured the cozy scene.

Picking up a framed photo of David with Kensington dressed up like a princess, she smiled and ran her finger over it, memorizing each detail. Another picture of an older couple with Kensington and two older boys stood next to it. She assumed they were David's parents and nephews. Emma picked up a small pink Bible and thumbed through it, stopping when she came to a picture of her holding Kensington at the hospital. David had written "Mama" on the photo. A sob caught in her throat, and she clutched her stomach as if she'd been sucker punched.

Kensington did know her—David had made sure of it. Tears of remorse and recrimination coursed down her face. She buried her face in the old bear, inhaling the scent of dreams given up and probably lost forever.

Chapter Eight

"*Who?*" Jennifer shrieked, her eyes snapping with surprised fury. "Angela, you and Kenzie go upstairs to your room and play. And don't be mean to your baby brother. Let him play, too."

"But he's a boy," the tiny, dark-haired girl complained.

When her mother gave her a look, she grabbed Kenzie's hand and left without another word.

David was always impressed by this ability and chalked it up to the double X chromosome. His mother had the same gift.

Jennifer turned back to David, slamming her hand on the counter. "What is *she* doing here? She hasn't had anything to do with Kenzie for over four years! Let me call Jimmy; he's a lawyer."

"No, I'll handle it." David didn't want Dylan's people getting involved. "I just need you to keep Kenzie for a while so I can talk to her. I don't want her seeing me upset or hearing what could turn into an ugly argument."

Jennifer huffed her exasperation.

"Please?"

"Okay. I'm sorry. I'm just in shock, and I don't want to see you or Kenzie get hurt." She gave him a quick hug and kiss on the cheek. "And I mean it. If you need a lawyer, let us know."

David trudged back to the cottage he'd rented from Jennifer and Dylan, wanting to hear—yet at the same time dreading—Emma's explanation for reappearing in their lives. He prayed for guidance and not to lose his patience before entering his home. Upon opening the door, the smell of warm cookies greeted him. His stomach rolled in protest. He didn't think he'd ever like the smell again. Looking around, his annoyance escalated.

Where is she? Did she run again?

A muffled sound came from Kenzie's room, infuriating him. But as he marched down the hall, concern tempered his resentment, and he leaned against the doorframe. Eyes closed, clutching Kenzie's bear, Emma was curled in a tight ball. A few tears remained on her flushed cheek. It was a familiar scene and one that brought back painful memories. Part of him wanted to take her in his arms and comfort her, but the part that wanted to throw her out of his home kept him rooted at the doorway.

She wasn't the same girl who'd left years ago. Her dark brown hair was shorter, just brushing the top of her shoulders. He liked the bangs; they softened her features. Gold hoops adorned her ears, and he saw no other jewelry. He didn't want to explore why not seeing a wedding band relieved him. Her soft wrap dress in muted earth tones hugged her body, revealing soft, inviting curves. Polished red toenails peeked from her sandals. Perversely, he wondered if she still had the awful gray hoodie.

"Emma."

She sat up with a start, her eyes wide. She still had the same stubborn little chin, the faint smattering of freckles, and those beautiful hazel eyes, now bright with tears. Running a shaking hand through her hair, she wiped her face and stood, bringing her hands in front of her stomach. David's heart sank, and a cold knot of fear settled in his gut when he remembered she couldn't have any more children. Maybe he did need a lawyer.

"I'm sorry. I just wanted to see her room. I should have waited on you." Emma tucked the picture of her with Kensington back in the Bible and placed the old brown bear on the bed. She smiled, timidly. "I see my old teddy bear is loved."

"Her favorite," David conceded and motioned for Emma to sit.

He sat on the floor with his back to Kenzie's bookcase as Emma positioned herself on the edge of the bed. They sat in a stony silence for a couple of minutes until David closed his eyes. Just the sight of her pained him.

"Kensington's beautiful." She spoke only slightly above a whisper.

"She looks like you," David admitted reluctantly. He opened his eyes and found hers misty, with the haunted look he remembered so well. When he could trust his voice not to break, he asked the questions that plagued his heart. "Why are you here? What do you want with *my* daughter?"

"I want to be a part of her life. I *need* to be part of her life." She spoke without hesitation, with a newfound air of self-assurance.

He found it unnerving. This wasn't the Emma he knew. "You didn't want her, or need her, when you ran out on her," he countered. "Why now?" *You left her. Me. Us.*

"I was lost, destitute, and unable to take care of myself, much less a child. I had no future. W-What kind of life could I have given her then?" She broke eye contact with him and shoved a lock of hair behind her ear.

His breathing eased. This Emma he knew — the insecure Emma, not the quiet, determined woman who wanted to insinuate her way back into their lives.

"That excuse won't work with me. I was here to help you. Mrs. Jordan, Jennifer, and Dylan were here to help you. *You refused.* Instead, you left me with a baby who needed her mother. Do you have any idea what you put us through?" David leapt to his feet and began to pace, four and a half years of pent-up anger and frustration simmering just below the surface of his control.

"I'm sorry."

He bit back a string of expletives. Words he never used suddenly came to the forefront of his mind. "*You're sorry?*" He ground his teeth together so hard his jaw hurt, and he couldn't curb the sarcasm. "That's it? You're sorry, so I should just let you march back in here and disrupt my life, *yet again?* You're sorry, so I should let you into Kenzie's life? What do you expect her to do when you can't deal and take off running again for God knows where? I will *not* allow you to break my daughter's heart. Do you understand me? Get out! Get out of my house and get out of our lives and don't come back! I'm calling my lawyer." He prayed his bluff would work as he shook with rage and fear, pointing at the door.

"I'm not leaving." She stood and faced him. "I have nowhere else to go. I'm thinking about moving here to Pine Bluff. I want to be part of my daughter's life. I'm a different person now. Let me prove it to you; let me show you." Her voice trembled, but she lifted her chin and looked him square in the eyes.

"No thanks. I didn't want your *services* back then, and I'm not interested now."

The resounding slap she leveled across his face echoed between them. Emma looked as startled by her reaction as he felt.

"Oh my God. I'm so sorry," she gasped, turning away, her hands covering her red face.

Guilt overtook his rage. Never in his life had he spoken so crudely to a woman. "No, I'm sorry. I shouldn't have said that. It was uncalled for, and I shouldn't have gone there."

"Is that what you think? That I'm still a prostitute?"

He shrugged. "I don't know. How would I know? Look, I can't bear the thought of Kenzie being hurt."

Shoving his pride to the side, he decided to beg. He'd do anything to keep Kenzie.

"Don't take her from me, Emma," he pleaded. "*Please don't take her.*"

"You think I'm here to take her?"

He shrugged. "You never contacted us after you left." David rubbed the back of his neck.

Emma walked to the window and looked out. "I never felt worthy or good enough…" Her breath hitched. "I wanted to—I truly did—I-I just had to get my shit together. I just couldn't, until Richard…"

"Who's Richard?" His heart felt heavy, ready to implode at any minute. Was this her husband? Did they have money? He didn't want to be any more beholden to Jennifer and Dylan than he already was, but he might need to accept her offer of a lawyer after all.

"He was the second-best thing to ever happen to me." She kept her back to him, staring out the window.

"What was the first?"

She turned toward him, smiling sadly. "Getting caught trying to steal a jar of peanut butter."

As her confession sunk in, a knock interrupted them. Groaning, David stormed out of Kenzie's room with Emma following. He flung open the door to find Dylan leaning against the frame, his arms crossed in front of his chest.

"I'm supposed to be here on some pretense or another. Got a cup of sugar or some other shit I could borrow?" Dylan asked. His steely blue eyes flickered toward Emma, and he gave a curt nod, not bothering to hide his curiosity. "Emma."

"Dylan." She held her head high, but her eyes were wide and her throat bobbled.

"Jennifer is too nosy and overprotective," David complained, closing the front door as Dylan came in.

"Really?" he asked with mock surprise and a chuckle. "Surely you jest. Not my Jen."

David was in no mood for humor and crossed his arms. "We're fine."

Emma retrieved her checkbook from her purse. Tearing a check out, she handed it to Dylan. "I was going to stop by later, but you saved me a trip. Thank you…*for everything.* This is my final payment, and I added interest to it."

"This isn't necessary," Dylan replied, his eyes cutting from David to the floor. He stuck his hands in his pocket and shifted nervously.

"I insist." Emma urged him to take the check.

Dylan shoved it in his pocket and nodded. He rocked on his feet, refusing to make eye contact with David.

"What's going on here?" David looked back and forth from Dylan to Emma. "Tell me what this is about." He shoved a hand through his hair and, with a grimace, wiped cookie dough off on his jeans.

"You haven't told him?" Dylan backed up a step.

Emma shook her head. "I haven't had a chance…"

"Oh shit." Dylan looked like a deer caught in the headlights, and he popped a piece of candy in his mouth.

David's eyes narrowed. "Someone needs to tell me what's going on, because I'm seriously about to lose it."

"It doesn't concern you. I've been paying Dylan back for the baby stuff his wife bought when Kensington was born."

"What part of *that* doesn't concern *me?*" David leaned against the kitchen counter for support, attempting to process what she'd just said. "She's *my* daughter!"

"I've been sending Dylan money to pay off my debt. Sometimes it was just a few bucks, but I paid what I could, when I could..." Her voice trailed off.

David shook his head and stared at Dylan. Realization dawned, and he spun to face Emma. "Wait a minute. Did you just say you've been paying *Dylan?* That's how you knew we were still here? How *nice.* Did you two exchange Christmas cards and penpal letters, too?"

When did I become so sarcastic and snarky? At this moment, he didn't like himself, much less the people standing before him.

"I made arrangements before I left..."

He slammed his fist on the counter, and she jumped.

"Before you left?" He turned, grabbed Dylan by the front of his shirt, and shoved him against the wall. "You knew she was leaving? You've known where she was all along? What did you make Emma do as payment for this so-called arrangement?"

"Calm down, and I resent the hell out of your implication," Dylan ground out, shrugging out of his grasp. "I've *never* been unfaithful to my wife. It wasn't like that. Now keep your damn hands off me."

David closed his eyes, took a deep breath, and stepped back. The thought of Emma with Dylan had made him physically sick. Even more disturbing was his relief when Dylan denied it. The walls of his home felt like they were closing in on him, robbing him of air.

"I've got to get out of here before I do or say something I'll regret. Don't be here when I return. *Either of you.*" He left, slamming the front door and sprinting through the woods toward the lake. Afraid, angry, and hurt, he ran until his heart felt like it would burst. Then he pushed harder, running as if his life depended on it.

"Why the hell didn't you tell me you were coming back?" Dylan roared. His eyes glinted with anger. "Couldn't you have made your final payment by mail like all the others? Do you know how much shit you've just stirred?"

Emma sank into a chair at the kitchen table and rubbed her aching head. "I'm sorry. I've made a terrible mess of this. I haven't been thinking clearly. Richard died, and two days later I found out my mother died of an overdose."

"Richard?"

"A friend."

Dylan blew out a deep breath. "I'm sorry. I didn't know about your losses. I'm just confused as to why you didn't give me any warning—not to mention what you've done to preacher man."

"Don't be sorry. She was a horrible mother, even worse than me. But with Richard's death and then hers, I realized I have no one except Kensington. Things are different. I'm a better person, able to hold my head up. Lately, whenever I think about my daughter, it feels like the hole in my heart is widening to the size of the Grand Canyon. I've obsessed over her. I just wanted to see her, to let her know I love her. I didn't think things through, just got in my car and here I am…"

Emma paused to collect herself. Twisting her hands together, she shifted uncomfortably as she struggled to find the right words.

"I'd always planned to give her up for adoption. I know leaving her was wrong, but at the time, I felt like I didn't have any other choice. David loved Kensington. I saw it every time he was with her. The thought of giving her to a stranger…I knew he'd take care of her." She pressed her fingers into her eyes. "I don't want to hurt either of them. God, I thought I was a better person, but now I see I'm still selfish. I shouldn't have come."

She stood to leave. "Tell David I'm sorry. I won't bother him again."

"Sit your ass down. You're not leaving. Tell me what happened after you left here. You've barely told me anything." Pulling out a chair, he turned it around and sat, leaning his arms over the back.

Emma swallowed her fear and regrets. "I actually need to start when I first arrived in Pine Bluff, more than four years ago. Three weeks before Kensington's birth, I'd made a run for it, to escape Scott—"

"Kenzie's father?"

"No, my pimp. Kenzie's biological father died overseas in a roadside bomb."

"Geezus, Emma. I'm sorry. And wait, you had a pimp?"

"It's a long, unpleasant story, so I'll hit the highlights. I hate using the term victim, but I was trafficked. Anyway, Scott regarded me as his property, and he wasn't pleased about my pregnancy. I ran off to avoid having an abortion. A few weeks later, he found me in Pine Bluff—apparently through a tracer he'd put on my phone. He beat the hell out of me for my 'disobedience and disrespect.' Lucky for me, he created enough ruckus at the hotel that someone called the cops, and I escaped. You know the rest of that story: David caught me shoplifting, Kensington was born. But I was afraid Scott would find me again if I stayed here. Or he'd do something to Kensington, so I left.

"I ended up on the run with my friend Angel. I tried to endure the pain and guilt of abandoning my baby, but I couldn't handle it. My depression spiraled, and Angel was strung out on drugs…Let's just say my life got a lot worse before it got better. But I survived, and I've worked hard to change.

"I've been in counseling. I've earned my GED and held down a real job. I made *good* friends. I had my life back—or rather I *had* a life. I'd been planning to contact David to apologize. I wanted to see if I could be part of my daughter's life. Ever since I left, it's always been my intention to return, to try to redeem myself. But I learned in counseling that I had to work on *me* before I could work on repairing my relationships…

"But then Richard—someone I cared deeply about—became ill and died. Then my mother passed, and Angel's gone. I realized I have no one. All my old insecurities flared, and I couldn't stop thinking about Kensington."

Dylan sighed. "I don't know what to say."

Emma went to her purse and pulled out three photos. "I've practically worn the ink off these pictures you sent me. Thank you. I know you didn't have to do it."

Dylan glanced at them and handed them back. "I sent more, but your address changed, and they were returned by the postal service…Shit."

"I know what I did was unforgivable, but I want to see if I can develop a relationship with my daughter. I want her to know it wasn't her fault I gave her up. I did it *for* her. Out of love."

"You should never have run in the first place." Dylan tapped the table with his thumb.

"I realize that now, but I didn't trust anyone…"

He sighed. "Dammit, you should've contacted me, and let me prepare David for this shock. And, uh, please don't mention the pictures to David or Jen. I'm in deep enough shit as it is. Jesus H. Christ, Emma. He's angrier than I've ever seen him, and trust me,

I've seen him angry plenty of times." Dylan rubbed a hand across his furrowed brow. "I don't even want to think about what's going to happen when Jen finds out we've been in touch. I may end up sleeping on the couch for the rest of my life."

"Sorry," Emma whispered. "I was afraid if I asked to see my daughter, the answer would be no. I don't know what I'm doing. I've fucked everything up."

What did I expect? That David would welcome me back with open arms?

Dylan ran a hand through his hair. "If David says no, where will you go?"

"I don't know."

Dylan stared at her for a moment and muttered, "I may regret this." He stood. "Look, come with me and we'll talk to Mrs. J. Maybe you can stay in the garage apartment until we get this mess settled. It's empty. David's usually the epitome of reasonable; maybe he'll come around. This will give me time to figure out how to explain all of this to my wife. Fair warning, Jen isn't pleased about your homecoming and will probably blow an amp when she learns we may be neighbors."

"Thank you, Dylan. I-I don't deserve this, but thank you." She nodded, breathing deeply and trying to tell herself it would be all right.

David leaned against the railing on the dock, shaking from the run, unable to breathe. He'd logged over ten miles, and it felt like a vise was squeezing his chest. He sank to his knees with his head against the railing and repeated the prayer he'd repeated almost nonstop since he saw Emma's face.

Please don't let her take my daughter from me.

Never had he felt so alone and scared. After a moment, he forced a deep breath and dragged himself to his feet, slowly making his way to Jennifer's. More than anything else, he needed to hold Kenzie, to feel her arms around his neck and hear her call him Daddy. He'd even take an eye roll.

As he neared the huge house the McAthies lived in, he heard shrieks of laughter from the backyard. Kenzie and Angela ran back and forth, playing tag. Jennifer's dark hair curled with perspiration as she watched the girls, and she laughed as she pushed Riordan in his baby swing. Jennifer was a natural when it came to mother-hood—loving, firm, and always there for her kids. Not at all like the woman who'd abandoned hers.

When Kenzie became aware of his presence, she ran toward him with a squeal. He knelt and wrapped his arms around her, holding her so tightly she squirmed.

"Stoooooop, Daddy! You're sweaty and stink! Lemme go. You're it," she yelled. He let her go and half-heartedly chased the girls until he caught Angela and tagged her. Collapsing in a chair next to the swing set, he closed his eyes. After a few minutes he became concerned when his sweating continued and his trembling didn't abate. He'd be in trouble soon.

"You okay?" Jennifer asked. Her brow furrowed.

"N-No," he replied, shaking all over. "Carbs."

"Watch Rory." Jennifer ran inside.

David managed to stand and give the baby a push in the swing. Riordan gave him a wide, drooling grin. Jennifer returned and handed him a glass of orange juice and some peanut butter crackers.

"Thanks." He downed the orange juice and ate to get his glucose elevated. Still thirsty, he turned on the hose and drank. Then he squirted the two little girls, making them squeal and laugh. Wiping his mouth with the back of his hand, he returned to the swing set.

"Where's Dylan?"

Jennifer's mouth thinned into a straight line. "In his studio, hid-ing. I'm not happy with our new neighbor, or my husband's involve-ment in all of this. I'm really sorry, David."

"New neighbor?" Tingling apprehension replaced his hypoglycemia.

"Afraid so. Dylan convinced Mrs. J to rent the garage apartment to Emma. I told them both they should've talked to you first."

Jennifer's eyes went wide at the expletive that left his mouth. He apologized and grabbed a reluctant Kenzie to march home.

Chapter Nine

"Where's Mama?" Kenzie asked, patting the bubbles in the bathtub.

"Too close for comfort," David muttered.

At his daughter's inquisitive look, he sighed, wondering how much to tell her. What could he tell her? He didn't really know much more than she did. He washed her face and handed her the washcloth.

"Remember how I told you about the best Christmas present I ever received?"

"Me! Mama gave me to you. She loved me, but she had to go away."

"That's right. And now she's back…"

And here's the million-dollar question, why? David rubbed his brow, unsure what to say.

"Does she like princesses?"

"I, um, guess so. Don't all girls?" He lifted Kenzie out of the bath and dried her off, helping her into her nightgown and panties.

"I bet she likes puppies. Puppies are fun. What about Barbie? Does she like Barbie? Books? I love books. Does she like ice cream? I hate peas. Does Mama hate peas?"

"I don't know." David plastered on a smile to hide his frustration and growing panic. "I love you, Kenzie McFrenzie."

She hugged his neck. "Love you more."

Not possible. He hugged her tight, wishing he could whisk her away and keep her safe in a tower like one of her beloved princesses.

"Go pick up your puzzle from the coffee table."

"Okay." She shuffled off—without an argument for a change.

Grateful for at least one thing going right today, David knelt and wiped up the mess in the bathroom. How one kid could slosh this much water out of a deep, claw-foot bathtub never ceased to amaze him.

When the knock on the front door he'd been dreading came, he closed his eyes for a moment, taking time to ask for help dealing with this situation. He heard Kenzie answer the door, and his heart stopped for a moment. What if Emma grabbed her and ran? He chastised himself for his paranoia when he heard the door close and Kenzie's nonstop chattering begin.

His heart hammered and his breathing hitched when Kenzie and Emma came to the doorway of the bathroom. He stood, feeling unsettled, and tried not to stare, still not used to the changes in Emma's appearance. She was prettier than he'd remembered, and her air of quiet determination only added to her attractiveness—which angered him. Why couldn't she be the distrusting, foul-mouthed girl who'd left him with a newborn? He knew how to approach that person.

She seemed almost relaxed in long khaki shorts and a blue tank top. Little, if any, makeup obscured the smattering of freckles across her nose. Her messy ponytail revealed a long neck he remembered kissing…

He hung up Kenzie's towel, schooling his face in disinterest before turning around.

Emma held a ready-made, covered veggie tray in her hands. "Hi. I come bearing gifts, perhaps a peace offering? I, uh, picked it up when I grabbed a few groceries." She gave him a tentative, hopeful smile.

Resigned, he looked at Kenzie. "Brush your teeth and get ready for bed, please."

"No, Daddy," Kenzie whined.

"Excuse me?"

"I wanna see her. *Mama.*" Kenzie pointed at Emma and gave him the smile she used when she wanted something.

An unmistakable look of longing crossed both ladies' faces as they stared at him, and shyly at each other. He blew his hair off his forehead and replied, "Brush your teeth and Em—uh, your mother can put you to bed tonight."

When he left the bathroom, Emma followed him, hot on his heels back to the kitchen.

"Thank you!" Her eyes shone with excitement as she placed the tray on the table.

Aware that little ears heard everything, he kept his voice even, despite wanting to punch a wall. "After Kenzie's asleep, we're going to talk, and you're going to tell me what your plans are for my daughter."

Emma nodded, her smile brightening her face. "Yes, of course. Again, thank you."

Kenzie walked in carrying the beloved Teddy. David squatted and held her hand, afraid of letting go. Was this the beginning of the end? Was he making a huge mistake? Hazel eyes, the mirror of her mother's, met his, full of trust and love.

"Kenzie, this is Emma. She's your mother." He swallowed the lump in his throat and added, "Mama."

"I know, Daddy."

Looking at her, he saw none of his conflicted emotions reflected in her face, just simple acceptance. He wished it could be that easy for him.

She reached out and cradled his cheek in her hand. As if sensing his fear, she said, "Love you."

"Love you more." He returned her smile and with a resigned nod, stood and escorted them to Kenzie's bedroom.

Emma watched Kensington climb into bed and scoot over so David could sit beside her. He gave her a kiss good night and one for Teddy as well. When he brushed an errant curl out of the little girl's face, she remembered him doing the same for her in the hospital all those years ago.

"Tell me something good about today." David's voice sounded strained and his back seemed stiff.

With a shy smile, Kenzie pointed at her. Emma caught her breath and returned the smile. David glanced over, pain etching his face, and her smile fell. She chewed the inside of her mouth. It wasn't her intent to hurt him. David meant more to her than he'd ever realize. He'd saved her life, raised her daughter, and shown her what unconditional love looked like. She was determined to erase his fear.

"And was there anything bad about today?"

"Rory pooped in his diaper. It was gross." Kensington's nose wrinkled.

David chuckled, but it sounded forced. "Boys are pretty disgusting, huh?"

Kensington nodded in total agreement.

"Keep that thought for at least another thirty years, okay?"

"Okay, Daddy. Except Connor, he's cute."

"Ah, yes, I suppose he is. He's also *way* too old for you." He tapped her nose and stood. "Mama's going to read you a bedtime story and hear your prayers."

Kenzie squealed and clapped.

Emma's eyebrows lifted. "Really?"

"One story and prayers. Don't let her coerce you into any more." Scrubbing a hand over his face, he moved so she could sit on the bed.

He stood in the doorway for a moment. His look of resignation and abject despair tempered her excitement.

Then he walked out, leaving her alone with her daughter for the first time since she'd left her in the hospital. Her hands shook as she picked up the fairy-tale book and turned to where the bookmark had been placed. Barely speaking above a whisper, she began the story of The Three Little Pigs.

"No, that's not right," Kensington interrupted, her lower lip pushed forward, in danger of becoming a full-blown pout.

"W-What?" Emma's heart hammered. *What did I do wrong? I can't even read a story right?*

"Make the voices."

"The voices?"

"Like this, Mama. The way Daddy does it." Kensington scrunched her face, drew her hands into claws and growled, "*Huff* and *puff.*"

Emma laughed nervously. "Oh, I see. Sorry." She started over and attempted different voices for each of the characters. She wasn't a great reader, though, and nervousness made her stutter in several parts. When she finished, Kensington said her prayers. Emma had to bite her lip to contain her emotion when her daughter thanked God for her daddy and mama. She then added a request for a puppy.

Emma leaned over and kissed her daughter for the first time in four and a half years, unable to contain the tears spilling down her cheeks. "I love you, Kensington. I always have."

Kensington's arms wrapped around her neck, and she kissed her damp cheek. "I know. Daddy told me."

Her heart felt ready to explode. Emma turned off the bedside lamp and rubbed Kensington's back until she fell asleep. She gave her another gentle kiss and reluctantly left to find David.

Stepping into the hall, she nearly tripped over him just outside the door. He sat with his arms wrapped around his legs, his forehead resting on his knees. When he noticed her, he jumped to his feet. She wondered if he'd worn the faded *World's Best Dad* T-shirt on purpose. Together, they walked to the kitchen. Instead of sitting, he stood at the sink with his back toward her and hung his head for a full, tense minute. When he turned to face her, he looked lost.

Emma stepped forward and looked up into his red-rimmed eyes, cupping his rough cheek with her hand. "I'm so sorry. I've done this so wrong…" She took a deep breath. "I came here for two reasons. To see my daughter, and to thank you for loving her enough for both of us…"

"Don't take her from me."

"Never," she gasped, stepping back. She wrapped her arms tight around her chest, forcing herself to maintain eye contact when all she wanted to do was sink to the floor and hide. Tears stung her eyes and slipped down her face.

He looked at the ceiling, his throat working up and down, before he pulled her into his arms. Relief washed over her and she sagged against him, crying into his soft T-shirt. Resting his cheek on top of her head, he patted her back.

"Shhh. Don't cry."

Emma stepped away and wiped her tears. "I'm sorry. I've been an emotional wreck today. I've caused you so much pain and worry.

I promise it wasn't my intention. I've made a horrible mess of everything. You're a wonderful father, and I just needed to see her, to tell her how much I love her. I don't want to be like my mother..."

"Calm down. You're babbling. To be honest, I'm still in shock, trying to process my feelings. You should have called me first. But please, stop crying and talk to me." David handed her a paper towel.

She drew in a ragged breath and blew her nose in a loud, most-unladylike fashion. David chuckled, and the tension between them lightened marginally. He started a pot of decaf and motioned for her to sit at the kitchen table. With his back to the counter, he crossed his arms in front of his chest.

"Why, Emma? Why did you leave? And why did you hang up on me that night?"

Emma met his gaze without flinching. She had to make him understand. "I knew I couldn't care for her. It had never been my intention to keep her...but then she came early. I was scared. I was broke. I was beat down. My brain was scrambled from...I didn't..." Emma took a deep breath and tried again. "I had planned all along to give her up for adoption. I told you that when she was born..." She dropped her gaze and clenched her hands together, struggling to keep her emotions in check. "I was alone and on the run, making a living any way I could."

"Prostituting." His voice was quiet, pained even, but held no judgment.

Emma lifted her chin and stared him straight in the eyes, but shame heated her cheeks. "Yes."

"Why?"

"I was trapped. I didn't have an education, and I didn't have any skills. It was all I knew." She shrugged and attempted to seem nonchalant, her old defense mechanisms kicking in to protect her fragile self-worth.

"Trapped?"

"I was a commodity. My pimp owned me; I did what I was told or I got beat."

The color drained from David's face. "Human trafficking?"

"Yes. I had run away, but I didn't get far. Two nights before you caught me shoplifting, my pimp, Scott, found me. He beat me—"

"Dear God, Emma..."

She didn't respond until she could speak without crying. "I wanted Kensington to have a better life than I did." *Hooker, whore, prostitute...*

She inhaled and exhaled, using the visualization tool her therapist had taught her to put a mental brake on her inner monologue.

"I didn't want her to feel unworthy of love—or worse, end up like me." Emma raised her chin again and forced herself to make eye contact. "You were so kind, you cared, and I knew you would never hurt her. You loved her. I saw it when you held her, when you talked to her. What I did to you was wrong, but I don't regret it. I did it for her sake. She's loved, and she's happy."

"I do love her. She's my life." David clasped his hands behind his head and tipped his head back for a moment. "I can't imagine my life without her. But you should've gone to the police. At the hospital, they would've protected you. I would've done anything I could to help you."

Emma nodded. "I know that now. But I'd seen things happen to others. I knew what Scott was capable of, and I was scared…After I left, I hated myself, hated what I was, what I'd done to you. It got so bad that I didn't want to live anymore with the guilt, the self-hatred. I attempted to end it all, but I even failed at that. That was the night I hung up on you…" She looked at the floor, unable to face him. "I was so lost," she murmured, more to herself than him.

She stood and walked to the sink, keeping her back to David. "I didn't truly believe I could trust you. Or anyone, for that matter. Crazy, right? I trusted you'd care for Kensington, but I didn't think I was worthy of love, of anyone caring about *me*. My own mother didn't want me; why would anyone else?

"A few years later, when I was safe in a shelter for girls like me, my therapist asked me what I wanted. And I realized I wanted what you had so freely given me. You treated me with respect. You didn't judge me. You treated me like a person, like someone who mattered. Because of your thoughtfulness, I wanted to change, but I didn't know how. Kensington deserved better than a mother who didn't even like herself. I had to learn how to be me, how to be a decent human being, how to love."

"I still don't understand why you ran away to do all those things." His voice had risen, but he quickly lowered it. "You never gave me a chance. I would've helped you…"

She sighed. "The day you showed me the nursery at Mrs. Jordan's, it completely overwhelmed me. No one had *ever* given me anything without expecting something in return.

"At the time, only two people had ever given a damn about me—Kensington's father, David Kensington—Ken, who died serving our country overseas and never even knew I was pregnant. And my best friend, Angel Sinclair, who to this day, repeatedly loses the battle with his demons and falls back to shooting heroin. I didn't know what to do. The kindness everyone here offered was too much. I didn't feel worthy of it, and it terrified me.

"Before I left, I went to Dylan and told him I wanted to pay him back. It was my desperate attempt to maintain a shred of dignity, and he seemed to understand I needed to do that. He wrote down the amount he'd spent on an envelope and gave it to me, but he didn't know I planned to leave. I don't think he really believed I'd pay him back. Over the years, I've mailed him money any time I could, even if it was just a couple of dollars." She rubbed the little finger Scott had broken one time when he'd caught her trying to steal two bucks.

"I'd like to kill Dylan."

Emma clasped her hands and pleaded, "Please don't blame him. Knowing I had this debt is the only thing that kept me going at times. I needed to pay it back for Kensington's sake. I prayed that someday I'd be good enough to come back and tell her in person how much I truly love her. I realize now I should have contacted you, or at the very least told Dylan when I'd decided to come back. I'm far from perfect, but I promise I'm trying to be better."

She poured two cups of coffee and handed him one.

"It's been more than four years…" David's voice cracked, and he slammed his fist on the table. "*Four years*, Emma! I need more. Give me every last detail. All of this impacts my daughter and her well-being."

"It's ugly—"

"No uglier than abandoning a baby." He dropped his head and blew out a slow breath. "Sorry. Please continue."

"After I left here, I hooked up with Angel. He was Ken's best friend, and now he's mine. A few months later, though, we ended up parting ways in Atlanta. He can't stay in one place for too long. Once I was alone again, Scott found me at a gas station, and being conditioned like a dog, I didn't resist him. I thought fighting would only make it worse. But this time was different. He was still furious at me for leaving…" She shuddered.

"Scott *who?*" David growled, clenching his fists.

"His last name isn't important. He's dead to me. Thankfully, last I heard he's serving time for tax evasion."

No way she'd ever reveal his name. Somehow, he'd find her and torture her before killing her. Or worse, he'd hurt Kensington, or David.

"I bided my time, earning Scott's trust enough to be allowed to get back out and work. I knew it was the only way I'd ever escape. There was a convention in Birmingham, and I, uh, finished my job one night, and as I was leaving, a woman approached me. I was terrified, but I knew that was my chance. She offered me hope, a safe place to stay. It was a shelter for women like me. I stayed for two years. There I learned I'm not a bad person.

"When I left the shelter, I found Angel again. No matter what, we manage to stay in touch. We were both in a good place for once. He was clean from drugs and got us jobs in a diner in Atlanta, where he grew up. But he was restless as usual, and once I got settled, he left. I wanted roots, someplace permanent. I was tired of being on the run. I thrived with the routine of a daily job, and it turns out, I'm a good waitress. I started feeling better about myself. I was finally good at something besides…" Emma shrugged. "You know."

David ran a finger along the grain of the wood table as he listened to her story.

"After a while I had a regular customer at the diner, a widower named Richard Raginhard. He always treated me like a lady. He'd come in every evening after work for supper. He called me Em, just like you used to, and his thoughtfulness reminded me a lot of you.

"At first I liked him because he tipped well. But as I got to know him, it was more than money. When he'd smile and say, 'Thanks for the great meal and company,' it made me happy." She warmed at the memory.

"One night, he didn't come in. I worried all night, wondering what had happened to him. As I locked up, he finally drove up and apologized over and over for being so late. He said he'd had a late meeting.

"He offered me a ride home. I told him I only lived a few blocks away and usually walked, which distressed him. He didn't think I should be walking alone that late at night. I found out later that Richard was an old friend of Angel's family, a law partner with his brother and dad. Angel knew he'd look out for me.

"When Richard and I got to my apartment, I invited him in and offered to fix him a sandwich. He seemed so sad that night. I knew he was a lonely man; he had often talked about his late wife. I wanted to make him feel better. So I offered him a meal and the only other thing I thought men wanted."

David raised his eyes to hers, not saying a word, but his face tightened.

"He turned me down. He was the second man to ever tell me no." She looked at David for a moment before looking away. "He told me I was better than that, that I deserved to be treated like a princess. That I didn't have to have sex with him to earn his attention." Tears streamed down her cheeks. "He gave me a kiss on the cheek and asked if I would consider dating an older man. I was shocked — not by the fact that he was thirty-two years older than me, but by the fact that he'd invited me on a date. I'd never been on a date in my life."

"Not even in high school? Or with Ken or Angel?" David asked.

"I didn't go to high school. My mother sold me for drugs." She spoke matter-of-factly.

"My God. How old were you?" he croaked.

"Twelve."

"Dear God," David gasped, covering his face.

His reaction made her miss Richard. He'd done the same thing when she told him. She shrugged. She wasn't looking for sympathy, just telling the story of her life.

"It's okay. I was drugged. I don't remember it," Emma lied, looking away. The first time had been horrific. But she'd soon learned not to show emotion. When she cried, she was beaten. But if she "behaved," she was rewarded with affection and a little freedom. Still, a small part of her had never been subdued. She'd always longed for something more…

Taking a deep breath, she continued. "And I didn't *date* Ken. It just happened — hormones, I guess. Angel and I never dated. Ken was his best friend; he'd never cross that line.

"Anyway, I told Richard I would like to go out on a date with him. Then he asked if he could stay the night on my couch. He couldn't face going home to his empty house. I gave him a blanket and a pillow. Later I heard him crying. I ended up holding him all night. I thought he was depressed because he missed his wife.

"We started dating—movies, out to eat, walks in the park. He insisted I complete the GED classes I'd started while in the shelter. He helped me study and took me to a fancy restaurant to celebrate when I passed. That night he told me he needed me. I assumed he meant he finally wanted to have sex." She sank back into her chair and looked at her clasped hands on the table.

"That wasn't what he meant at all. He needed me to care for him because he was *dying*. The night I'd held him as he wept was the day he'd learned he had an inoperable cancer…a brain tumor. And then he told me he wanted to take care of *me* and asked me to marry him." Her lower lip trembled, and she covered her face, trying to contain her grief.

"Did you?"

"No. It felt like another form of prostitution. I cared for him, but I didn't love him like a wife should, and I refused to take advantage of him. But we remained friends, and I was there for him at the end. We would talk, and I told him *everything*. He encouraged me to contact you. He said it was important for me to find out if I could establish a relationship with my daughter, especially since I'd have no one after he died."

Emma took a deep breath. "I should have listened to him. He'd kick my ass if he knew I'd surprised you like I did…"

David blew out a deep breath, still studying the table.

"Because Richard needed me, I put aside my developing plan to contact you. It had already been close to four years, and truthfully, I still didn't know what to say, how to ask…So I focused my attention on him and continued with my therapy and worked my job. He didn't have anyone but me, and he didn't have much time left. The last month of his life, he suffered horribly. I quit my job to take care of him full time along with the hospice staff." She drew in a shaky breath. "He died two weeks ago, and suddenly my plan to find you and Kensington returned to the forefront of my mind. I couldn't make myself wait anymore, but I promise that's all I want from you. I'd just like to be part of my daughter's life. Richard left me a little money—some in cash, and the rest I'll get when his estate is settled. It's enough for me to re-locate and not worry. He wanted me to reunite with Kensington."

She swallowed a few times. "I know I've made a terrible mess of coming back here. I acted on impulse, and I'm sorry. It was never my intention to hurt you. I'm not here to take Kensington from you. I just hope you can find it in your heart to let me be a part of her life. Please?" The last word was whispered like a prayer.

David didn't answer right away. He stared at the table, not looking at her.

He's probably disgusted…

Weariness lined his face when he finally looked up. "Thank you. I'll consider your request, but I can't answer you right now. I'm sorry about everything you've been through. And I know it wasn't easy for you to share, but I need time to think and pray."

Emma nodded and stood to leave. At the door, she looked back at him. He sat at the table, staring at nothing before covering his face with his hands.

She sighed. Richard was wrong; so was her therapist. She hadn't changed at all. She was still selfish and impetuous. Scott was the one who really knew her, and it was just like he'd always said: she was unworthy of anything good.

Chapter Ten

David put his head on the table, too emotionally spent to move. He needed to pray, but for what? What was he supposed to do? Yes, Emma's story was sad — more than sad. It was horrific. Yes, she was Kenzie's mother, but it had been her *choice* to leave. All his plans had been ripped out of his control the day Emma walked out. When she'd listed him as Kensington's father on the birth certificate, his dream of attending seminary had vanished like an early morning mist.

David had decided early on that the less people knew about his business, the better. After threats and begging, Mrs. Jordan, Dylan, and Jennifer had respected his wishes. His family had been horrified and disappointed in him, thinking he'd derailed his future with a slip in judgment. But after the initial shock, they'd come around and loved Kenzie as much as their other grandchildren.

Though his family situation had no official bearing on his fitness as a teacher, a schoolteacher in a small town had to be squeaky clean — preferably not accused or suspected of *moral turpitude*. Because he was unwilling to answer questions about his relationship to Kenzie and Emma, he'd nearly lost his job as well. A single man caring for an infant, with the mother not in the picture, had sent the gossipmongers into overdrive. Lydia Meadows had been the first to cast aspersions on his reputation. She'd seen him with Emma at the hospital, and remained unhappy with her daughter's grade.

Luckily, he had influential friends in the community who gave character references and stood behind him to point out the limits of the morality police at the hearing with the school board. But the experience had been brutal and left scars of mistrust. He never let his guard down now, keeping a strict wall of formality between himself and most people, especially students and their parents. Though friendly to everyone, he had few true friends. And he hadn't dared to date in four and a half years.

On one thing, Emma was right. He'd loved Kenzie even before he'd shouldered the responsibility of her care. She was his life. *And now Emma wants to waltz in here and be Mother of the Year?* Frustrated, he shoved the plate of cookies he and Kenzie had baked this morning—before Emma showed up and ruined everything—off the table.

That was stupid. He cleaned up the mess, angry at Emma, and angry at Dylan's betrayal. *How can I get past this?*

He paused. He wasn't being fair. This situation wasn't Dylan's fault. Along with Jennifer, Dylan had always been there for Kenzie. They were her godparents. He replenished his coffee, uncovered the tray Emma had brought, and perused it. Picking up a celery stick, he poked it in the spinach dip. What if the dip was poisoned? If he was dead, she'd stand a better chance of gaining custody. *I need to review my will…Idiot, it's store-bought. You just opened it.*

Exhausted, he rubbed his eyes and sighed. His mind was not in a good place. Truthfully, could he fault Emma for running? Her own mother had *sold* her into slavery…Feeling nauseated, he tossed the celery stick in the garbage. The depth of depravity Emma had experienced in her life was beyond his comprehension.

This brought up another concern, and he groaned at the weight of his decision. What kind of mother would Emma be? True, she wasn't the same tough, distrustful girl he'd known in the past. But how much trauma had she endured? And what had been its impact on her? Her best friend—this Angel character—was a junkie, for crying out loud. Aside from therapists, this Richard seemed to be the only person who'd been a stable influence in her life. And Richard was dead and had left her money—something he had very little of. If she tried to take Kenzie from him through the legal system, he'd have to beg, borrow, and perhaps steal. And he'd do it, too. But whoever Richard had been, he'd cared for Emma, wanted to marry her…

David shoved aside his feelings about Richard, unwilling to explore the myriad of emotions that situation stirred up. He didn't like to think he was jealous of a dead man, but there it was, rearing its ugly, warped head and staring him in the face. Four and a half years ago, he'd felt something for Emma…right up until she abandoned her baby and ripped his dreams to shreds. He'd always had the thought in the back of his mind—what would he do if she came back. And now she was here. And he had to put Kenzie first. And his daughter was curious about her mother.

David put the vegetable tray in the refrigerator and turned on the television, keeping the sound down so as not to wake Kenzie. *Wonderful,* he thought sarcastically as he scrolled through the channels to find a soft-porn flick playing—not what a self-imposed celibate needed when the woman who'd haunted his dreams was back in his life. He switched to the news channel and closed his eyes, unable to pray for the first time he could ever remember.

David let out a painful *umph* as forty pounds of elbows and knees jumped on him, nearly leaving him singing soprano.

"Wake up, Daddy!"

"I'm awake," he mumbled, rubbing his eyes and wincing at the crick in his neck. He'd slept on the couch. "What's for breakfast?" he asked, giving Kenzie a kiss on the forehead.

"Ask Mama."

David sat up with a start, looked around, relaxing only when he was sure Emma was nowhere to be found. He glanced at his watch, surprised to find it was already past nine. "Mama isn't here, Kenz."

Kenzie rolled her eyes. "Go ask her, Daddy."

This foreshadowing of more eye rolls from Kenzie in the future made him feel old and lost in the sea of parenthood. He attributed it to genetics. Emma was certainly a champion eye-roller.

"You want your mother to come eat breakfast with us?"

She nodded vigorously, curls bouncing. "She lives next door!"

"How do you know this?" He really needed coffee.

"Because Angela and I heard Jennifer yelling at Dylan about it. She threw a magazine! And it hit him! We got in trouble for laughing."

Kenzie sat on his chest, holding poor Teddy in a choke hold. David sympathized with the hapless bear. Not so much with Dylan.

"Does Mama have a puppy?"

"I don't think so." *Good God, I hope not. I'm not sure she can take care of herself.*

He had no one to blame but himself for Kenzie's interest in her mother. He'd kept Emma's memory present in his daughter's life with the few pictures he had and their nightly prayers.

"Please, Daddy?" The hopeful, excited look on her face reminded him of Emma staring at the fireworks.

He sighed. Now that Emma was present in the flesh, he needed to make the transition as smooth as possible for Kenzie's sake; he had to put his own fears and feelings aside. With some ground rules, maybe he and Emma could make this work. If not, he'd call a lawyer. Or maybe he'd call one anyway, to be safe...

Picking up the phone, he frowned. He hadn't thought to ask Emma for her phone number.

"Fine, go put some shoes on, and we'll walk next door and invite her."

Kenzie bounced off his chest, shoving an elbow into his solar plexus.

"Yeow!" Fatherhood wasn't for the weak. He sat up, rubbing his sore stomach, then went to brush his teeth. After running a comb through his hair, he slipped into his shoes. Kenzie came back wearing her red sneakers, blue nightgown, and purple fairy wings.

"All right, Miss Fashionista, let's go."

They sauntered through the woods, up the hill toward Emma's. Already hot and humid, the sweat trickled down his back as he listened to Kenzie's nonstop chatter. Then a bloodcurdling scream made the hair on the back of his neck stand up. It had come from the garage apartment.

Grabbing Kenzie's hand, they ran up the hill. When they reached Mrs. Jordan's backyard, he commanded, "Go get Mrs. J."

Kenzie nodded, and he sprinted to the back of the garage apartment. His heart dropped to the pit of his stomach as he looked up in horror. "Emma!"

Soaking wet and wrapped in a towel, she hung from the window ledge by her fingers. Although the garage with the apartment was built on the side of a hill, the window was high enough that dropping to the ground wasn't an appealing option. Shaking, she looked down at him, fear on her face.

"Emma, calm down and just let go. I'll catch you."

"Oh my God! Go away, David! I'm practically naked!" she screeched, her eyes wide as she struggled to hold on.

"Mama?" Kenzie giggled.

"K-Kensington?"

"I'll catch you. Let go now!" he ordered sternly. Without taking his eyes off Emma he asked, "Kenzie, didn't I tell you to go get Mrs. J?"

Instead of answering, his daughter laughed harder. "What's Mama doing?"

"Why are you and Kensington here?" Her casual tone of voice was totally at odds with the desperation on her face.

"We came to invite you to breakfast. Why are you hanging out the window? Most folks use the door."

"I'm not most people. You should know that by now. I can't even count how many windows I've snuck out of."

"I'm here, and I'll catch you. Just let go," he coaxed again.

"No! I c-can't."

"For heaven's sake. What made you sneak out this time?" He didn't want to sound impatient, but he was about to have a heart attack if she didn't get down. Plus, he couldn't watch her and Kenzie at the same time.

"S-Snake." Emma shook harder, and her hold on the window slipped a bit. She shrieked as her towel fell to the ground.

David stared at the naked beauty dangling above him. His mouth went dry, and he prayed neither girl noticed his physical reaction as he tried to focus on Emma's safety. Forcing his gaze to her face he asked, "What snake?"

"In my hallway! I'd just finished my bath, and when I stepped out of the bathroom to get dressed, I saw it slithering toward me! Close your eyes, David!"

"I can't close my eyes and catch you. Trust me, honey. I'll catch you. Just let go."

"N-No, I'm scared. I c-can't."

She whimpered and wiggled in an enticing manner as she tried to regain her hold on the window. Even if she wasn't doing it on purpose to drive him crazy, he found it difficult to be a responsible adult male in this situation. He had to get her to let go—whether it was for her sake or his, he'd never be sure.

"Emma, what if the snake slithers up over the window ledge? *Let. Go. Now!*"

She released her hands with a scream.

He caught her, and the feel of his arms around her completed her undoing. She should have trusted him.

I do trust him.

Emma threw her arms around his neck as her heart pounded out of control. No longer trembling over the snake, or her fear, Emma held on tight, rocked by the slow epiphany made clear in his strong arms. She had put her trust in David, and he hadn't let her down. *Ever.*

"I've got you, Em. You're safe," he whispered. "Kenzie, hand your mother the towel."

David set her on her feet, and she pressed her face deeper into his shirtfront, embarrassed by her nakedness. This was a new feeling. She'd been naked in front of men more times than she cared to remember. She hoped David hadn't seen her greatest shame, the permanent reminder of her past. Kensington handed her the towel, and she wrapped it tightly around her body. Heat infused her skin when she noticed the bulge in David's jeans.

"Th-Thank you." She looked away from David and smiled down at her beautiful daughter with the flyaway, uncombed curls. The fairy wings she wore flapped slightly in the morning breeze.

"Okay. Let's go snake hunting." David's voice sounded strained as he looked everywhere but at her.

Her eyes widened, and she backed up a step. "Oh, hell no. I'm not going back in there."

David ran a hand through his hair and sighed. "Language check, please. Okay. I'll go in, get you some clothes, and you and Kenzie can walk back to my house. I expect a full pot of coffee and breakfast as payment for snake corralling. Deal?"

"Deal, but what if the snake gets you?"

"Then I expect a moving eulogy about me dying a hero," he replied with a grin. "Kenzie, stay with Emma and behave."

"Okay, Snake-Killer Hero Daddy." She gave him a sharp salute, and her eyes danced with mischief.

"Great. I'm raising a stand-up comic," he mumbled. He grabbed a hoe from the garage and jogged up the steps.

"Be careful," Emma cautioned.

In a few minutes, he tossed her clothes and shoes down to her.

Emma slipped on her tennis shoes as Kensington tugged on her hand. "Hurry, Mama, the snake might get us!"

The thought terrified her, and she glanced around the path for the snake's relatives. Still clad only in a towel, holding her clothes with one hand and Kenzie's hand with the other, she hurried with Kensington through the woods toward David's home. Halfway home, the little girl stopped in the middle of the path and tore off her wings, nightgown, and underwear.

Emma's eyes bugged, and she gasped. "What are you doing?"

"I wanna be naked, too!" She squealed with laughter, putting her wings back on. Running ahead down the path, she looked like a bare-bottomed cherub.

"Wait!" Emma grabbed the nightgown and underwear and took off running after her.

David will not *approve of this.*

She caught up to her, and together they stepped from the canopy of the woods into the yard — just as Dylan jogged by in a pair of shorts, earbuds plugged into his phone. His shaggy, sun-kissed hair hung damp in his face, and he glistened with sweat. *Great.* Emma tried to hurry Kenzie into the house before he noticed them. But he did a literal double take as he jogged by and spun around. *Busted.*

Unplugging his earbuds, he looked them over. "Morning, Emma, Kenz. Interesting attire for a stroll through the woods."

"A big snake scared Mama, and she was naked, and Daddy's at her house! And I'm naked, too!" Kenzie squealed, dancing around with excitement. "I'm the Naked Fairy!"

"I see. We're calling *it* a snake, are we? Well, Emma, I wouldn't think seeing you in the buff would scare a *snake*," Dylan replied with a wink. "But then again, we're talking about the deacon."

Emma was quite sure her cheeks matched the color of Kensington's sneakers. "There's a snake in my house, and he's trying to kill it. I didn't have time to get dressed."

Good grief, my version sounds worse than Kensington's.

"Anyway, please excuse us, Dylan. Have a nice run." With her shoulders squared, chin held high, she pulled Kensington toward the house.

"You wanna come get naked with us?" Kensington asked as Emma dragged her off.

Dylan laughed. "I better not. And hey, Emma, we need to talk about that check you wrote me, *soon*." He looked at her pointedly, and she nodded as he took off at a run toward her apartment.

David walked out of Emma's apartment with a three-foot rat snake in his hands as Dylan came running up the steps.

"Damn. I didn't know Methodists got into snake-handling," Dylan noted, admiring the snake.

"Very funny. Somehow this got in Emma's apartment, but I'm not killing it. It's a good snake."

"I ran in to your girls on my morning run. Is there a nudist colony around here now? Or have your girls become pagans, dancing in the forest?"

"Huh? Emma is *not* my girl," David retorted, a bit more harshly than necessary. He was still embarrassed by how his body had reacted to her. There was a very cold shower in his immediate future, and he wondered how he'd ever be able to look her in the face. She had to have known he'd been aroused.

"So, things okay?" Dylan asked as David released the snake into the woods.

He shrugged. "I'm not happy with *your* role in all of this, but she's here. Kenzie's besotted with her. I'm just going to bide my time to see if she runs again and be ready to pick up the pieces."

Dylan had the grace to look sheepish. "Sorry. Look, it's your call on Emma. Jen and I are here for you if you need us. See ya, deacon." He headed back down the path.

"Hey, Dylan, why did you ask about a nudist colony?" *I'll kill him if he saw Emma naked.*

Dylan stopped and turned. "Emma had a towel around her, and your kid was naked except for her sneakers and fairy wings. Kenzie invited me to get naked with them, but I declined. If you want, I'm thinking we can book a double room at the convent for our daughters. I thought they'd be sixteen before we'd need it, but now I'm not so sure. Angela's already talks about how cute Luke Tyler is—like I'd let any daughter of mine date a Tyler. She's not even five! I'm telling you, David, we dads have to stick together." He laughed and waved before running back through the woods.

David scowled as he walked home. These days Kenzie could be naked and running around at the drop of a hat. Was it genetics? Maybe it *was* time to think about putting her in a convent.

He opened his front door to the smell of something burning. Kenzie was chattering nonstop, unaware of his appearance in the doorway. Emma glanced at him and blushed, even though she was now dressed in a pair of jeans and a red T-shirt. Kenzie sat on the counter in her nightgown, covered in black toast crumbs.

"Mama burned the toast. Did you kill the snake, Daddy?"

Emma blanched at the mention of the snake.

"I took care of it," he hedged.

"Did you squoosh its guts out?"

When did my daughter become so bloodthirsty? He chose to ignore the question so he wouldn't have to lie. "Breakfast smells, uh, well-*cooked.*"

"Sorry." Emma looked worried.

"Not a problem, I like crunchy toast." David laughed and opened the window above the sink. He poured a cup of coffee and went to check his blood sugar.

When he returned, Emma had breakfast on the table. Sitting down to a Southern breakfast of scrambled eggs, scraped toast, sausage, and lumpy grits, he asked, "When did you learn to cook?"

Emma laughed, and he smiled at the sound.

"You mean when did I learn to burn toast? When I was in the shelter."

David nodded and took hold of their hands, offering a quick blessing. When her soft palm squeezed his, an electrical current of desire shot through him, and the image of her warm, naked body messed with his head. He nearly groaned aloud. What was wrong with him?

I'm getting horny during a blessing over the food? Seriously? Am I that desperate, or does God just have a sick sense of humor?

He yanked his hand away, picked up his fork, and took a bite of his breakfast. "This is delicious." It felt strangely natural having her here, and he smiled as she refreshed his coffee.

"Thank you. You're being generous."

Kenzie smacked her hand in her eggs, making a mess.

"Don't play with your food, Kenzie."

Kenzie rolled her eyes. "I'm not."

"Don't roll your eyes at me, young lady."

She quickly flicked her tongue out instead.

"I saw that!" He frowned, bewildered by her behavior.

"I didn't roll my eyes this time," Kenzie replied with a saucy smirk.

What's with this attitude? "If you can't apologize, go to your room. When you can act civilly and not be disrespectful, you may come back and join us for breakfast."

Kenzie's lower lip pushed out into a pout, and she shot a look of *help me* to Emma, who twisted her napkin, shifting her gaze between Kenzie and him.

"David, I think—"

"Don't go there, Emma," he warned. "You don't have the right." He looked at Kenzie and raised an eyebrow. "Kenzie." He tried to ignore Emma's narrowed glare as he waited for his daughter's response.

"I'm sorry, Daddy."

"Sorry for what?"

"Being dis-diswespec—" She struggled for the word, wrinkled her nose, and huffed. "You know."

"Disrespectful?" he encouraged.

She nodded and smiled, melting his heart.

"Thank you. Now eat your breakfast."

The remainder of the breakfast passed in relative peace and quiet, although Emma picked at her food. When a knock at the front door broke the silence, David excused himself. He'd opened the front door only a fraction of an inch before Jennifer barged in.

"Will you please explain to me why Emma walked practically naked through the woods to your house?" she asked as she stormed through the house. "Dylan told me about it! Why haven't you sent her packing yet?"

"Won't you come in, Jennifer?" David asked. He put a finger to his lips and motioned toward the kitchen, but Jennifer ignored him, too worked up with indignation.

"I don't like her being here, and I don't trust her. I told Dylan and Mrs. J this was a huge mistake. I could see letting her stay a night or two, but now this? She's nothing but trouble—"

Emma came to the doorway of the living area, her eyes blazing. "Thanks for getting rid of the snake, David. I'm going to take my troublesome self back to my apartment and finish *unpacking*. I left my phone number on the kitchen counter." She slapped the dishtowel she'd been holding into his hand as she glared at Jennifer. The door slammed behind her.

David blew the hair out of his eyes. Dylan had the right idea about a convent. At the moment, he wished he'd converted to Catholicism years ago and become a monk. It would have saved him all kinds of trouble.

Chapter
Eleven

That afternoon, Emma made the last trip from her car into the apartment with her arms full. She'd left most of her things in her car since she'd arrived, too emotionally exhausted to think, much less feel confident enough to unpack. Fortunately, having had very little for most of her life, she didn't have much. And she still wasn't sure how long she'd be here…

Her phone rang, and she struggled to put her things down and dig it out of her pocket. She trembled at the unknown number, fearing the worst.

"This is David. Here's the deal," he began when she answered, not bothering to say hello.

"Deal?" she asked, sinking to the couch. Was he changing his mind? She forced herself to take a deep breath.

"You can have supervised visits with Kenzie."

"O-Okay, thank you," she choked.

He hung up without saying goodbye. Hugging herself, she grinned and hurried to put things away. This was now her *home*.

Placing a photo of Richard on her dresser, she smiled sadly, missing his gentle spirit and wise counsel. How she wished she could talk to him, ask his advice, and even tell him he'd been right. She tucked the only picture she had of her with Ken and Angel into her mirror, along with the picture of her with David and Kensington from the hospital. The few pictures Dylan had sent her of Kensington over the years she placed in her dresser drawer, out of sight.

She moved to the window and looked out into the woods. Her skin tingled as she recalled the warmth and strength of David's arms around her this morning. She'd felt so...*safe.*

Her cell phone rang again, and this time she smiled, recognizing the number.

"Hello?"

"How's it going, Emmanuelle? Sorry I missed your call earlier. I was in court." Only Damien Sinclair, Angel's brother, called her Emmanuelle. He loved to tease her about having such an exotic, "porn star" name, as he was unaware of her past. Angel and Richard had kept her secrets.

"It's been difficult, but I'm making it. Kensington's beautiful, and she knew me! It's still hard for me to believe, but David kept my memory alive for her. I'm so grateful for that." Her heart expanded when she mentioned David's generosity.

"That's great. So no problems? Nothing I need to handle? It will take months before the estate is settled, but you know Richard put money in that savings account for you. It's yours, so use it as you need to while you're getting settled and finding a new job."

"No. I'm fine. I'm renting an apartment next door to David and Kensington. I like the proximity to my daughter. And I did write the check I spoke to you and your father about, for my final payment to Dylan McAthie."

Damien sighed. "He didn't need the money. I know you're adamant about paying it back, but Dad and I still think it foolish. That money is a drop in the bucket to McAthie and could've helped *you.* You need to be frugal," Damien cautioned.

"I'm in the backwoods of Alabama—it's almost like *Deliverance* country. The only thing I might splurge on is a speedboat so I won't have to paddle. You know how I hate to exercise," she teased.

Damien laughed. "All right, sweetheart. Call me if you hear banjos playing or need me."

"Thank you. I will. Any news on Angel?"

"Nope. We are incommunicado."

The bitterness in his voice made her sad.

"Meaning you haven't attempted to contact him?"

"That would be correct. *I'm working a step.*" His tone was derisive this time.

"Everyone deserves a second chance, even your brother."

"You can be the bleeding-heart liberal; you haven't had to deal with Angel's shit. And trust me, he's on — at the very least — his twentieth chance. Talk to you soon."

"Bye." She hung up, not mentioning that Angel was out of rehab and clean. Although contact from him was sporadic with his nomad's lifestyle, he always managed to touch base with her. She'd made sure he had her cell number. She needed to give him her official new address next time he called.

A knock at her door startled her, and she braced herself. She sincerely hoped it wasn't Jennifer. *It would be a pity if Kensington had to come visit her mama at the county jail this early in our relationship.*

When she opened the door, she found Dylan leaning against the railing, his mouth settled in a grim line. He flipped her check toward her as he walked in without an invitation. Emma crossed her arms but then dropped them to her sides, refusing to be intimidated.

"May I get you something to drink?" she offered politely, motioning for him to sit on the old brown couch and refusing to take the check.

"This check is ridiculous; I'm not accepting it."

"My attorney assured me it would more than cover the remainder of what I owed you for the baby things, plus reasonable interest." She lifted her chin, perching on the edge of the chair opposite the couch.

"I should've ripped it up or given it back to you right away…" Dylan's eyes narrowed. "Wait, what? *You* have a lawyer?"

"Yes." She bristled.

"Emma, I don't want this money. I don't need this money. I probably have more money than God. As a matter of fact, I want to give back what you've already paid me. *It was a gift.*" He again extended the check toward her, motioning vaguely. "I'm sure you need this to set up house or something." He paused. "Or leave town?"

She shook her head. "I'm not leaving. At least not until David tells me to. I'm paying off my debts. What I can pay off financially, I mean. Nothing, of course, can repay what everyone has done for Kensington."

He sighed. "I didn't think you were leaving. Jen made me ask." Dylan offered the check again. "Put this in a college fund for Kenzie."

"No, my lawyer is already working on setting that up." Emma crossed her arms. "Do what you want with the money; I don't want it. It isn't even my money. It was Richard's."

Dylan pursed his lips.

Anger coursed through her veins, and she jumped from the chair, her hands fisted at her sides. "I didn't prostitute myself for it, if that's what you're thinking. I already told you, I took care of a dying man. *That's it.*" She held her head high.

His brows knit as he shook his head. "I didn't think that, Emma."

She relaxed and nodded. "I-I'm sorry. Thank you. I really couldn't blame you if you did."

"Actually, I was thinking how much you've changed. You have confidence now, and it becomes you. I still don't want the check. So it seems we're at a stalemate." He smiled and once again offered it to her, but she refused.

Dylan sat back, stretching his arms over the back of the couch, and crossed his foot on his knee. Out of habit, she stared at the floor. To control her fidgeting, she moved her hands to behind her back, weaving them together.

"You know, you can't pay David back for everything he's done. He wouldn't want the money anyway. The man has pride. It would've been so easy for him to deny the information you provided on the birth certificate and put Kenzie into the system. We even offered to pay the expenses for the blood test." Dylan put his foot down and leaned forward, resting his elbows on his knees. "David didn't do that. Why? Because he *loved* Kenzie and *wanted* her. Understand?"

Emma swallowed the lump forming in her throat and nodded. "I know, but I feel like I should do *something*. I'm trying to make amends somehow. Wrongly, it seems…"

Dylan stood and pocketed the check. "There's only one thing you need to do. Don't break Kenzie's heart. And just so you know, I'm not the enemy. Neither is Jen. We were willing to adopt Kenzie if David hadn't stepped up to the plate. But you should know…Jen and preacher man have a history. Do I like it? Not really. She's protective of him, so it's gonna take her a while to come around." He walked to the door and turned back to face her. "Welcome home, Emma. I plan to donate this money to charity. Any preferences?"

"It's your money; I'll trust your judgment. Thank you, Dylan, for everything."

"Okay, the snake farm it is." He winked at her and left.

A shiver ran up her spine, but after a moment she smiled. She closed the door and thought about her future, here in Pine Bluff.

She'd need a job. She wanted to earn her own money, legitimately. And a job would keep her from intruding too much on David and Kensington. They should take things slowly and give everyone time to adjust. She wasn't a fool; she knew she walked a tightrope with David's generosity. But she was determined not to fall.

He had agreed to supervised visits. She didn't dare hope for any more than that, knowing her heart couldn't take the disappointment. Damien had wanted her to pursue Kensington through the court system, but she didn't want to do things that way. Biology aside, she didn't feel like she really had the right to. David had raised her, and she couldn't bear the thought of causing him any more pain. But now that she'd seen Kensington, she couldn't consider not being part of her life. That child was all she had left in the world. Without her, she might as well not be here.

Just as Emma was considering what to eat for dinner, someone again pounded on her door. Her heart matched the staccato beat as unpleasant memories surfaced. Jumping up, she cracked the door, only to have it thrown open as David stormed in. She instinctively moved to put the couch between them.

"You have a lawyer?" he roared.

Damn you, Dylan McAthie!

"Please, calm down and let me explain."

"Calm down? Are you kidding me? So help me, if you try to take my daughter, I'll fight you to my last dime, to my last dying breath. Do you hear me?" he yelled. He paced, fisting one hand in his palm. "I should have known better than to trust you."

Emma watched him, ready to bolt for safety. "I can explain—"

"Shut up." He stopped pacing and looked at the ceiling, his fingers interlocked behind his neck.

She remained quiet, gripping the back of the couch for support.

"You said you weren't here to take her…" He threw his arms up. "Why do you have a lawyer? Answer me."

"You told me to shut up. Which do you want?" she snapped.

Instantly horrified, she dropped her gaze, waiting for the beating. Her smart mouth always got her in trouble.

"Sorry," he muttered.

Timidly, she looked up. His shoulders sagged, and he blew out a ragged breath, motioning for her to sit.

Swallowing her fear, she perched on the arm of the couch, ready to run. Her knee bounced as he sat beside her.

To her surprise, he reached out and placed his hand on her knee, stilling it. "I'm sorry. I shouldn't have overreacted and scared you."

"Thank you."

He removed his hand and covered his face. "But the fact remains, you *are* scaring me. Why do you have a lawyer?"

He looked at her, fear in his eyes.

"Damien, my attorney, is a friend. He's Angel's brother. Richard worked in the same firm. After he died, Damien handled the estate. That's all. I'm not good with money, never having had any, so he's helping me. I won't lie—he's offered to help me where Kensington's concerned, but I told him no."

"Why?" He stared at her, opening his mouth and then shutting it. Finally he asked, "Why *wouldn't* you fight for her?"

His incongruity would have made her smile if he weren't so sincere. "Because she's *your* daughter, David. But, maybe…"

"Maybe what?"

"Maybe someday we'll both think of her as *our* daughter. I want to…what's the term? Co-parent *with* you. Not against you."

They sat in silence, as if contemplating a move in a chess game.

"Swear to me on whatever you hold dear that you won't take her from me."

"I swear on Kensington's life. You can trust me on that."

David nodded. "I hope so, Emma. I truly do." He stood to leave, but paused at the door and mumbled, "Thank you."

Chapter
Twelve

Emma's feet ached. Three weeks ago, getting a job as a waitress had seemed like a good idea. She now worked part-time at the Mug and Cone, a diner not unlike the one in Atlanta. This one was affectionately known as the Hug and Moan by the local teenagers. Wiggling her toes in her shoes, she decided she must've gotten soft during her stint taking care of Richard. Twelve-hour shifts used to be a piece of cake.

"Order up!" Frances yelled from the kitchen.

Her boss, Frances Kelton, was a well-known busybody. People came to the diner as much for the gossip as the food. During her initial interview, Emma had politely skirted questions other than those required by law to be hired. She worked hard, which had earned her the respect of her new boss—and in all fairness, Frances was kind, if somewhat nosy.

Emma glanced at her watch, counting the time until her shift ended. The restaurant was empty except for a few giggling teenaged girls lingering over French fries and Diet Cokes. They wouldn't tip much, but she was fine with it, just ready to go home and soak in the tub. They ignored her, their attention focused on the boys skateboarding outside. She placed their second order of fries on the table.

"Anything else?" she asked.

"No, thanks," one of the girls answered without a glance.

Emma looked out the window and watched the boys turn and flip their boards in an obvious effort to impress the girls. Her heart skipped a beat when she saw David walking toward the diner, holding Kensington's hand. His worn jeans and black T-shirt enhanced his rugged good looks, as did the scruff on his face. Bouncing beside him in jean shorts, sandals, and a yellow T-shirt with a bumblebee on it, Kensington waved at the skateboarders. Two pigtails and a gold crown completed her outfit.

A woman holding a cardboard box ran across the street and approached David. Kensington started jumping up and down, tugging on David's shirt. He shook his head and placed his hands on his hips. Kensington clasped her hands as if praying or begging, and her lower lip quivered. The woman laughed, reached into the box, and handed Kensington a squirming ball of brown fluff. Kensington squealed when the puppy licked her face. Stooping beside her, David talked to her a moment before he placed the puppy back in the box. Kensington held David's hand, but she turned and watched the woman walk away, looking heartbroken.

David pointed to the restaurant, and Emma crossed her fingers. He hadn't been to the diner since she'd started working here.

During her daily supervised visits, he'd started out pleasant, but reserved. He'd watched her like a hawk. But as the days went by, and Kensington took everything in stride, they'd both begun to relax. He no longer hovered when she visited. And a couple of times, she'd found him staring at her — not in a bad way.

To her surprise and joy, yesterday he'd left her alone with her daughter for a couple of hours while he cut the grass. When he'd come in hot and sweaty, she'd had a glass of iced tea ready for him. He'd thanked her, and when his fingers brushed hers as he took the glass, she'd blushed like a schoolgirl.

The skateboarders greeted David, and he stopped to talk, smiling and laughing at something they said. Crying, Kensington broke free from her father's hand and launched herself into the arms of one the boys, pointing toward the retreating back of the woman with the puppy. The teen picked her up, threw her in the air, and caught her, turning her tears to giggles.

To Emma's surprise, David accepted a skateboard and helmet from the boy holding Kensington and took a run, making two successful 180 ollies. When he finished, he flipped the board up into his hand. Emma chuckled as fist bumps circulated.

Then the bell on the door rang as he and Kensington entered the diner, and she took a deep breath, wishing her heart would quit pounding. The teenaged girls at the table giggled when David walked past.

"That was sick, Mr. Patterson," a vivacious brunette offered.

"Thanks, Jocelyn." David gave the table a small smile of acknowledgment, which caused twitters of nervous laughter. Choosing a booth by the window, David frowned as Kensington stood on the seat to watch the boys outside.

Nervous, Emma's hand shook as she placed their water and silverware on the table and handed David a menu. The smile he gave her made her stomach flutter, but this time it wasn't from nerves. *He's so handsome.*

"So, are you a true skater or just a poser?" she asked, grinning.

David leaned back in the booth and laughed. "Shh, don't give my secret away. I'm pretty much a poser."

"Daddy isn't as good as Connor," Kensington commented. Kneeling on her knees in the booth, she stuck her straw in her water and blew bubbles.

David placed a hand on her back in a silent signal to stop. "It's hard to be a hero when Connor's around," he admitted, motioning to the young man who'd thrown Kensington in the air. "He goes to our church and *someone…*" David grinned at Kensington "…is smitten." He winked conspiratorially.

If she were struck dead right now, Emma knew she'd die happy. She felt like part of their family, as if she belonged. She flashed them a wide smile.

"If I promise to keep my room clean, can we have Molly?"

David sighed.

"Molly?" Emma asked.

"The puppy in the box. She needs a home!" Kensington bounced in her seat.

"I told you I'd think about it, Kenzie."

"Puh-lease, Daddy?"

When he didn't answer, she cut her eyes toward Emma and smiled. "Mama wants a puppy!"

Emma shook her head, not getting in the middle of this one.

David sighed. "If you keep asking, the answer will be a definite no. Now, sit down and behave."

"Do you know what you want to order?" Emma asked.

"Chicken fingers and a strawberry milkshake!" Kensington yelled. Turning her back on her father, she pressed her nose to the window, bouncing and grinning as she watched Connor do a run.

"Make that two chicken fingers and a Diet Coke for me with an order of fries." David frowned at his daughter. "Sit down before you hurt yourself, Princess Kenzie McFrenzie."

Ignoring him, Kenzie pounded on the window. When Connor waved and winked at her, she hid her red face behind her hands, peeking through her fingers.

David rubbed his brow and gave an exasperated groan. "I'm already dreading the teenage years, aren't you?"

Surprised, Emma dropped her order pad. David picked it up and handed it to her.

Emma wanted to scream and bounce like her daughter. *He just included me in Kensington's future.* "I, uh, I'm kind of looking forward to the teenage years." She smiled, watching her daughter giggle and make faces at Connor. "I don't want to miss any other milestones in her life." She hurried away, grinning and humming as she turned the order in.

Frances gave her a curious glance. "You okay, hun?"

"Yes, just glad my shift is almost over. My feet are tired," she said.

"Hey! I forgot to tell you. The other day when you were off, some guy asked about you."

Emma glanced nervously to the table where David laughed, teasing Kensington. "Did he give a name?" Goose bumps skittered across her arms.

"No, he's been in here a couple of times. Just an ordinary guy, for the most part pleasant. He was upset he didn't get a refill on his tea and said you were a better waitress than Randi. Which is true," Frances replied with a laugh. "That girl never can remember to refill glasses or take ketchup to the table." She nodded toward David. "That one would be a good catch. Every single female in the county—and some not-so-single—has her eye on him."

"He's just my neighbor," Emma lied smoothly.

Fifteen minutes later, with her shift officially over, she brought their food to the table. "Do you need anything else?"

"No, we're good, thanks. Kenzie, sit down and eat."

"After we eat can we go get Molly?"

David frowned. Kenzie gave him a kiss on the cheek to further her cause, making Emma laugh.

"Enjoy your meal." She turned away, taking off her apron.

"Em, is your shift over?"

She spun around and faced him, glancing toward Frances, who watched as if they were her favorite reality television show. "Yes."

"Want to join us? I'll share my French fries," he offered.

Emma wanted nothing more than to sit and enjoy their company, but not enough to give Frances a chance to spread rumors.

"No, thanks. I'm beat. I'll see ya later."

"Is Mama going to Bible School with us?"

David shifted in his seat. "I, uh, don't know. Um, if she wants to, I suppose…"

Me in church? The roof would probably cave in on us. "No, I think a hot bubble bath is in my future. I'll see you soon, though. Have fun."

Grabbing her purse from behind the counter, she waved casually to Frances and walked out the door, stopping in front of the skateboarders.

Emma walked over to her daughter's crush and pointed at the board. "Mind if I try it?"

Connor frowned and blew the hair out of his eyes. "Not if you know what you're doing."

Emma smiled. "It's been a while, but I'd like to give it a go."

Dropping her purse on the ground, she accepted the board and a helmet, and with a quick glance at David's stunned face in the window, took off. She took a moment to get a feel for the ride, and when she felt confident, she popped the tail of the board, slid her foot up and did a 360 high ollie, gliding through the air. *I've still got it!* When she landed, she gave an air pump of triumph with a loud whoop. Ken would have been proud.

She kicked the board to her hand and grinned. The surprised look on the boys' faces made her laugh. From the window, she could see

David's mouth hanging open for a moment and Kensington jumping up and down, clapping and squealing. Feeling lighthearted, she took a bow.

After walking to her car, she paused as she unlocked it, shaken by the feeling of being watched. Her dormant street-survivor instincts roared to life, but when she looked around, no one was there. Perhaps the evening sunlight made the shadows appear ominous. The skateboarders rounded the corner laughing, and she relaxed, chiding herself for her silliness.

A clap of thunder shook her apartment, followed by a bright flash of lightning. Emma put down her book and pulled her knees to her chest. She remembered another storm and gave silent thanks that her daughter had David.

On her sixth birthday—the birthday when she'd received the teddy bear—a storm had awakened her, the rumbling thunder so loud it had tumbled books and pictures to the floor. Terrified and crying, she'd made her way to her mother's bedroom, only to be shocked by the sight of a half-dressed man grunting and groaning on top of her mother. Running to the bed, she'd tried to stop the man from hurting her mama. Without bothering to zip his pants, he'd climbed off her mother and slapped her across the face, screaming at her to get lost. Frightened, she'd run back to her room and hidden under the covers. It hadn't been the last night she'd cried herself to sleep clutching her teddy bear for comfort.

Another crack of thunder sounded, and Emma shot out of bed. The clock said it was only nine. Pulling on a pair of yoga pants, she slipped into her shoes.

Kensington! Is she scared?

The urgent need to check on her daughter overcame her fear of the storm. She didn't bother with a flashlight; lightning arced through the sky, lighting the path through the woods. Emma took off at a run through the pouring rain toward David's house. Wet branches slapped her face, and thorns pricked her arms.

When she reached the edge of the woods, lightning hit the transformer and sparks flew with the explosion. The noise was so loud and unexpected, she screamed. David's house went dark. More thunder and another bolt of lightning snaked across the sky. The front screen door opened, and David peered out into the rain.

"David!" She stumbled toward him.

He ran, meeting her in the yard. "Emma! What are you doing?" He grabbed her hand, yanking her toward the porch.

Slipping in the mud, she fell and cried out. He picked her up and carried her the last ten feet to the safety of the screened in porch. He held her for a moment, soaked and gasping for breath, before she slid down his body to stand on her own two feet, her heart hammering.

He pulled away and grasped her face. "What are you doing here? You could've been killed." Another bolt of lightning revealed the worry on his face.

"Kensington," she gasped. "Is she okay? Is she scared?"

"She's spending the night at the McAthies'. I'm sure she's fine. Jennifer invited her over after Vacation Bible School because of the storm warnings and to give me a chance to get Kenzie's surprise." He opened the front door. "Hold on, let me light the candles. I was preparing for a power outage when I heard the transformer blow."

Emma waited as he fumbled in the dark with the lighter. The first candle sputtered, and he lit two more. He smiled, and her heart did a strange flip-flop. He stood before her, clad only in a pair of wet jeans, and the candlelight nicely defined his six-pack abs and cut biceps. His damp hair fell rakishly onto his forehead, and his scruffy beard gave him an alluring, almost wicked look.

Her cheeks heated as he looked over her wet body with anything but a saintly expression.

"Come in."

Said the big, bad wolf to Little Red Riding Hood.

She entered, and his eyes flickered. She looked down to realize her wet white sleep shirt hid nothing. Self-conscious, she covered her chest with her arms.

"I'll be right back," he croaked. He seemed to have difficulty tearing his gaze away, but he turned and walked down the hall with one of the candles.

She heard a whimper from a box by the fireplace. She knelt and smiled, petting the puppy she'd seen earlier outside the diner. Emma shivered and rubbed her arms, looking around the room. An open mystery novel lay on the coffee table next to a bowl of popcorn and a beer.

She looked up as David returned, wearing dry jeans and a plaid shirt. Smiling, he held out some dry clothes for her.

"Oh." She looked at the clothes and stood, backing toward the front door. "No, that's okay. I just panicked thinking about Kensington in the storm. When I was her age, storms terrified me. This was silly of me—of course you know how she reacts in storms; you're her father. I'll, uh, just head back home." *Quit babbling.*

She shut her mouth and turned to leave. In an instant, he stood behind her, his right hand holding the front door shut. His breath whispered across the back of her neck, sending tingles down her spine.

"Don't go."

"I-I think it would be best." Her mouth tasted like cotton, and every nerve in her body was attuned to the man standing behind her.

"Probably. But don't go." His lips nearly brushed the back of her neck, and a longing spiraled down to her core.

Gripping the doorframe, she looked back over her shoulder. Her breathing hitched at the intensity in his eyes.

"Don't leave. Stay. We'll be able to carry on a conversation without being interrupted by Kenzie. Usually when you're here, she gets all the attention, which is as it should be. But I don't really feel like I *know* you. I don't even know if you like ice cream—or peas."

"I, uh…" She hesitated. "Chocolate and no. Peas are gross. Do you?"

"I don't eat ice cream, and I love 'em. Now, go get in some dry clothes." He nodded toward the bathroom.

Her gut told her to run. Her heart begged to stay.

The puppy whimpered, and David chuckled.

"See? She wants you to stay, too."

"What made you break down and get the dog?"

"Call me a sucker for a sweet face." He brushed the back of his fingers across her jaw.

Heat flooded her cheeks.

"Stay. Please? If you stay, I'll let you play with the puppy."

"That's the strangest pick-up line I've ever heard." She smiled. "What's her name?"

He laughed. "Is it working? Molly. Don't ask me why. Kenzie named her when she saw her earlier."

"I like it." Emma took the candle and clothes. "Okay, let me change." She scooted past him to the bathroom. Memories of the last time she'd borrowed clothes from him made her shaky. Gazing at her reflection in the mirror, she sighed. The girl staring back was still the same scared, dirty, unloved girl…just a little older.

No, that's not true!

Richard and her counselor at the shelter had both believed in her. The new therapist she'd visited in town had told her thoughts like this were her worst enemy. She squared her shoulders, bolstering her flailing confidence. Now in dry clothes, she fled the bathroom without looking back.

David stood when she entered, and she dropped her gaze to the floor. The candle flame flickered from her trembling. "You don't have to stand for me."

"I can't help it. I was brought up to stand when a lady enters a room."

Emma raised an eyebrow and laughed self-consciously. She sat on the couch, curling her feet under her. "We both know I'm no lady."

"Don't." His voice sounded firm—the one he used when reprimanding Kensington. He sat beside her and stretched his arm across the back of the couch.

"Don't?"

"Don't put yourself down." He drank a swig of his beer.

Emma looked away. "I'm merely stating a fact. You're not supposed to drink, are you? Didn't you go to Vacation Bible School tonight?" she murmured, deflecting his comment. "Have you checked your sugar?"

"I'm not perfect, and occasionally I indulge in a beer—sometimes even on a Sunday. And especially after Vacation Bible School. Do you know how many times I've had to listen to Kenzie sing 'Jesus Loves Me'? I can just about guarantee God isn't going to strike me dead for drinking it. Would you like one?"

"Yes, please."

Returning from the kitchen with the beer, David tapped his bottle to hers. "To parenthood. United we stand, divided we'll fall."

"Th-Thank you," she stammered, putting the bottle down with a shaking hand. Her gratitude threatened to spill down her cheeks. She pinched her leg to keep it in check. He'd just offered her more than forgiveness. He'd once again acknowledged that he expected her to be here in the future. This was what she had prayed for, a second chance. She turned away to get her emotions under control.

"Emma? Please, don't cry. This a fresh start, a new beginning. Kenzie needs her mother. I need help raising her. Together, we can figure this out."

"Thank you." Impulsively, she hugged him.

She pulled away, but their foreheads remained together. Before she could move, his hands cupped her face, his thumb grazing across her lower lip. *Do his lips feel the same as I remember?*

His erratic breathing mirrored hers. Almost of their own volition, her lips sought his, tentatively at first, then more possessively as he responded.

Her hands weaved into his hair, and she inhaled his soft aftershave and clean soap, fueling her desire. He brushed her hair from her face almost reverently. Impatient, she explored his mouth, and her tongue danced with his. Using her teeth, she tugged on his lower lip. His answering moan escalated her desire, and she moved in closer, deepening their kiss. Moving her hands to his shirt, she fumbled with the buttons as she kissed him, wanting to feel his warm skin against hers. He cradled her face in his hands, whispering her name as he pulled away. Emma tried to bring him back, but he grasped her hands in his and shook his head.

"No." He leapt from the couch. By the flickering candlelight she saw conflict cross his face. He closed his eyes and stood for a few seconds with his hands clasped behind his neck.

"David…"

He raised his hand to stop her before turning his back to her and stretching his arms out against the fireplace mantle. He dropped his head.

His rejection was like a cold bucket of water thrown in her face. Shivering, she pulled her feet up, wrapping her arms around her knees, making herself as small as possible.

"Oh God, I'm so sorry," she breathed. *I've just ruined everything.* Placing her hot face on her knees, she took a few seconds to pull herself together. Beyond mortified, she rose from the couch, grabbed the candle, and raced to the bathroom.

She didn't dare look in the mirror as she ripped off the borrowed dry clothes before struggling back into her wet, clingy garments. She already knew her cheeks were flushed with shame. As she folded the dry clothes, she jumped at the knock on the door.

"Emma, I'm sorry. Please come out. We need to talk."

She opened the door to find him blocking her way, a hand on each side of the doorframe. The dim lighting didn't prevent his gaze from dropping to where her wet T-shirt clung to her hardened nipples. She crossed her arms in front of her chest. Not trusting herself to lay hands on him again, she stared at the floor, waiting for him to move.

"Please…" he croaked.

Emma looked up. His eyes were closed and his Adam's apple bobbled.

"Please…I'm only human, and you're a beautiful girl. Please, put the dry clothes back on. Show me some mercy."

"I'm going home. I'm terribly sorry. I don't know what I was thinking. Never mind—obviously, I wasn't thinking. I mean, why would you be interested in someone like me? You know what they say; you can't make a silk purse out of a pig ear or something like that. Leopards don't change their stripes. Don't put pearls before swans…"

Dammit, I'm chattering like a crazy woman.

She attempted to duck under his arm, but he caught her. The candle remained in the bathroom, and she couldn't see in the dark hallway. He pinned her against the wall and kissed her neck.

"Shut up."

"W-What?" she gasped.

He quit kissing her neck and chuckled softly. "You have a terrible grasp of idioms and totally mistook my reaction."

"W-What?"

"And now you have a stutter," he teased. "Or Tourette's."

"I don't understand." She placed her hands on his chest. Despite being cold from her wet clothes, heat stirred in the pit of her stomach. The darkness and his nearness unsettled and sharpened her senses. His breathing was ragged, she could smell him, and beneath her hand, his heart pounded.

"I want you, Em. God knows I do. But I'm not wired that way. Things were about to escalate a little too fast."

"W-What?" She didn't seem to have another word in her vocabulary. Moving her hands from his chest, she covered her eyes, mortified. Her brows knit together and she peeked through her fingers at him. "Wait, I'm confused. Are you interested in me as Kensington's mother or something more?"

David snickered, which soon turned into a laugh and then became a hold-on-to-the-wall guffaw. He reached into the bathroom, still laughing, and picked up the candle. "Confused is an understatement." He took her hand and walked her back to the living area. Her teeth chattered from cold, wet clothes and nerves. Thunder shook the house.

David placed the candle on the coffee table and grabbed an afghan off the back of the couch. He wrapped it around her, sat, and pulled her into his lap. Underneath her thigh, she could feel his interest—clarifying things considerably—but before she could think about that, he kissed her—a mind-blowing, toe-curling, hungry kiss. She couldn't remember the last time a kiss had affected her like this.

Liar. It was the kiss she'd shared with this very man that fateful New Year's Eve…

After exploring her mouth for a moment, he gave her bottom lip a light nip. "We're both a little confused, but I'm definitely interested in *you*," he whispered. "I just don't want to move too fast. I want to treat you with the respect you deserve, okay?"

Stunned, she blinked and stared at him. *Respect? Me?*

"Breathe, honey, before you pass out."

Emma wondered if she should pinch herself. Surely she was dreaming. Sucking in a breath, her brain fog cleared. *What am I doing? He's a good man…*

She sighed. "Look, I'm not the girl for you. You need a nice, virgin, Christian girl." She tried, without success, to keep the bitterness out of her voice.

David's laughter rumbled with the thunder outside. He tapped her nose with his index finger. "I dated the nice Christian girl. She dumped me for the bad-boy rock star. I think it would be best if you go change back into the dry clothes and come talk to me. Please?"

"I should go home." She puzzled over the jealousy she felt at the thought of David dating Jennifer.

"Probably. But don't, for Kenzie's sake." He looked deep into her eyes, and his voice took on a husky timbre. "For *our* sake…to see where this might go."

She caught her breath at his implication, not daring to hope.

David rubbed his eyes and blew out a slow, torturous breath. Dealing with Emma was like approaching an unbroken horse or an abused dog. Skittish didn't begin to describe her. Thank God, she'd gone to change. That wet T-shirt had accented every glorious inch of her beautiful breasts.

Although the glimpse had been brief, visions of Emma naked had plagued his dreams since the infamous snake incident a few weeks ago. Tonight, his resolve to build their relationship on more than a physical attraction had rapidly deteriorated. Was he that weak a man? He'd wanted to throw her down on the couch and make love to her, which would have been a colossal mistake. Her relationship with their daughter was progressing better than he could have hoped. He could tell Emma loved being with Kenzie, and the feelings were reciprocated. Awkward at first, Emma now seemed more comfortable in her role of mother. And he found himself looking forward to her daily visits. He'd been a bit jealous on more than one occasion when Kenzie received all her attention. He'd found his interest in Emma to be more than her as the mother of his child.

Her confusion was his fault. But he needed time.

Time to get his raging need for her under control.

Time to make her understand he wasn't like the creeps she was used to.

Time to be sure having her back in Kenzie's life was the right thing.

Time to make sure she wasn't going to ditch him and Kenzie and run again.

Time to make sure she was ready to accept love and be in a healthy, full-fledged relationship. He still wasn't sure how much her past had affected her. He didn't want to add to her trauma. Maybe he should seek counseling, too?

Plus, his own self-doubt permeated his thoughts. Jennifer had left him for Dylan. But it wasn't like he didn't know the mechanics of what to do. Sex was like putting together Kenzie's dollhouse: tab A goes into slot B. He groaned, rubbing his eyes.

I'm losing it, comparing sex to putting together toys. Really? Loser.

He stood and paced, running a hand through his hair. Deep down he was terrified Emma would recognize his lack of experience and find him deficient, which would be deflating, in more ways than one. He collapsed with a sigh onto the couch. *Pathetic.* It was the only word that applied.

He looked up when Emma strolled back in and perched on the chair facing him. She picked up her beer and closed her eyes to take a long drink. He watched her lips around the tall neck of the bottle.

Pathetic and horny.

Stop it, you jerk!

Shifting uncomfortably, he moved the embroidered pillow his mother had made onto his lap, covering his erection. He'd hated that pillow until this moment.

Emma needs to go home before I humiliate myself like an adolescent teen.

No, I don't want her to go.

A crack of thunder shook the windows, reminding him that the storm still raged. He couldn't send her home in this weather — it provided a viable excuse to keep her here anyway. He gulped a big swallow of his beer and decided conversation would be a plus. It would be better than lusting after her and thinking of all the things he wanted to do that didn't include one bit of dialogue.

"So, where do you see yourself in ten years?"

Emma grabbed a handful of popcorn and furrowed her brow. She took a moment before answering. "Honestly?"

He watched her nibble on the popcorn. *Do her lips taste salty?*

"Yes, of course." *Please stay with me. In my bed. No! Stop it you, douchebag. I mean with us, with Kenzie and me.* David took another draw off his beer. He needed to get a grip.

"I can't think that far ahead." She looked at him, a puzzled expression on her face. "Is that odd?"

"No, I imagine it has to do with having to live moment to moment for all those years," he offered.

She smiled and appeared to relax. "Where do you see yourself in ten years?" Her gaze met his, unwavering. Tonight her eyes appeared green rather than brown, and as usual, their changing color fascinated him.

"Oh, that's easy. I'll be a harried father with a loaded shotgun, arguing with Kenz and dealing with eye rolls," he replied with an exaggerated sigh.

Emma giggled. "Yeah, I can definitely see that." She pulled her knees to her chest and wrapped her arms around them, staring at the candle. Only the sounds of the snoring puppy and rain broke the silence.

"Where are you, Emma?" he asked softly.

She smiled, but her face remained pensive. "Kenzie will be in a much better place than I was in my teens." Her eyes glistened in the candlelight. "Thank you. Thank you for saving my daughter."

They sat in silence, staring at the dancing flame. David got up and retrieved two more beers from the refrigerator. Handing her one, he folded himself on the floor in front of her chair. "Thank *you*."

"For what?"

"For the best Christmas gift ever. Thank you for giving me my daughter." He leaned his head back against her knee, drawing happiness from simply being here with this fascinating and frustrating woman. She leaned forward and hugged his neck. He held on to her arms, rubbing them with his thumbs and wishing this moment could last forever. When she tried to stifle a yawn by making a funny face, he laughed and let her go.

"You should go to bed, sleepyhead." He stood and held out the candle to her.

"I should go home."

A crack of thunder made her jump and shriek. She laughed nervously.

"No, not in this storm. You can stay here, in Kenzie's room." He motioned down the hall with his head. He wished he could trust himself to hold her all night…

Hesitantly, she took the candle and looked up when their fingertips touched. Was it his imagination? Maybe it was just a flash of lightning. No, he was positive sparks had flown between them. Spinning on his heels, he headed down the hall with Emma following.

At the doorway, he stroked her cheek with the back of his fingers and placed a gentle kiss on her lips. "Good night, Emma."

It was hard to ignore the look that flickered in her eyes, which were now dark green. He wanted her on so many levels.

"Good night, David." Whispery soft, her voice tickled across his heated skin.

With a rapidly declining resolve, he shut the door and made his way back to the living room, smiling when he didn't hear the lock click. He finished his beer and decided to have one more before turning in for a restless night, a night he knew would be filled with images of Emma naked, her mercurial eyes dark with desire as he'd just seen them.

Chapter
Thirteen

"*I love you, Em.*"

Emma fought waking up, still reveling in her dream of dancing with David on the dock under the moonlight. She opened her eyes and gazed around the room. Her happiness faltered. Although he was kind and seemed interested, could David ever fully forgive her? She'd never been in a truly healthy relationship. Was it even possible? *What if last night was a fluke—a combination of alcohol and ambiance?*

Reality sucked.

Yawning, she rubbed her face and got up when she heard Molly whimpering.

She found her pawing at David's closed bedroom door. Picking up the whining dog, she nuzzled her.

"Shh, he's still sleeping. Come on, I'll feed you and take you outside."

The power must've come back on after they went to sleep, and she turned off the lamp, puzzled to find six empty beer bottles. She'd only had one and part of a second…Poor David. He might be waking up with a nasty hangover. When she put Molly down, the dog ran back to his door, whining.

Quickly, she retrieved the puppy and took her outside. Molly sniffed around her new surroundings, and it took Emma fifteen minutes to get her to do her business and come back in. Her paws were muddy, but that mess would have to wait. Emma needed coffee. The dog went back to whimpering outside David's door.

Picking up the beer bottles and the stale bowl of popcorn, Emma moved into the kitchen to start a pot. Quietly rummaging through the refrigerator, she decided on eggs and bacon for breakfast. Cooking him a meal was the least she could do to thank him for letting her stay last night. Maybe she'd manage to not burn the toast this time.

The dog continued to paw at his door and bark. *How is he sleeping through that?*

Twenty minutes later, with the coffee brewed, bacon fried, and bread ready to pop in the toaster, she tried once again to stop the dog from scratching at the door. Biting her lip, she rapped.

She knocked again when he didn't answer and cracked the door. Wearing only pajama pants, David sat on the side of the bed, hands over his face. The dog shoved her way in and began barking more insistently.

"Stop, dammit!"

His curse shocked her. *He must really be hung over.*

"David? Are you okay?"

"Go away," he mumbled.

"I beg your pardon?"

He looked up, his face haggard.

"Are you hung over? Do you want some ibuprofen and coffee?" she asked.

"No, what I want is for you to leave." He stood up and swayed. The dog grabbed his pants leg and growled. He swatted her away, but she wasn't to be deterred.

Emma winced. "Leave?"

"That's what I said."

"What's wrong? This isn't like you—" She hung by the door, unsure of what to do. She'd had plenty of experiences with men who were hung over, and not many of them were good. But something was off…

"This isn't like me, huh?" He threw his arms up. "No, of course not. Good old David's a patsy everyone can run over. Anyone can take whatever they want from him, even if it kills him, because he'll do the Christian thing and turn the other cheek. Well, I'm telling you, I want you to leave. I don't feel well. And if you don't leave, I'll throw you out myself."

He shook off the growling puppy, gripped his stomach, and shoved past her toward the bathroom, staggering and heaving.

Emma raced after him and handed him a wet washcloth as he vomited. "Let me help you. You shouldn't have drunk—"

"You're not my mother. Just go away. It's what you do best, isn't it? Leave?" His voice trailed off as he once again vomited. He appeared to pass out, slipping to the floor.

"David!" She knelt with him, cradling his head in her hands as she tried to get him to respond. His eyes fluttered, and she noticed a strange, fruity smell on his breath.

"Oh my God! You need to go to the doctor."

"No." He shrugged out of her grasp, struggling to get up, but his eyes rolled back, and he slumped to the floor.

Emma ran and grabbed the phone, relieved to see he had Jennifer's number on speed dial. Her hand shook as she hit the button.

"Good morning, David." Jennifer answered cheerfully, the sound of children chattering in the background.

"Something's wrong with David. He's really sick and passed out," Emma shouted, frantic. "Hurry! Please, hurry!" Dropping the phone, she ran back to David and wiped his face with the wet cloth. Molly circled them, whimpering.

The front door slammed open, and Jennifer raced down the hall, her robe over her nightgown billowing in her wake.

"Find his glucometer! Dylan called an ambulance," she ordered. She frowned as she assessed David. "What has he eaten?"

Emma handed her the glucometer. "N-Nothing. I was cooking breakfast. He drank beer last night. At least four, I think."

Emma blushed and crossed her arms in front of her chest when Jennifer's eyes narrowed.

"Oh, David. You know better," she scolded, checking his glucose and casting a murderous glance toward Emma. "It's too high," she muttered.

"Go away," David groused. "I'm fine." He batted at her hand as she checked his pulse.

"You're not fine. You're an ass, and you're going to the hospital."

"Do I need to go stay with the children?" Emma chewed her lower lip, wringing her hands.

"No, Dylan's with them. They're fine." She shook David. "Can you hear me? Breathe deep for me. Did you take your insulin last night?"

"I can't remember. No, I don't think so…" he mumbled.

"I'm going to kill you when you feel better."

"I run faster," he rasped.

His attempt at humor gave Emma hope as she kept the whimpering, insistent puppy at bay.

"Stop, silly dog," she whispered.

"That's odd. It's like the dog knows he's sick," Jennifer said.

The wail of the ambulance coming down the long driveway brought Emma to her feet, and taking the dog with her, she ran to greet them at the door.

Once inside, the EMTs worked fast and started an IV. Jennifer gave them as much medical history as she knew, supplemented by Emma's recounting of last night and this morning.

As the ambulance pulled away, Jennifer looked at Emma. "They started his IV pretty easily. That's a good sign, because it means he wasn't totally dehydrated. Can you drive yourself to the hospital, or do you want to wait on me to change?"

"What about Kensington?"

"Leave her with Dylan. She'll be fine. No need to worry her. She can come see David later. I'll have Dylan check on the dog, too."

"Thanks. I'll go home, grab my purse, and go straight to the hospital." Impulsively, she gave Jennifer a hug. To her surprise, Jennifer hugged her back.

She ran home, her heart pounding.

David has to be okay; Kensington needs him.

I need him…

Emma's leg bounced as she sat by David's bedside, waiting on him to wake up. At least she was in the room now. She'd dawdled a full thirty minutes after the nurse told her she could come in, too nervous to do so. His harsh words from earlier echoed in her mind.

"Stop," he mumbled, shifting in the bed.

She stilled and stared at the floor.

"Look at me, Emma. I know you're upset. Your leg is bouncing. And I'm sure I was less than polite with you this morning."

She looked up at him, clenching her hands together.

"You didn't do anything wrong. It's the DKA that made me so irritable."

She shook her head, silently questioning him. She didn't understand.

"DKA is diabetic ketoacidosis. My mind gets fuzzy, and I get belligerent and nasty with everyone. Ask Jennifer. Or my mom—she has plenty of stories from my adolescence. Now that I'm an adult, it doesn't happen often, but this was totally my fault. I was careless. You did nothing wrong. As a matter of fact, you did everything right in getting me help. Thank you. Can you forgive me?"

She nodded and looked away. *Forgive, yes. Forget, not likely.* The things he'd said to her this morning had reinforced all of her insecurities.

"Kiss and make up?" he asked with a faint smile.

Her jaw went slack, but before she could respond, the door opened.

"How's the king of beers?" Jennifer entered, holding Kensington's hand.

"Ready to sign a temperance pledge," David replied hoarsely. He struggled to sit up and gave Kensington a weak wave.

She peered at him from behind Jennifer's leg, keeping a death grip on Teddy. Her eyes were wide as she surveyed the hospital room.

"Is Daddy okay?"

Emma smiled. "Of course he is. Daddy just has to eat right and take his medicine."

Jennifer played with the curl of Kensington's pigtail. "I'll be right back. I need to go get her car seat so you can take her home after her visit."

"Me?" she gasped. She looked to David and back at Jennifer.

Jennifer smiled, but suspicion lingered in her eyes. "David told me on the phone this is what he wanted."

Emma turned to David, wondering if this was a dream. He nodded.

"She's welcome to stay with us. We can even take care of the four-footed, you-know-what..." Jennifer's voice trailed off when David shook his head. "Okay, then I'll be next door if you need anything, Emma."

"Thank you." For the first time, she didn't feel like a complete outsider. Jennifer's willingness to support his decision boosted her confidence. "That is, if it's okay with Kensington." She held her breath as she waited for the answer.

Kensington nodded, her pigtails bouncing. Emma's heart swelled.

"I'll be back in a jiffy with the car seat." Jennifer closed the door behind her.

"I brought you Teddy." Kensington handed her bear to her father.

David grinned. "Thank you. You sure? I'll be fine. He might miss you."

"He'll make you feel better, Daddy."

"You make me better, Kenz." He looked up at Emma. "Both my girls do."

Emma's heart stuttered with cautious happiness, and she bit her lip. *Both my girls?*

She turned toward David. "Who's going to stay with you tonight? Jennifer? Your mother will be here tomorrow." As much as she hated giving up time with Kensington, she owed David too much not to offer. "Or I could stay, and Kensington could stay with the McAthies."

David rubbed the heel of his hand over his eyes. "No, I'll be fine by myself. I can't get into much trouble. I wish you hadn't called my mother." He pulled one of Kensington's pigtails and smiled when she tried to climb over the bedrails to get to him.

"I didn't. I, uh, didn't think about it. Jennifer did." Emma lowered one bedrail and carefully sat Kensington on the side of the bed. "Now sit still, okay?"

Kensington nodded and looked with wonder at the IV tube. "What's that for?"

"Medicine to make me feel better. Maybe you'll grow up and be a doctor or a nurse and make people feel better too."

She rolled her eyes. "No. I wanna be a skater like Connor."

Emma snickered.

"I'll let this eye roll slide. I'm too tired to worry about it and happy to see you." He opened his arms.

Kensington slid in and snuggled under his chin. Emma felt a slight twinge of jealousy and then felt like a bitch.

"I love you, Daddy."

He kissed Kensington's forehead. "Love you more. And when you get home, there's a special surprise for you."

"When Jennifer gets back with the car seat, we'll leave and let you rest," Emma told him. "And I'll make sure the house is clean and ready for your mother." She bit her lip to keep from laughing when David rolled his eyes. *And he wonders where Kensington learned it?*

"About my mother. She may not be…exactly friendly toward you."

"I understand. I wouldn't be either." She looked up when Jennifer returned. "Give Daddy a kiss goodbye," she told Kensington. "We need to let him rest." Kensington kissed David on the cheek, and Emma picked her up. "We'll see you in the morning. Are you sure you don't want to wait and give Kenzie the surprise yourself?"

"No, this will help take her mind off me." David's eyes looked tired, but he smiled. "You two behave."

"You behave, Daddy!" Kensington replied.

"Will do. Don't you want to take Teddy?"

She shook her head.

Emma gave his hand a squeeze. "I'll take good care of her, I promise."

"I know you will. Thank you."

As the door closed behind Emma and Kenzie, Jennifer perched on the edge of his bed.

"Please don't start." David closed his eyes, not wanting a lecture about his health, or Emma.

"Sticking your head in the sand isn't going to work." Jennifer's tone was the one she used with the kids. "What were you thinking? Drinking? *Really?* You were in diabetic ketoacidosis, and you know how dangerous that is! And allowing *her* to spend the night? You're a father with responsibilities—"

"Stop. It isn't what you're thinking. I forgot my insulin last night, and yes, I drank too much. It was a stupid mistake, and one I regret. You can put your nurse hat away." He motioned for her to leave.

"And Emma? Was that another stupid mistake? What happens if she walks out on you again?"

Jennifer had just voiced his deepest fear, the one he wasn't up to facing right now—not with his thinking still fuzzy. "I'm not discussing Em with you. It isn't any of your business."

"I'll ignore your tone of voice and chalk it up to your DKA. My concern is for you and Kenzie." She huffed and crossed her arms.

"I know, I know. I'm sorry. Look, if I can find it in my heart to give Emma a second chance, can't you?"

Jennifer frowned and didn't respond.

"Please? She's important to me."

"How important?" Jennifer's frown deepened. "No, don't answer that. I'm pretty sure I don't want to know." She sighed and threw up her hands. "Okay. But if she hurts you, I'll pull her hair out in the most horrendous catfight you've ever seen."

"Only if you two go at it in the mud—now that I'd like to see." He chuckled.

Her mouth dropped. "David Michael Patterson! You've been hanging around Dylan way too much. I will pray for your wicked soul tonight," she teased, giving him a quick kiss on the forehead. "Rest and don't give the nurses too much grief."

"I won't. Promise." Before she reached the door, he called out to her. "Hey, Jennifer?"

"Yes?"

"Take Teddy to Kenzie. I know she'll have a meltdown without him, and check on my girls for me, okay? Kenz is in an awful testing phase. I don't want Emma overwhelmed."

"That isn't how Daddy does it." Kensington glared at the sandwich and wrinkled her nose. She leaned over and played with the puppy.

Emma clenched her jaw to keep from yelling. If Kensington had said it once, she'd said it a hundred times since they'd returned to David's.

"It's fine. It's just a grilled cheese sandwich. Leave the dog alone and eat, please."

Her daughter huffed and rolled her eyes.

"Kensington, what has Daddy told you about rolling your eyes?"

Her eyes narrowed, and Emma quickly regretted pushing her.

"My name is Kenzie!" Her lower lip stuck out in a full pout.

Molly sat up, her tail wagging.

Kenzie tore off a bite and threw it to the begging dog.

"Fine, *Kenzie*. Eat. And don't give it to Molly. It will make her sick." Emma pinched the bridge of her nose and counted to ten.

"No, I don't want it. It will make me sick, too. That isn't how Daddy does it." She swung her feet back and forth, watching Emma, waiting. A smug look flitted across her face.

Emma closed her eyes and mentally added scheduling an appointment with her therapist to her to-do list. When she spoke, she tried her best to keep her tone firm, but even. "You need to eat, and then you can take your bath so we can read a story before bed."

"I want it like Daddy does it!"

"I don't know how your daddy does it," she ground out.

God obviously knew what He was doing when I had to have a hysterectomy. I don't know jack-shit about being a mother.

"Because you weren't here."

The words echoed in the cavern of Emma's tight chest and bounced off her self-loathing and fear. She knew the words weren't malicious, just honest. Which almost made it worse. To top it off, she tripped over the eager dog.

"Dammit!"

Kenzie laughed. "You said a bad word. I'm telling Daddy."

Emma sucked in a deep breath and bit her lip to keep from crying. "Show me what you want, Kensing — Kenzie."

Kenzie held up four fingers and pointed at the sandwich cut in half. Emma cut the sandwich into fourths, but Kenzie shook her head no.

"Now what?" *Am I such a horrible mother I can't even make a simple goddamned grilled cheese sandwich?*

"They don't look right." Kenzie glared and pursed her lips.

Emma's patience was at its limit. "If you don't want to eat, you can take your bath and go to bed hungry."

"Fine! I hate you! I want my daddy!" Kensington jumped down and ran to her room, slamming the door shut.

Stunned, Emma sank into a kitchen chair and dropped her head onto her crossed arms, taking a moment. She twisted the tablecloth and held it like a life rope. What had made her think she could step in and fill David's shoes as a parent? She possessed all the mothering skills of…Dammit, she couldn't even think of an animal species with bad mothers.

I'm officially the worst mother on the planet, aside from my own. Molly's sad puppy eyes seemed to confirm it.

The muffled sobs from Kenzie's bedroom only increased her guilt. She might be a horrible mother, but she was the only parent here right now.

A knock on the front door made her bolt upright, and her heart hammered. Had the bad-parent police already been notified of her piss-poor parenting skills? She cracked the door and resisted the urge to roll her eyes.

Is eye rolling genetic or learned behavior? Both?

Jennifer smiled and held out Teddy. "David was afraid Kenzie might change her mind. Was she surprised to find Molly?" Jennifer's brows knit together as Kenzie's wailing intensified. "What's going on? Are you two okay?"

"Y-Yes, everything is…" Emma stopped and shook her head, motioning Jennifer inside. She hated asking a woman who didn't like her for help, but now wasn't the time for pride. They walked to the kitchen.

"Why is Kenzie crying?"

"I don't know if I can do this." Emma picked up the uneaten grilled cheese sandwich and handed it to Jennifer. "I can't even make a damn grilled cheese sandwich right."

"It looks okay to me." Jennifer placed it back on the table.

Emma continued. "It isn't how her daddy makes it." Emma air quoted the remark and walked to the sink, hanging her head in defeat.

"David isn't a gourmet cook. A grilled cheese sandwich is a grilled cheese sandwich. Don't worry about it. She's just being a bratty almost-five year old. Trust me, I have one. They're horrible at times."

"She pointed out that I didn't know how to make the sandwich right because I haven't been here." Emma dashed away the tear slipping down her cheek.

Jennifer grimaced and blew out a deep breath. "Ouch."

"I can't fault her for her honesty. She's right. I think maybe I've made a huge mistake coming back here. I just wanted..." She threw her hands out and shrugged. "I don't know how to do this...mothering stuff."

Jennifer's face reddened. Through clenched teeth, she spat, "So help me, if you leave —"

Emma clasped her hands. "No. No! I'm not leaving! I'm just horrible at this, and I feel so bad for Kensington. I'm sorry. I shouldn't be venting."

Emma paused, wondering how much she should reveal. But Jennifer was here, and she didn't have anyone else to talk to.

"I don't know how much you know. When Kensington was born, I had to have a hysterectomy. She's the only child I'll ever have. Which is probably for the best, now that I think about it...Anyway, that fact really hit home a couple of months ago. A dear friend lost his battle with cancer, and my mother died of an overdose. I've never felt so alone." She paced, not daring to make eye contact. "I'd always planned to come back and make amends, but suddenly I couldn't wait any longer. Showing up here unannounced was selfish on my part. I just wanted Kensington to know I existed, that I loved her. Obviously, I didn't think my plan through, and I didn't listen to those who counseled me to take different steps. What was I thinking? That I could just show up and be a mother? I don't know how—"

"Oh..." Jennifer sighed. "I'm sorry about your losses. I understand the pain of losing a parent. I just worry about Kenzie and David."

Emma held up a hand and shook her head. "Please, no sympathy for my mother. She wasn't a nice person. I never wanted to be like her, but sadly, I'm realizing perhaps I am. I didn't consider how disruptive my presence would be to David and Kensington. But I promise, it's never been my intention to take her away from him. I just want to watch her grow up to be a beautiful young woman. The type of girl I wish I'd been..."

Jennifer met her gaze with tears in her eyes. "I can't imagine not being a part of my children's lives. I understand why you wanted to come back. The thing is, I never understood why you *left* in the first place." She paused, as if weighing her words carefully. "David was devastated when he read that note and realized you were gone."

Emma hung her head, guilt squeezing her chest so hard she couldn't breathe.

Jennifer clasped her hand. "Hear me out. He seems to have made peace with you being back. And it's obvious both he and Kenzie care about you—even if you don't make a sandwich right." She smiled. "I *want* to try to be your friend, for his sake and for Kenzie's. However, if you hurt them again, I'll wash my hands of you forever."

She squeezed Emma's hand. "Start over? As friends and moms who need to stick together to survive? After all, they'll be teens before we're ready."

Emma smiled and nodded. "Yes. Thank you."

Looking down at the plate, Jennifer giggled, pointing at the cold grilled cheese. "Triangles."

Emma frowned. "What?"

"David cuts a sandwich into four triangles, diagonally. That's what you did wrong."

Relaxing, Emma blew out a breath. "Triangles. Got it. I can do this."

"You can. She's testing her boundaries. David even mentioned his concerns about that. Plus, I'm sure she's scared. She's never experienced anything like this before. It's the first time David's been in the hospital in more than ten years. She's just experiencing a little separation anxiety. Most kids go through it at some point in time.

"As for the way she's acting out—there have been a few times I've had to walk away from my children to keep from going stark raving mad. Dylan swears Angela isn't dead because we don't get mad at her at the same time. One parent usually remains calm when the other one can't think straight. Unfortunately, it will probably get worse before it gets better."

Emma shook her head. "I can't imagine you ever losing your cool. You seem like the ultimate mom. David's already fretting about Kensington growing up and the teen years, and I wonder too. She has my genes, after all." Emma offered a self-deprecating smile.

Jennifer patted her arm and squeezed her waist as they walked toward the door. "Don't worry. I think Dylan already has plans in motion to reserve two places at a nunnery for those girls. And I have my moments of self-doubt like every other parent. Just be firm and loving. And you have to make sure to follow through with discipline. You can do it. David has faith in you."

With one last squeeze, Jennifer turned to go. "Call me if you need me. And if she goes to bed hungry, it won't kill her for one night." She grinned. "But I bet she'll come out once she calms down and her tummy growls."

The puppy whimpered from her box. Jennifer sighed. "Angela wants a dog now. I'm hoping for a cat; they're more self-sufficient. I already have three children to pick up after, if you include Dylan."

Emma laughed.

Jennifer closed the door behind her, leaving her alone.

The sobbing from down the hall had subsided, and she secretly hoped Kensington had fallen asleep. *Coward.* Taking a deep breath, she knocked on the door, but there was no answer. Emma cracked it open, and Kensington squeezed her eyes closed, ignoring her. She sat on the bed and brushed the hair out of her little girl's tear-stained face. Leaning over, she kissed her cheek.

"I'm sorry I got upset with you." She handed her Teddy.

"I want my Daddy." Kensington hugged her bear.

"I know you do, but Daddy has to feel better first. He'll be home soon."

"Promise?" Two hazel eyes met hers, full of cautious hope.

"Promise. Meanwhile, we need to clean house for a special guest. Don't you want to come eat your sandwich? We have a lot to do tomorrow."

Kensington sat up, hugging Teddy. "Who's coming?"

"Your grandmother. She's worried about Daddy, too."

Kensington's eyes lit up. "Nana? Is Papa coming too?"

"I don't know, but we have to clean the house."

"Okay." Kensington threw her arms around Emma's neck.

She inhaled the scent of Kensington's soft hair. "I'm sorry I wasn't here for you, baby. I love you. I've always loved you." A tear slipped down her cheek, and she held Kensington tighter.

Kensington wiped the tear off Emma's face.

"Don't cry, Mama. Daddy will be okay. I love you."

"Love you more."

Emma felt immediately lighter. Taking her daughter's hand, she walked her back to the kitchen to start over on supper—this time with triangle-shaped grilled cheese sandwiches.

Chapter
Fourteen

"Nana!" Kensington threw herself into the arms of David's mother. A plump woman with graying light-brown hair and pale, greenish-gray eyes, Vivian Patterson picked Kensington up and hugged her close, smiling widely.

"My goodness, you're getting so tall and heavy. Is Daddy feeding you rocks?"

"No, Nana. That's silly." Kenzie laughed and squealed when her feet once again touched the ground. Grabbing her grandmother's hand, she pulled her into the house. "Me and Mama cleaned for you. Daddy gets to come home today." She danced and twirled with excitement.

"Hello, Mrs. Patterson." Emma looked her in the eyes and attempted what she hoped was a warm smile.

Mrs. Patterson's wide smile faded to a thin, straight line. One eyebrow rose a fraction and her gaze swept Emma from head to toe. Emma wished she'd kept her mouth shut.

"So, you're *Emma*." Mrs. Patterson didn't bother to hide her derision.

"We made cookies for you and Daddy." Kensington tugged on her grandmother's hand, urging her toward the kitchen.

"You made a *diabetic* cookies? A man hospitalized because of his diabetes?" Her face flushed. "Are you trying to kill my son? Is that your plan?"

Kensington's mouth popped open as she stared up at her grandmother. Emma's cheeks heated as her temper flared, but she kept a lid on it for her daughter's sake.

She held out her hand. "I'm Emma Devine, Kensington's mother."

"I know who you are," the woman snapped in return. "Vivian Patterson, David's *mother*." She hesitated a moment and glanced at her granddaughter before shaking Emma's hand.

Taking Vivian's suitcase, Emma held her head high as she walked toward David's bedroom. She'd spent last night and this morning cleaning the house from top to bottom in anticipation of the white-glove test from David's mother.

"I have your room ready for you. David's being released from the hospital today, and I know he'll be happy to see you. He insisted you sleep in his room, and he'll take the couch." She deposited the suitcase on the bed and turned to face his mother. "And the cookies are sugar-free. As I'm sure you know, David has a terrible sweet tooth. I thought they might cheer him up a little. Kenzie enjoyed making them for her father."

"I can't imagine you know that much about my son. You haven't exactly been a presence in his life or *his* daughter's."

Emma flinched but held her tongue. She ran a hand through her hair, wishing the butterflies in her stomach would calm down.

Vivian pulled a book out of the suitcase and handed it to Kensington, giving her a kiss. "This was one of your Daddy's favorite books. He can read it to you when he comes home."

"Thank you, Nana." Kensington danced around with the book. "Look, Mama!"

"That's a great book. Why don't you go look at it while I help your Nana get settled?"

"Okay. I'll show it to Teddy." Kenzie raced out of the room.

"That child goes ninety to nothing," Vivian murmured. Her warm smile turned icy.

"Is there anything I can do for you before I leave to get David?" Emma folded her hands together as Vivian continued to unpack.

She slammed the suitcase shut and turned to face Emma, her arms crossed in front of her chest. "Yes, there is something you can do. Leave. *Period.* Go back to wherever you've been all these years."

Emma forced herself to maintain eye contact and keep her voice even. "I know you're not going to like what I'm about to say, but I want to be very clear and put my cards on the table. I'm here to stay, to be a part of my daughter's life. This is with David's blessing. I hope we can get along for the sake of your granddaughter and son, but it's your choice. I can't make you like me. I won't be rude to you. But I'm not *leaving.*" Emma shoved her shaking hands behind her back, squeezing them until it hurt. The knowledge that David wanted her here helped keep her feet in place.

Mrs. Patterson started at her for a few seconds, as if sizing up an opponent.

"Actually, my son hasn't told me much about you. From the beginning, he's been very close-mouthed about how you became involved in his life. All I knew, until moments ago, was your name and the fact that you gave birth and *abandoned* your child. What kind of mother does that? Do you have any idea what you put my son through? He had a bright future ahead of him with plans to go to seminary!" Her voice escalated with her agitation, but she broke off angrily when Kenzie ran back into the room, peering at them with concern.

"What's wrong, Nana?"

"Nothing, darling. Go read your book. Emma and I are just talking."

Kensington glanced back and forth between them, her face suspicious. "Don't you want to come meet Molly? She's my dog!"

Emma nodded and gave her a reassuring smile. "We're just talking; we'll be done in a moment. Go play with your puppy."

Kensington blew an exaggerated sigh before leaving the room.

At a lower volume, Vivian continued. "I know David isn't her father—not her biological father." She held up her hand when Emma tried to interrupt.

"He has never denied nor confirmed it. He tells me simply that he's Kenzie's father, but *I know my son.* He would never take up with someone *like you.* You tricked him somehow. I don't need to know you. Your actions spoke volumes about your character when you deserted your baby. You're a cold, heartless little witch—only concerned about yourself."

Vivian's assessment echoed in the room, reigniting the doubt in Emma's soul. David's mother grabbed the suitcase and placed it under the window before turning back to Emma, her hands on her hips. "Well?"

Emma stood with her arms wrapped around her chest, feeling like everything Vivian said was probably true. Her mouth was dry, and she found it difficult to swallow. The woman was right; she didn't deserve David's forgiveness or Kensington's love, but she was trying to do the right thing now, to make amends.

"Aren't you going to say anything?"

Emma shook her head. She refused to add lying to her list of character defects. Taking a deep breath, she paused a moment before speaking. She dug deep and remembered that she did have worth. Her efforts on her daughter's behalf mattered. She looked Vivian straight in the eyes, refusing to allow the cowering, shamed girl who still lingered within her an outlet.

"Everything you said is true. There's nothing I can add to your character assessment except to stress the fact that I love my daughter. I don't deny that I've made some serious mistakes. Now, if you don't need anything, I'll go get David. Would you like to spend the time with Kensington? If not, I'll be happy to take her with me. She's anxious to see her daddy."

Emma straightened her shoulders despite her inner turmoil. The only thing keeping her from collapsing in a puddle of guilt and shame was the knowledge that David believed in her. Like Richard and her therapist, he saw something redeemable about her.

And Kenzie loved her, which was the most amazing thing in the world.

Vivian looked taken aback. "I'll spend the time with Kenzie. I'm only here for a couple of days, to make sure David's okay."

"I know he'll be pleased to see you." Emma turned and walked away, speaking to Kensington on the way out.

She waited until she was alone in the car to dissolve into tears.

"You don't have to hide it from me, Emma. I can see you've been crying," David said as they settled in the car.

"I'm fine," she replied, tight-lipped.

He sighed and looked out the window. "I'm sure my mother gave you a hard time. She's a little overprotective, and I apologize if she said anything out of line." He rubbed a hand down her hair, regarding her with concern. "Hey, talk to me."

Emma shrugged away from him. "Your mother didn't say anything that wasn't true." Keeping her face blank, she started the car. She refused to comment further. It wouldn't be fair to put him in the middle. His mother was justified in trying to protect her son, and she understood Vivian's misgivings. She wouldn't want her child involved with someone like her either.

"Hey." He grabbed her hand and gave it a squeeze. "If it makes you feel any better, she never thought my brother-in-law was good enough for my sister when they were dating. Now she adores him."

"We're not dating. She has good reasons not to like me. I don't blame her at all. And she knows you're not Kensington's biological father." Emma stared straight ahead at the road. They drove in silence for a few moments.

"We could be," David offered.

"Could be what?"

"Dating. Tell me about Kenzie's father." David stared out the window, scanning the horizon with a furrow in his brow.

It was the moment she'd known would come, sooner or later. How was she to explain Ken? Dear, sweet Ken.

Emma pulled off the road into a parking lot. When she looked up, she found it ironic that they were in front of his church. *What better place for true confessions? And dating? Is he on some kind of medication that's messing with his mind?* She turned off the car and sat for a moment, staring at a stained-glass window of Jesus with a lamb.

"I've told you a little about him before. His name was David Kensington. But he never liked being called David, so he went by Ken. I met him at a truck stop outside of Birmingham. I, uh, mistook him for my john. He played along with it and walked me to his car. Angel was in there waiting when we arrived.

"Before getting in, I told Ken I charged extra for another person. He said, 'Sure, sure, just get in before we get bagged by that cop over there.' I hadn't realized there was an undercover cop watching us, but sure enough, he sauntered over and asked what we were doing. Ken told him I was his little sister and he was late picking me up.

"The cop seemed suspicious, but he let us go. Angel thought the whole thing was hilarious. Ken said it was 'the balls.' He was from Boston, so he had a funny accent and used slang I'd never heard before. As we drove away from the truck stop, Ken confessed that he was not the person who'd hired me for sex, and he hoped I was good with a road trip. I don't even remember where he and Angel were going that night, but I knew their destination had to be a lot better than what mine would've been."

She sighed. "Ken was funny, in a quirky kind of way, and I fell hard for him. He had a cowlick and a scar on his jaw from a barroom brawl. And when he laughed, his eyes would twinkle and he'd start snorting…" Her voice drifted off as she remembered her first love.

"Writing was their passion—graffiti writing. Ken and Angel lived for it, and I'd act as their lookout. On occasion, I'd help do a throw up if it was a stencil, but I wasn't very good…Actually, I sucked at it. Ken was good, but Angel was hands down the best. He's the king. That boy is so talented." She smiled at the memories, but her heart felt heavy, wondering if Angel was okay. She hadn't been in touch with him in a few weeks…

"From the moment he rescued me that night, Ken was good to me. He protected me and loved me, even knowing my past. He was the first man to ever take an interest in me as a *person*. He and Angel taught me how to laugh. It was a whirlwind relationship, but we packed a lifetime of experience into seven months. His family hated me and refused to acknowledge I existed. I still remember the day he called and told them about me." She shook her head. "Your mother isn't the first woman to find me unacceptable for her son. His parents called me a gold-digging whore and said I wasn't good enough for him. They didn't particularly like Angel either, but his family has money, so they tolerated him." She shrugged and stared at her clenched hands.

"We just traveled around from city to city. They took me places I'd never imagined visiting—New York, Boston, Philadelphia. Me, Ken, and Angel: we called ourselves the three amigos. We'd do odd jobs, scraping by as best we could. We'd shoplift if we got really hungry. Well, the boys did the shoplifting. You witnessed firsthand that I wasn't any good at it. They were protective of me and didn't want me getting into trouble; I'd already been in enough. If things got too bad, I'd slip off and make a little money and lie about it. I didn't want to be a burden." Heat rose in her cheeks as memories swirled around her.

"Go on…" David interrupted her musings.

"Eventually Ken got busted for graffiti and disorderly conduct. It wasn't his first brush with the law. His parents pulled some strings and had him enlist in the army instead of going to jail. A couple months later he died overseas in a roadside bomb blast. Instead of paying some dumb fine or serving time, he ended up with a death sentence. And I found myself pregnant and alone, except for Angel. You pretty much know the rest.

"I know people don't understand the life I've led. Some of it wasn't my fault, and some of it was poor decisions on my part, even selfishness. But I accept full responsibility for the terrible things I've done, and I'm trying to make amends, to redeem myself."

She sighed. "Your mother has every right to be concerned about me being in your life. Don't blame her. She just wants to protect you and Kenzie. I'm incredibly grateful for your generosity and can never repay you."

David sat for a moment, deep in thought, gazing out the window. Emma waited, wondering if he had changed his mind about her being around Kenzie. Her chest hammered. If he forbade her from seeing her daughter, she'd abide by his decision. But her heart would shatter into a million pieces, and she didn't know how she'd ever put her life back together again.

He reached over and held her hand. "I'm sorry about all the crap that's happened to you. But I'm happy that circumstances brought you and Kenzie into my life."

Raising her hand to his lips, he kissed it, as if she were a princess in one of Kenzie's fairy-tale books. She stole a look at him from under her lashes. The warmth of his lips sent shockwaves to her core, and the heavy fear that hung like a funeral pall over her life lifted. In his face, she saw hope, bright and full of color. She pulled in a deep, cleansing breath.

"Me too," she whispered with a smile.

Chapter
Fifteen

Emma finished loading the dishwasher and looked around for something else to do. She dreaded going into the other room to face David's mother and her cold, critical looks. For his homecoming, Vivian had cooked his favorite meal: meatloaf and mashed potatoes. Emma had offered to help, but she'd insisted the meatloaf recipe was a family secret and refused to allow her in the kitchen.

Taking the coward's way out, Emma had volunteered to do the dishes. Being alone doing a mundane chore had calmed her nerves after the tense meal. Folding the kitchen towel, she smiled when she heard Kenzie ask her grandmother for more stories about "when Daddy was a bad boy."

Emma walked into the living area, easing toward the front door. "I'll just say good night. Thank you again for dinner, Mrs. Patterson."

David stood, as he always did, when she entered the room. He gave her an apologetic look and rolled his eyes behind his mother's back.

"Kenzie, do you want to walk with me to take your mother home?" he asked.

"No. I'll stay with Nana. She's telling me about when you were bad." Kenzie giggled.

David frowned. "I was never *bad*—mischievous perhaps, but never bad."

His mother snorted. "Mischievous? Do you remember the time you threw Carole's cat out the second-story window to see if the poor thing would really land on his feet?"

"That was a science experiment. I'll be back in a few minutes. I'm going to walk Emma home while you entertain Kenzie with these exaggerated tales."

"Emma's a big girl. I'm quite sure she can make it next door without assistance," his mother replied with a sniff and a frown. "It isn't like she hasn't been on her own before."

Emma dug her nails into her palms to the point of pain. If she stayed one minute longer, she'd either bite her tongue until it bled or slap David's mother.

"I agree. Emma's quite capable of taking care of herself, but you raised me to be a gentleman, and I'm walking her home. I'll be back soon. Kenzie, mind your grandmother." David placed a reassuring hand on Emma's lower back, escorting her out the door.

Once outside, Emma shrugged her shoulders to relieve the knot of tension in her back. "Your mother's a polite southern lady. However, I wish she'd just tell me straight out she hates my fucking guts instead of taking cheap shots."

David's eyebrows lifted, and he grinned.

"Sorry about the language." She shook her head. "Not that I blame her, but seriously, she acts like I'm going to lead you down the road to hell or steal her damn meatloaf recipe and sell it to the Food Network."

"Road to hell, huh? Sounds like quite an adventure. I've never been there. Do you have a road map in case we get lost? I left my phone with the GPS back at the house."

"Not funny."

He nudged her arm with his elbow and chuckled. "Come on, lighten up and just laugh about it. Just imagine all the passive-aggressive torment we can inflict on her as payback. And by the way, the secret ingredient in her meatloaf is chili sauce."

"Chili sauce? I'll be damned. I never would have guessed that. I hate to admit it, but it really was delicious. Anyway, it's easy for you to laugh. She doesn't hate *you*."

He grabbed her hand and squeezed it. Her heart flip-flopped.

"Besides, don't you think meeting me is torment enough for your mother? Are you sure you're okay? Seeking revenge doesn't sound like you at all."

Emma tried not to stare at the beautiful man strolling beside her. Despite his recent illness, the fading sun made him god-like, even in jeans and a T-shirt. His dark eyes seemed to simmer with passion when he smiled at her. The wind mussed his hair, giving him a sexy, unkempt look. He'd scared her more than she thought possible when he lay on the bathroom floor pale and listless.

"I guess you don't know me as well as you think. You can ask my sister. I was a tormentor extraordinaire in my younger days. Now, for the task at hand, let's see…For starters, I'll take my time getting home. Make my mom wonder what we've been up to." He wiggled his eyebrows at her with a conspiratorial grin.

"No! Good grief, David. She'll think I've captured and murdered you. Or worse, seduced you."

"That wouldn't be so bad," he murmured.

Shivers of desire moved through her. "What?" Emma turned and stopped so abruptly on the trail he ran into her. She caught her breath when his arms wrapped around her waist.

"You've already captivated me," he whispered against her forehead.

"Captured. I said captured, not captivated," Emma croaked. Lifting her face, she stared at his sensuous mouth. *Kiss me!* She caught her breath when he did exactly that, his mouth teasing her bottom lip. She tangled her fingers in the curls at the nape of his neck.

He pulled her closer, holding her tight, their foreheads resting together. She couldn't have moved if she'd wanted to. And she didn't. Staring into his eyes, she saw her desire reflected in their dark depths just before his lips found hers again.

From the back of his throat came a soft growl of need. His tongue delved into her mouth, exploring and playful. He tasted of peppermint, and she dreamily wondered if he had *planned* to kiss her. Her nipples hardened in response, and she whimpered with an overwhelming longing for more, not wanting him to stop though her mind screamed to put on the brakes. David's lips moved to her neck, leaving a trail of warmth and desire.

"Stop. We should stop," she murmured, gripping his firm biceps. Her legs felt like jelly. Desire zipped through her like she'd been struck by lightning, her skin tingling in response. "Maybe we should stop…" She tried again without much conviction as his arousal pressed against her. His warm hands slid under her T-shirt to her lower back.

"Stop?" he murmured against her lips.

"Don't stop. I mean, we have to stop…" She couldn't stop.

"I know, I know." He let out an anguished groan. Moving his hands from her back to her arms, he leaned forward and nipped her lower lip one last time. Gazing down at her with a decidedly whimsical smile, he murmured, "What have you done to me, Emma Devine? This is surreal, like one of Kenzie's princess stories. I believe you're a temptress weaving her spell."

Heat rose in her cheeks, and it wasn't from the setting sun. Her heart raced so fast she couldn't catch her breath, and she knew if she didn't leave now, there would be no going back. She'd tackle him right here on the path through the woods.

"I have to go. I'll see you when your mother leaves." With reluctance, she disentangled herself from his grasp and darted up the hill. She paused at the sound of crunching leaves behind her.

"Hold on, Em. I can't run, not yet. Wait for me."

Guilt washed over her. *Dear God, he's just been released from the hospital!* She ran back to him and cupped his face in her hands. "I'm sorry. Are you okay?"

"I'm fine, honey. A little worked up, but fine. Let me walk you home. You don't want a snake getting you, do you?" He smiled and kissed her palm. The heat from his lips sizzled down her arm to the pit of her stomach.

"I've walked home a million times on my own. I think I can make it the last ten yards," she replied, breathless.

His warm brown eyes crinkled with his smile. "But I want my good-night kiss. You know, as a reward for being a gentleman."

"What the hell do you call what we just did?" she asked, still flushed and shaky.

"A preamble?"

"A preamble to what? Are you insane? Holy crap! David, do gentlemen kiss like that?" Heat infused her cheeks, and she fanned them.

David stepped back and scratched his head as if in deep thought. "I don't know. I've never kissed one. You tell me."

"You know my history; I don't think I've kissed many either…" She wrapped her arms around her chest and looked at the ground.

David tilted her chin up. "Look at me. Your history is only important in that it has made you the strong, resilient woman you are now. I mean that, Em."

She found his naïveté endearing. Her past impacted her entire life. Through her counseling, she was learning to move forward, but it would always shadow her outlook on the world, her relationships with people. Trust would forever be an issue she had to work on. But because of this man, she was willing to consider it now…She swallowed the lump in her throat and wrapped her arms around his neck.

She kissed his cheek. "Thank you."

"You're welcome," he murmured, pulling her in for another kiss.

Emma reluctantly stepped back. Grinning, she pushed a lock of hair out of his eyes. "Your mother's going to know what we've been doing. Look at you. Your hair is a mess. I guess you could walk me home and borrow a comb."

The smile he gave her was the one she'd seen him use when indulging Kenzie in some silly notion.

"Okay, whatever." He wrapped her hand in his warm, firm grasp as they continued toward her place. Once inside, David followed her to the bathroom where she handed him a comb. Haphazardly, he ran it through his hair and turned to face her.

She laughed. "You made it worse. Sit." She pointed to the closed lid on the commode. He sat with an exaggerated sigh. With horror, she realized she'd left the book she'd been reading next to the bathtub. David glanced at the title, *Parenting for Dummies*. He raised an eyebrow and smirked. Emma felt her cheeks flush, but ignored his amused look as she combed his unruly hair. She caught her breath when he pulled her close, resting his head against her stomach, his arms wrapped around her hips.

"David, stop. You're supposed to be making yourself look presentable."

"I don't want to go home," he whined, a convincing imitation of their daughter. He looked up at her and smiled. "Please don't make me."

"What do you want me to do? Call and ask your mother if you can spend the night?" She laughed.

"Would you?" His eyes danced with mischief, and his grin widened.

"No! Do you need to check your sugar? What's wrong with you? You're usually so...so *responsible*."

He stood up, chuckling. "Take it easy. I'm just kidding. We haven't broken any commandments." He pinched her nose and winked at her. "Good night, honey." He barely made it to the front door before she ran after him.

"David, wait!" Emma's heart raced with her recklessness, but she didn't want him to leave, at least not without another kiss. She was as crazy as he was.

Turning, he looked at her with a smoldering gaze, "Yes?"

"What about that kiss good night?" she asked a little breathlessly, holding on to the front door for support.

He leaned down and gave her a soft kiss. "Good night, Emma."

"Good night," she sighed with ill-disguised disappointment. "I'll see you when your mother leaves."

"In that case, I hope I can convince her to go home tonight," he called over his shoulder with a wave.

She slammed the door.

I'm falling in love with Emmanuelle Summer Devine.

He'd tried to ignore the feelings, but there was no doubt about it. During the long days in the hospital, he'd had plenty of time to dissect his convoluted thoughts. The word *home* no longer meant just him and Kenzie. Home now included Emma. A moment ago, he hadn't been kidding when he'd said he didn't want to leave. He wanted to stay, and it wasn't just because of their growing sexual attraction—although granted, that was *definitely* there.

Emma fascinated him. She was like a puzzle, and he had most of the pieces, but didn't quite know how to complete the picture. An enigma. That was the word to describe her. The wall of protection around her heart was so thick he wondered if he'd ever be able to penetrate it. He desperately wanted to know everything about her, to make her smile, and to hold her when she was sad. To show her he could be trusted to take care of her in every way possible.

To make her understand she's worthy of love.

He entered the house and headed toward the sounds of giggling and splashing in the bathroom. He stood in the doorway and watched as his mother wrapped a towel around his squirming, wet daughter, who giggled with careless abandon at her own silliness. His mother was soaked, her hair in disarray. She shot him an inquiring, suspicious look. Molly barked, adding to the pandemonium.

"Daddy!" Kenzie jumped into his arms, still wrapped in her towel, wiggling like a basketful of wet puppies. He hugged her tight, inhaling the smell of her bubble bath on her warm skin, brushing his cheek against her damp curls.

"It's so good to be home. I missed you, Kenzie McFrenzie."

"I missed you, too. So did Nana and Molly." She gave him a resounding kiss on the cheek with her typical enthusiasm. He put her down, and she wriggled into the nightgown his mother held for her. As she brushed her teeth, she chattered the entire time, and he wondered if she'd ever settle down. After two bedtime stories and her nightly prayers, she finally closed her eyes, falling into an exhausted sleep with Molly at her feet.

He picked up the dog and took her outside, delaying the confrontation he knew was coming. His mother came to the door and called his name.

Reluctantly, he scooped Molly into his arms and followed his mother into the living area.

"I forget how old I am until I spend a day with a grandchild." She laughed, collapsing on the overstuffed chair.

After sniffing her surroundings, Molly settled in her bed.

"If I could harness Kenzie's energy into something constructive, I could amass a fortune instead of being a broke schoolteacher," he agreed with a tired yawn. He stretched out on the sofa and closed his eyes, glad to be home.

"Did you check your glucose?"

David smiled without opening his eyes. "Yes, ma'am. I'm on the money. Supper was delicious. Thank you. No one makes meatloaf like you do."

"Good."

The ticking mantle clock and his mother's drumming fingernails were all that broke the uncomfortable silence. With a sense of dread leftover from his teenage years, he waited for the lecture. Avoiding this conversation was as unlikely as a summer snowstorm in Alabama.

"She's going to break your heart. And Kenzie's."

Leave it to his mother to get straight to the point. He knew her words weren't meant to hurt, but were spoken with love and concern for her family. Understanding this didn't make it any easier.

"Possibly." There was a chance his mother was right.

"How can you let her back into your lives so easily? She abandoned her *baby!*" The sentence ended with a bleat of frustration.

"She didn't abandon Kenzie; she entrusted her care to me, and now she's back," he countered.

"Take the blinders off, son. Don't defend her. I was there to help pick up the pieces, remember? She ruined your life."

David bolted upright and glared at his mother. "You're wrong. My future simply changed. I took a different course than planned, but I can't imagine my life without Kenzie. And I would hope you feel the same way." He spoke with conviction. "God knows I love you. But I'm an adult capable of making my own decisions. Even if they prove to be colossal mistakes, they're mine to make."

"Don't you take that tone with me, young man. You know I love Kenzie. She's my granddaughter." She huffed with indignation.

"And Emma is her mother," he replied, holding his ground.

"What are you saying?" She pushed a strand of hair out of her face.

"I'm saying I wish you'd give Emma a chance. She's in our lives — I hope permanently."

"You can't be serious. You're going to *marry* her?"

His mother's horrified gasp irritated him. Tired, he didn't feel like arguing with her tonight. "I haven't thought that far ahead. I meant she's Kenzie's mother, and therefore in our lives. But if our relationship progresses as I'd like, and if she'll have me, then yes, that could happen."

"If she'll have *you?* Are you sure your sugar's okay? You're obviously not thinking clearly. That woman doesn't *deserve* you or Kenzie. She's a heartless, selfish little witch who left you to care for a newborn baby without a thought for you, or her child," his mother screeched. "She destroyed your dream of attending seminary, and you nearly lost your job! You're too good for her —"

"Enough." He spoke firmly and held up a hand to stop her tirade. "Mom, I love you, and I respect you. And I know you've been stressed about my hospitalization. But stop. Let's call it a night before one of us says something we'll both regret. I'm not going to listen to you attack Emma. Is she perfect? No. I'm not perfect, either. She was scared, homeless, and young. Life has not been kind to her. Was her decision after Kenzie's birth the right one?" He shrugged. "The one thing I *do know*, her decision gave me my daughter.

"I'm falling in love with Emma—" He paused and shot his mother a warning look. "Regardless of whether or not we marry, she's going to be involved in our lives as Kenzie's mother. I want you in my life, and in Kenzie's. Please, don't make me choose between you and Emma." Hurt flashed in her eyes and he softened his voice. "Please, Mom, for my sake and Kenzie's, give her a chance. You're my mother and my rock."

He took a deep breath and continued. "This is the only time I'm going to say this. No more passive-aggressive, hateful statements about Emma. And don't be rude to her. And absolutely, you are not to malign her in front of Kenz. If you can't, at the very least, be civil and try to get to know her, I will be forced to respectfully ask you to leave my home." Exhausted, he stood up to go shower.

"David…" His mother grasped his hand and beseeched him with her gaze.

"Good night, Mom. I mean what I said. Please give Emma a chance. She didn't have a great mother for a role model, like I did. In fact, she's endured horrible, disgusting things you and I could hardly imagine. If I can forgive her, surely you can." He kissed the top of her head and left her alone to think.

Chapter
Sixteen

After an excruciating forty-eight-hour visit, David's mother had now been gone for five days. But due to staff shortages at the restaurant and her counseling sessions, Emma hadn't had time to see Kenzie or David. At last, as of now, she had four glorious days off. She missed her daughter and found herself hurrying through the woods to see if David would allow Kenzie to spend the night with her. She'd never had the nerve to ask before, but he'd allowed her to stay at his house while he was in the hospital, so maybe he'd trust her again. Truth be told, she missed her daughter's father, too. The shadowing of the trees provided little relief from the unrelenting heat, and the cloying humidity made her clothes stick uncomfortably to her skin.

Sweat poured down her face. Tugging on her shirttail, she attempted to dry off and make herself presentable. Mosquitoes swarmed, and she swatted them away, now wishing she'd stayed home until it cooled off later in the evening. She entered the screened porch, jumping—as she always did—when the door closed behind her with a *thwack*. Blowing her damp bangs out of her eyes, she knocked on the door. Her heart raced in anticipation of seeing David.

Kenzie, not David...Okay, both.

She waited a minute and knocked again, pulling at her shirt, trying to cool herself by flapping it. Shifting nervously on her sweaty, tired feet, she waited for someone to answer the door.

What a dumb idea. I should've just called. She huffed with growing irritation.

A niggling fear made her hesitate before leaving. David's car was parked in the driveway. What if he was sick again? Feeling like a burglar, she opened the unlocked door and peeked into the living area. Semi-dark, the cool room provided an oasis from the suffocating heat. Muted strands of light crept through the old-fashioned Venetian blinds. Molly picked her head up but settled back to sleep with a doggie huff. *Some guard dog.*

A loud snore signaled that David was far from dead. Tiptoeing closer to the couch, she bit her lip to keep from laughing out loud. Asleep with his right arm thrown over his eyes, he was oblivious to her presence. His left arm wrapped around Kensington, who napped curled into his chest, holding Teddy. A pink bow perched in his hair and purple glitter polish smeared his fingertips. Emma smiled. Was there anything more attractive than a man who loved his daughter so much he played dress-up?

Emma moved to slip back outside, but Kenzie stirred and opened her eyes. Awake in an instant, she grinned and waved. David let out another loud snore. Kenzie rolled her eyes and covered her ears.

"Kiss him, Mama. He's Sleeping Beauty," Kenzie whispered.

Emma knelt beside the couch. Leaning in, she gave David a quick peck on the lips. Kenzie giggled.

David opened his eyes and smiled lazily at Emma. "Hey you." Gruff with sleep and sexy as hell, his voice made her glad she was already on the floor. Her weak knees might not have held her up.

"Hello, Sleeping Beauty."

"Awakened by my true love's kiss." He stroked her cheek with the back of his fingers.

True love? Under the spell of those warm eyes and sleepy smile, her natural defenses fell. Emma longed to climb on top of him with Kenzie and snuggle. She wanted to feel as warm and secure as her daughter in David's arms.

"Now kiss me! I'm Sleeping Beauty, too!" Kenzie squeezed her eyes shut and pretend snored.

Emma gave her daughter a kiss and tickled her. Soon they were all tickling, laughing, and squealing. Kenzie rolled to the floor on top of Emma. Molly joined in the fray, barking and running around in circles.

"My girls. I'm a lucky man." David rubbed his eyes and yawned before propping his cheek on one hand. "You just get off work?"

"Yes, why?"

"My favorite perfume, cheeseburger and fries," he teased.

Emma grimaced. "Ew, I'm sorry. I get so used to the smell, I didn't realize I stunk." She felt her cheeks flame.

"Hey, they say the way to a man's heart is through his stomach."

She rolled her eyes, and he laughed.

"I'm teasing. But if you want a bath, be my guest." He motioned toward the bathroom down the hall. Examining his purple-glittered nails, he frowned. "Or we could all go swimming in the lake."

"Swimming!" Kenzie scrambled off Emma and ran down the hall with Molly on her heels. "I'm getting my swimsuit, Daddy!"

Emma swallowed nervously and rubbed her thigh. "I don't have a swimsuit."

"Just wear what you have on. You're going to have to wash those clothes anyway."

Emma looked down in dismay. "But I'm in jeans and a T-shirt."

David grinned. "I'd suggest skinny-dipping, but my resolve wouldn't be able to take it, and Kenzie would get terrible ideas. She's already almost five going on twenty-five." He sat up and removed the pink bow from his hair with a puzzled frown.

She clenched her legs together at the thought of swimming naked with David. "I'll just watch you two swim." She turned and laughed when Kenzie came barreling out of her room stark naked, waving her swimsuit and jumping up and down.

"Look, we can do something else, something we can all do as a family," David offered. He stood and grabbed the neon pink Minnie Mouse suit from Kenzie and calmly helped her into it.

He said as a family! Her heart melted faster than homemade ice cream.

"Let's go," Kenzie shouted, grabbing her parents by the hand.

"Swimming it is. I'll just go as I am," Emma said with a laugh, caught up in Kenzie's excitement.

"Okay, just give me a minute. Kenz go find your life jacket. You know the rule." He disappeared into his bedroom.

"No life jacket, no swimming!" She tore over to the hall closet and ran back, swinging it above her head. "Can Molly go, too?"

Emma smiled. "I think Molly's too little. She's just a puppy and needs to take a nap. Let's take her outside first, so she doesn't have an accident while we're gone."

Outside, Emma laughed as Kenzie shouted for the dog to hurry because it was time to swim. Ten minutes later, they returned to the living area and found David waiting for them. The pup settled into her bed, done with the excitement.

David wore a pair of sunglasses and blue swim trunks and had an armful of towels and sunscreen. Emma grabbed the sunscreen out of his hand—to keep from staring—and started to slather it on Kenzie. She'd never seen him this close to naked before, and it was quite unsettling. Only the fading bruises on his arms from his hospital stay marred his perfection.

"Stop, Mama, I'm slicky and sticky." Kenzie wrinkled her nose, trying to rub some of the lotion off.

"Oh, sorry." Emma mumbled. She had indeed overdone it with the sunscreen while daydreaming about David. She rubbed some on her own face, neck, and arms before handing the bottle back to him.

He squirted sunscreen in his hand and began smoothing it over his arms and chest. Emma watched as it soaked into his skin, defining every damn muscle he had. Her hands itched to explore his body, and she began to sweat all over again. The burning in her cheeks went from warm to downright hot.

"Do you mind?" he asked.

"I-I'm sorry; I didn't mean to s-stare," she stammered, tearing her gaze from his six-pack. She knelt and began to buckle the life jacket on Kenzie.

When she stole a glance back at David, he looked like the Cheshire cat.

"I meant would you mind getting my back?" He waved the bottle in front of her. "With the sunscreen."

Snapping to attention, she gave herself a mental shake. "Oh. Oh!"

Good grief, what must he think of me?

"Sure, of c-course," she stuttered with a gulp.

David handed her the bottle and turned around with a knowing smirk. She applied the sunscreen to his shoulders, resisting the urge to press her lips everywhere her fingers moved. Oh, how she wanted to wrap her arms around him and rake her nails across his chest. Truly, she actually did. *What's wrong with me?* This is David, the preacher wannabe, upstanding schoolteacher, and terrific father.

So? He was also a handsome, sexy, delicious example of manhood. And she was a woman. *Able to make my own choices and love whomever I want.* The freedom of this last thought was exhilarating.

She worked the sunscreen into his back like a deep tissue massage as her imagination took flight. His soft moan of pleasure brought her to her senses.

"That feels great," he murmured in a strained voice.

Yes, he does. She wanted to devour him from head to toe.

"Come *on*, let's go *swimming!*" Kenzie stomped her foot.

Embarrassed, Emma handed the sunscreen back to David. He now held the towels carefully draped over his arm and the front of his swim trunks. Her body had betrayed her as well. Flushed, she closed her eyes and took a step back, needing a minute to pull her shit together.

As if he could read her mind, he handed her a towel, which she threw over her shoulder. If asked, she would attribute her hardened nipples to the air-conditioner.

They walked down to the dock, swinging Kenzie between them, much to her squealing delight. David dropped the towels and threw off his sunglasses before diving into the water. He surfaced, slinging water out of his eyes and holding his hands up to Kenzie, who jumped to him, shrieking with glee. David and Kenzie played in the water, begging Emma to join them, but she declined, feeling self-conscious.

However, after sitting on the dock for over an hour watching them, the relentless sun took its toll. Spots danced in front of her eyes, and a tinge of nausea made her lightheaded.

A bit unsteady, she stood and called to David. "I'm getting a little overheated. I think I'll go home." Was it the sun or David that had her so unbalanced?

"Don't go, Mama! Come in and swim."

"The water's perfect. Just jump in, Em. You can swim, can't you?"

"I'm not the best swimmer in the world, but I won't drown." The water did look inviting, and she wanted to join the fun…Why not? *Just do it.* She shucked off her socks and shoes and jumped in with a satisfied moan as the cool water hit her hot, sweaty skin. When she surfaced, Kenzie and David both grinned at her.

"See? Doesn't it feel great?" His smile soothed her skittishness. "If you're going to live on the lake, you need a swimsuit."

A swimsuit wasn't an option for her…Shoving the memory aside, she smiled back at him, feeling shy and hyperaware of the desire coursing through her veins as she stared at him.

"It does feel nice." Emma kicked back to float with her eyes closed.

As David gave Kenzie swimming instructions, she listened to their muffled laughter and splashing. A rare sense of peace permeated her troubled soul, and she relaxed, drifting in the soothing water. A few minutes later, her self-preservation kicked in when she realized it was much too quiet. There was no splashing, no muffled voices. Keeping her eyes closed, she turned her head a little so she could hear.

"Dunk her, Daddy!" Kenzie stage-whispered.

Emma opened one eye. "Dunk me?" She splashed her daughter gently, causing her to squeak. A playful water fight followed, and she found herself giggling like Kenzie, feeling carefree and young.

David dunked her, and she surfaced, spewing water with a bubble of laughter. When David captured her with an arm around her waist, she squealed with surprise. Kenzie splashed happily, firmly held by her father's free hand. Emma's gaze locked with David's. His powerful kicks kept them buoyant. He stared at her lips, and a seductive smile spread across his face. She loved the laugh lines creasing his eyes.

Mesmerized, she watched the water drip down his cheek from the brown curl on his forehead. A clearing throat from someone on the dock stopped her from doing something reckless. David sighed and let her go, his lips thinned with annoyance.

"Dylan!" Kenzie squealed. "Come play with us."

"Having fun, little mermaid?" Dylan leaned against the rail. "Jen tried to phone. She wanted to know if Kenzie could spend the night."

"Yes! Say yes, Daddy! I wanna go now and see Angela."

Dylan shrugged. "I don't mind taking her so you two can have some alone time." He winked.

"No, that's okay." Emma slowly treaded water and moved a foot away from David, not meeting either man's eyes.

She'd forgotten to ask David if Kenzie could spend the night with her. She wouldn't spoil Kenzie's excitement now. She took a deep breath and swallowed her disappointment.

"Sure, that would be great." David grinned at Emma. He grabbed Kenzie and helped her up the dock ladder, just avoiding a kick in the nose.

"Nice nail polish, deacon. I used to wear black myself. Never thought about trying purple glitter. I'll get Kenzie's overnight bag later. You two behave, and don't do anything I wouldn't do." Dylan laughed and gave a wave as he walked away with Kenzie.

"That probably wouldn't leave much," Emma muttered, and David roared with laughter.

"So…" He swam around her like a shark circling a seal.

"So?"

"Since I'm kid free tonight, let's go on a date."

"Oh, don't be silly." *A date? How ridiculous.* A date meant being alone…and could lead to intimacy, which meant tackling subjects she wasn't ready to discuss.

"Do you have to work tomorrow?"

"No, but—"

"No buts allowed. Go on a date with me. Please?"

"I don't date."

"You dated Richard. What did he have that I don't, aside from a gazillion dollars?"

Emma sucked in a breath. *Is that what he thinks? That I just went out with him for his money?*

Pain and fury washed over her. She swam away, but David was a powerful swimmer and caught up with her. Treading water, she glared at him.

"Leave me alone."

"What? What's wrong with you?"

"Me?" she gasped. "Just leave me the hell alone, David."

"What did I say?" he asked, his brow furrowed.

"I know I was a prostitute, but I did *not* date Richard for his money. I didn't even know he had money when I met him. He was a good friend, and we were friends *only*. I know that's hard to believe of a whore, but it's the truth. Just go away. I need time to think." She moved away from him again, dog paddling toward the ladder on the dock. She knew she was overreacting, but she couldn't seem to get a handle on her fear.

"Emma, that isn't what I meant at all. I was just teasing you because you *have* been on a date before. Honey, I'm sorry. I know Richard hasn't been gone that long. Forgive me."

His apology slowed her, and she turned back to face him.

"Don't leave. I'm sorry. I didn't mean it the way you took it!"

An apology. Her exhaustion allowed other memories to surface.

Scott used to apologize after he'd beaten me "for your own good."

Empty words. Empty promises…

David isn't like Scott. He's different.

She loved David's wit, his engaging personality, his kindness, and his compassion. But how could this ever work? She had too much baggage. As she battled herself, the murky water and blue sky melded together in a swirl of psychedelic color.

Her limbs felt like lead, and she had difficulty keeping her head above the water. David's face blurred through her tears.

Help me, she silently screamed as she slipped under.

Chapter
Seventeen

Angry and irritated with himself, David wondered why he cared so much — and why Emma didn't seem to care enough — about their growing relationship. He wanted to move forward and thought he'd made that perfectly clear. Why did she continue to fight him and fight her feelings? Fuming, he watched her tread water in an almost trance-like state. The circles under her eyes seemed more pronounced in her sun-tinged face. His heart pounded in his ears. Something wasn't right.

As she gazed into the distance, her eyes grew heavy and unfocused. The rare look of peace settling on her beautiful features sent a gut-wrenching fear into his heart. Her arms moved slower and slower, barely keeping her head above the water. Looking at him, her mouth opened in a silent plea before she disappeared under the water. In two powerful strokes, he grabbed her waist with one arm, treading water with the other.

"I've got you Emma. You're safe."

Tears illuminated her eyes and clung to her dark lashes. She wrapped her arms around his neck and sobbed, "Help me."

"Let me." He closed his eyes for a moment, scared she would slip away from him. "I'm not letting go; do you hear me? I'm *never* letting go. And you're damn well not leaving me again."

She nodded and clung to his neck as he swam them toward the dock. David helped her up the ladder, and she collapsed into a fetal position, motionless with her eyes closed. Her face appeared pale and ethereal under a slight pink sunburn.

David grabbed a towel and threw it around her as he dragged her into his lap. He rocked her and brushed the top of her wet hair with kisses. "Don't ever scare me like that again, Em. You mean too much to Kenzie and me. We need you. And this may not be the time or place, but hear me out. I do *not* think of you as a whore or a prostitute. You were trafficked; it wasn't your fault."

Emma gave a slight nod and held on to him, shaking despite the heat. He felt her relax, and she gave an almost imperceptible sigh. Her head fell back as she gazed up at him, her hazel eyes a dark, turbulent green.

"I'm sorry I overreacted. I'm exhausted, and I scared myself," she confessed in a hoarse whisper. "I'm so incredibly tired of being me."

"I know, honey. I know." He didn't really, but he didn't know what else to say. Would he ever truly know her? David closed his eyes and buried his face in her neck, afraid to let her go. They sat for a few more minutes until he could breathe normally. He shuddered, not sure if it was fear or his blood sugar.

"You're okay now, but we need to get you hydrated. And I have to eat before my blood sugar tanks."

He helped her to her feet. "Let's go home. Can you walk, or do you want me to carry you?"

"I can walk." She still seemed dazed and a little off-kilter, but she managed to slip on her shoes.

Grabbing their things from the dock, he didn't mention the date again, unsure what emotions he'd trigger in her current state. The last thing he wanted to do was leave her alone, but he felt like she needed time to collect herself.

Why did everything have to be so complicated? Emma's mixed signals drove him nuts. He'd make progress on getting through her shell only to have her pull away, frightened. And now this episode had scared him witless. Had she just been tired, or was she more damaged than he realized? He vowed to love and protect her. Through his actions, she'd learn to give credence to his words.

He held her hand as they walked silently toward her apartment. Mrs. Jordan stood watering her roses by the side of her house and gave a friendly wave.

David stopped at Emma's bottom step and turned her to face him. "Emma?"

A weak smile curved her lips. "Yes?"

"You wouldn't…I mean, you're not going to do anything foolish…" His voice trailed off, unable to verbalize his greatest fear.

She frowned for a moment, brows knit together. As understanding took hold, she shook her head. "No, no. I wouldn't. Promise. I'm just tired—physically and, well, mentally, I guess. I'm trying, David, I promise. I'm terrified I'm going to do something wrong, or let you or Kenzie down…"

"Honey, you're doing fine. This is still new for all of us. Just relax. Will you be okay? I'll stay if you want me to."

"I'll be fine. I'm going to drink some water and catch a quick nap before we go out. What should I wear?" Her eyes found his and color bloomed in her cheeks.

He smiled. "You sure? What would you like to do? We can go see a movie, dinner, dancing, or all three. Whatever you're comfortable with. We can even stay home and just watch TV or something."

She raised her eyebrows. "Or something, preacher?"

Heat infused his cheeks. He stood there silent, tongue-tied and confused by her mercurial mood changes.

She sighed and seemed to force a smile. "I'm trying to make a joke. Whatever you decide, what time should I be ready?"

She handed him his towel, and his eyes zeroed in on her hard nipples beneath her wet T-shirt. *What am I, fourteen?*

"Six? And dress comfortably. We won't do anything too fancy schmancy."

Her smile widened, and he found himself staring at her lips.

"Fancy schmancy?"

He winked and shrugged as he walked backward toward his home, enjoying the look of her in wet, clingy clothes. When she noticed him staring, her cheeks brightened, and she turned and ran into her apartment.

"Do I need to turn this hose on you to cool you off, David Patterson?" Mrs. Jordan called.

David laughed. "Maybe!" He gave her a wave and jogged down the well-worn path toward home.

Littered with the seven different outfits she'd tried on and discarded in disgust, Emma's bedroom looked like a tornado had struck. She looked in the mirror with a critical eye and stepped out of the black dress—one she'd bought to go to the symphony with Richard. It looked too "fancy schmancy."

What the hell should I wear?

Overwhelmed by the decision, she sank on the side of the bed and covered her face. She jumped when she heard a knock and glared at the clock. *Dammit, six o'clock on the dot.* Heart racing, she shrugged unto her robe and ran to the front door.

David grinned down at her. Dressed in a white button-down shirt with the sleeves rolled up and jeans, he was the epitome of laid-back handsomeness. "I know I said casual, and your robe looks great, but that might be a bit too casual to go out for dinner. Did you decide to stay in? I don't mind. We can order a pizza or something."

"No, I want to go out. I just didn't know what to wear. My bedroom's a mess…" Flustered, she danced back and forth as she ran a hand through her carefully curled hair, which was already falling flat.

"I had help dressing," David confessed. "Jennifer came over to get Kenzie's overnight stuff and made me change into this shirt. She bought it for me for my birthday last year. I think it's a little pretentious, with the logo thingie." His finger circled the embroidered logo. "I was quite comfortable wearing my Atlanta Braves T-shirt and thought I looked fine. It isn't like we're going to church, just out to grab a bite to eat," he grumbled.

Emma gave him a genuine smile. "Well, now that I see what you're wearing, I can get dressed. Make yourself at home. There's diet soda in the fridge. I'll be right back. Was your sugar okay when you got home?"

"Yes, ma'am," he drawled. "Why, Em, someone might think you actually care about me."

"I do care. I mean…I, well…" Her face heated, and she scampered off to dress. She remembered locking this very same bedroom door years ago, scared David wanted to have sex with her. That thought was no longer completely unappealing. But she wasn't quite there yet. Not until she came totally clean about her past. She threw on jeans, changed into a strapless bra, and pulled on a white peasant-style blouse that left her shoulders bare.

Emma reapplied her pale pink lip gloss and sighed. Why had she bothered to curl her hair? The results had already dissipated. Kenzie was lucky to have inherited Ken's natural curls. Taking a deep breath, she squared her shoulders and decided she was as ready as she'd ever be.

David stopped pacing and smiled when she entered the living area. He appraised her from head to toe. His hair stood on end where he'd run a hand through it, which gave her a small measure of comfort. At least she wasn't the only one nervous. She reached up and finger-combed it, taking in the smell of his aftershave, the warmth of his sun-kissed skin, and the laugh lines next to his dark eyes.

"You look great, honey."

His words sent a tremor through her body. She loved it when he called her *honey*. No one had ever called her that before, and she'd never heard him call anyone else that, either. He took her hand as they walked out the door, and his fingers squeezed hers. She stopped and looked up at him.

He gazed at her with concern. "What's the matter? You're not backing out on me, are you? You *do* feel okay, don't you?"

"Yes. No, I just…" She took a deep breath. "Are you sure you want to go out with me? I mean, in public? W-What if someone…I mean, I don't want to hurt your reputation." Her voice trailed off, and she bit her lip as she stared at the buttons on his shirt.

"We have nothing to be ashamed about. We're just going to dinner. Besides, we're two adults, and eventually it will be common knowledge that we share a daughter. People will put two and two together and come up with whatever answer they want. Don't let it bother you. Besides, I'm sure people are going to stare at us, regardless."

He brushed a stray strand of hair off her cheek. She looked up at his smiling face.

"Why wouldn't they stare? I'll have the prettiest girl on my arm." He took her hand and kissed her temple before pulling her toward the car.

How could she resist? "Where are we going?" she asked as he held the car door open for her.

"Did you sleep any this afternoon?" David asked. The brush of his fingertips on her bare shoulder made her skin sizzle like butter in a frying pan.

"Not much," she confessed with a blush, glad to be hidden from his gaze as he closed her door and walked to the driver's side.

"We're going to be out late, but plans are loose and can be changed if you get too tired."

"No, I'll be fine." As nervous as she was, there was no way she'd get sleepy.

"Do you like Japanese food?"

"I don't know. I've never had it, but I love Chinese food." Her anxiety made the thought of food turn her stomach, but she wouldn't dream of disappointing him.

"Good. We'll drive into Birmingham. Is that okay? This will be like Chinese food, but it comes with a show. It's a lot of fun, and I think you'll like it. Kenzie loves to eat there and goes nuts when the guy tosses the food in the air. It never fails, sometime over the few days after, she emulates the Japanese chefs at home, and I end up cleaning a mess. Someday soon, if you like it, we'll both take her."

The thought of returning to Birmingham was unsettling. *What if...* She squelched her fear and stole a glance at him. "Sure, I'm game." *How can he appear so relaxed when I'm twisted in knots?*

A song about a guy waiting for his girl came on the radio, and David sang along softly with the chorus. Emma watched the side of the road speeding by, thinking about how many times today he'd made references to them as a family. It both pleased her and scared her. David reached over and held her hand. Startled by the contact, she jumped.

"I will, you know."

"Will what?"

His thumb circled her palm. He had warm, strong hands. *Hands I want all over me.* She blushed and stared out the window, praying he didn't know where her thoughts had wandered. *Do respectable girls have these kinds of thoughts?* She'd have to ask her therapist.

"Wait for you. As long as it takes." He squeezed her hand, and she turned, staring at him for a full moment, trying to process what he meant.

She pulled her hand from his, crossing her arms in front of her chest as she gazed at the road, unsure of how to respond. Her emotions pinged like a pinball machine. If not careful, she was in danger of tilting. He sighed, and she stole a glance at him, her bottom lip between her teeth. At this rate, she wouldn't have any lip gloss left when they got to the restaurant.

He stared straight at the road, disappointment furrowing his brow.

"Why would you wait for *me?*" she asked in a small voice. "Because of Kenzie? I've promised I'm not going to take her away."

A breath hissed from between his teeth. "You don't give yourself—or me—much credit, do you?"

"I, well…" She paused, confused. "I don't know how to do this. I'm not girlfriend material. I guess I'm an okay person now. I mean, I know I've changed, but I'm not exactly loveable…" She motioned expansively and sighed. "I mean, if you just want to scratch the itch, I guess I'm good with that. It's been a long time, but I…" *I'll just make sure it's in the dark.*

"What? No! I mean, yes I want to do that, but—" He slapped the steering wheel. "Why won't you believe me? *I* think you're loveable. *I* love everything about you. *I* think you're positively divine, Emma." He glanced at her with a smirk.

Emma stared at him with her mouth hanging open.

"I admit, I was stunned—angry even—when you came back. But now, I can't imagine you *not* being here. I'm hoping you feel the same way. To be honest, you send mixed signals, honey." He again looked over at her, his eyes hopeful as he tapped the steering wheel in time with the music.

Emma looked out the passenger window, suddenly wishing she were anywhere but in this car. How was she supposed to answer that? Clenching and unclenching her fists, her breathing sputtered.

"I'm sorry," she croaked, unsure if he'd even heard her as she stared at her lap.

A long, uncomfortable minute passed.

"Sorry as in you don't want to be in my life?" he asked.

She looked up, startled.

"N-No. No! I'm sorry I send mixed signals." Biting her lip and staring at her folded hands, she admitted, "I don't mean to; it's just that I get so scared I'm going to fuck everything up." She blew her bangs with frustration. "See? I already have. I know you don't like language like that. I'm sorry." Reaching over, she placed a timid hand on his knee and held her breath. When he took her hand in his and placed a gentle kiss on her fingers, she sighed so loudly it caused him to chuckle.

"You'll learn to curb the language; Kenzie will see to that. I can handle scared. As a matter of fact, I'm a pro at handling scared. I can even scare off snakes and the bogeyman. I have references; ask our daughter." He grinned at her, and the tension in the air lifted slightly.

"But what if the bogeyman is real?" Emma whispered, digging her nails into her palm. She knew he was too real, and she prayed she never crossed paths with him again. It was her greatest nightmare.

"Then stand strong. And know you'll never be alone. I'm no superman, but I would die for you and Kenzie," he replied.

"You're not just *any* man, David," she said. "I *want* to be in your life and in Kenzie's. But I don't want to be the reason you can't, or don't, pursue your dreams. I don't want to hold you back. I-I've ruined your life enough."

"You didn't ruin my life; you changed my life. *For the better.* We both made choices based on our situations. Like I told my mother, I'm very happy with my life. I have a beautiful daughter, a job that can be challenging, but also rewarding, and hopefully, a woman who wants me as much as I want her."

She looked out the window just as they passed by the BJCC arena—a place she'd often worked in her previous life. A chill washed over her, and she realized she hadn't responded.

"You want me?" she managed. Images of faceless men climbing on top of her, sweating and grunting, came to mind. She closed her eyes in shame, her stomach tightening into a knot.

His fist smashed against the steering wheel, and she jumped, facing him with alarm. She reached for the door handle.

"Quit going there. Don't. You. Dare. Go. There. I want you for so much more than what you're thinking. *Don't you know me better than that?*" he ground out. "And so help me, if you open that door, I'll stop the car, chase you down, and drag you back—kicking and screaming if I have to. You will not run from me again. Shit!" He hit the brakes as someone cut him off.

She wrapped her arms around her stomach, shaking.

David pulled onto the shoulder and turned the car off. The traffic continued to race past them. "I'm sorry, Em. I didn't mean to scare you or make you feel unsafe. Shh…Slow, deep breaths…" His stroked her hair and, unbuckling his seatbelt, wrapped his arms around her, murmuring reassurances. She clung to him, gasping for air, fighting her drowning fear.

"How can you throw me in with those kinds of men?" he asked. "Have I ever given you reason to?"

She shook her head. "I'm sorry," she whispered. "I'm damaged, David. I know all of it wasn't my fault, but I'm afraid I come with a lot of baggage. Being back in Birmingham…this area—I *worked* here. It was a panic attack. I have them at times…"

"I'm sorry. I didn't think about Birmingham being a trigger for you." David shook his head. "You need to tell me when I accidentally push the wrong button, Emma. I want all of you, not just your body. I want your trust, your love, your bright mind, and your passion. I want you by my side raising our daughter, and maybe more children. I want you to share my life. If you'll let me, I'll help you carry this baggage and lighten your load."

"You know I can't have any more children…" She choked, "I-I wasn't even capable of raising one; God knew what He was doing when He made it so I couldn't have more."

"Stop it. God didn't do that. Circumstances caused that."

"True. It was my fault. I didn't take care of myself," she said, a catch in her voice. She buried her face in his neck.

"I didn't say it was your fault." David pulled her face toward his. "It wasn't *anyone's* fault. It just happened. Bad things happen to good people. It's a fact of life. But it's how you respond that matters. When will you let go of the past and start to live? And giving birth isn't the only way to have children. I think I'm testament to that—you know how much I love Kenzie. Dammit, Em, I love you, too. When will you accept that as well?" He sighed. "I'm sorry. I shouldn't have cussed. I don't talk that way, especially in front of a lady. I just want you to be brave and move forward with your life—preferably with me by your side."

Emma bit her lip and smiled. If he only knew, she loved him best when his foibles revealed themselves. His words soothed her battered soul.

"It's okay, I've said a lot fuckin' worse." She gave him another small smile.

He chuckled and kissed her forehead. "True. My potty-mouth princess. Should we go home?"

"No." She squared her shoulders. "No, I want to try Japanese food." *I want to be brave.*

Silence reigned as he pulled out to continue their drive toward the restaurant. Emma thought about what he'd said. Everything she'd learned in therapy was falling in to place. It was like solving those anagrams David liked doing. She'd been given the clues and now she had the answer. She'd always shouldered the blame for the poor decisions in her life. But some of it hadn't been her fault. She could no longer use blame and shame as a shield to protect her fragile heart. Now was the time to be brave and face life openly. She had everything she needed to move forward. Besides, her self-imposed defenses were already cracked after relentless attack from this kind, loving man.

David loves me.

And maybe I could love him.

Yes, maybe it was time to surrender, to emerge from her dark world and enter his. Or, as her therapist would say, *fully engage in life.*

"Now," she whispered.

"What, honey?" He leaned closer, keeping his eyes on the road.

"Now," she said it louder this time and found her breathing easier, her chest lighter. "I want to start now. Living my life." She swallowed the anxiety lodged in her throat. "With you and Kenzie."

"Good." He smiled. "Perfect." His smile widened, and he held her hand, not letting go until he pulled into the restaurant parking lot.

When he opened her car door, she stepped into his arms, and he held her tightly.

"Thank you for giving me a chance, Em. For giving us a chance." He gave her a sweet kiss, and Emma melted into his arms, home at last.

Pulling away, she scanned her surroundings, still unable to shake her queasiness at being back on her old turf.

Chapter
Eighteen

David smiled at the snores from the passenger seat. They weren't loud, more like a soft purr. Emma had slept all the way home from the restaurant, and he didn't have the heart to wake her. The tranquility on her face while she slept reminded him of their daughter. At ease, she finally looked peaceful. Once inside the restaurant, she'd begun to relax. The Japanese chef's flipping knives and spatulas had captivated her, and when the fire leapt up from the food volcano, she'd applauded, just like Kenzie.

It had taken her a while to get the hang of using chopsticks, but after several amusing attempts, she'd learned how to operate them. In a way, he regretted teaching her; he'd loved seeing her blush when he fed her with his. Silly as it sounded, feeding her seemed almost erotic — not that he had much experience in that department. He'd been thankful the table hid his obvious discomfort.

Pulling the car onto the ridge overlooking the lake, he grinned. There weren't any other cars on the bluff. He had one more surprise for Emma tonight. He turned off the ignition and chuckled when another snore escaped her lips. A kiss to her warm, bare shoulder made her stir.

"Wake up, sleepyhead."

Emma jerked upright and scrunched against the door. "Where are we?" She looked around.

"I didn't mean to startle you. I've brought you to where all the kids hang out to, uh, you know, be away from adult supervision."

"What?" She looked around at the darkness surrounding the car. "David?" The octave jump when she said his name betrayed her nerves, and he chuckled. He kind of liked surprising her, but he hoped this wasn't another panic attack.

"Rest easy. We're just going to do some stargazing. C'mon, it isn't often I have a babysitter." He popped the trunk. She shot out of the car before he had time to walk around to her door.

He retrieved the blanket, flipped on a flashlight.

"I would have opened the door for you," he chided, holding out his hand. "Without the glare of city lights, you can see forever, and it's positively magical."

"You really just brought me here to look at the stars?"

"What? Were you afraid I planned to take advantage of you? *Tsk, tsk.* Such a dirty mind you have, Emma Devine."

She giggled nervously and punched his arm.

"You good?" he asked, just a little worried.

"So I've been told."

"Did you just make a joke?" He laughed and unfurled the blanket.

"Yeah, I think I did."

They collapsed on their backs. He cut off the flashlight, and they gazed at the velvet sky dotted by millions of stars. The sound of the water lapping below, the soft breeze in the trees, and low trill of frogs accented the night.

"Oh, wow," Emma whispered. "This is as pretty as fireworks. Do you know the different constellations? Can you show me some?"

"Sure." He pointed into the vast expanse of stars. "Over there is the Little Dipper. It's also called Ursa Minor, or the Little Bear. It starts with that star, right there. The North Star, or Polaris, and it's the start of the handle. See it?"

"Yes! I see it!" She followed it with her finger in the air.

"And over there is Ursa Major, the Big Bear, which contains the Big Dipper. The handle is the tail."

"This is incredible. How do I know you're telling me the truth and not just making this up?" she teased, nudging his shoulder.

He grinned with surprise at her sudden lightheartedness. "I guess you'll have to trust me." He rolled to his side and nuzzled her neck.

"I do," she whispered, her fingers in his hair. "I really do."

"Good. As for my credentials, I'm the faculty advisor for the astronomy club at the high school. This is nothing. We'll come back in August and bring Kenzie for the Perseid meteor shower."

"I'd like that. The three of us."

"Me too."

David pointed out several more constellations, and a shooting star streaked through the sky.

Emma gasped.

"Quick, close your eyes and make a wish," he whispered.

As she did, he leaned in and kissed her. Slowly, he deepened the kiss, exploring her mouth with his tongue.

"Tell me what you wished for." He nuzzled her bare shoulder and trailed kisses up her neck back to her lips.

Emma whispered, "It just came true. I wished you would kiss me." She smiled against his lips. "You always taste of peppermint."

David chuckled and dug a peppermint out of his pocket. He popped it in her mouth and kissed her again. "I see why the kids like this place." A raging need for her had developed deep within him, and he knew he should stop.

"David?"

He loved the way she said his name after he kissed her, all soft and breathless. Kissing her forehead, he smiled. "Yes?"

"I'd, um, like to do what you said. Move forward…We could go back to my place. I mean, it would be more comfortable." She cupped his cheek in her hand and nibbled his jaw.

"More comfortable for stargazing?" he teased, knowing full well what she meant. And knowing it wouldn't take much for him to accept the offer. But she still seemed a little fragile—earlier she'd downright scared him.

"A different type of star gazing. I can make you see stars," she purred, her warm breath fanning across his cheek.

"Emma, I, uh, we can't." David sat up and ran a hand through his hair, pulling in a ragged breath as he tried to maintain control.

"Is it me? You told me to embrace a new life. I'm doing this all wrong, aren't I?" The hurt in her voice tugged at his heart.

"No. Yes. Heck, I don't know. I want you. For heaven's sake, I'm in actual physical pain right now. But I love you, and I respect you. I'm not going to make love to you until you marry me. I want to prove I'm different from...others."

Emma sat up and huffed, "You don't have to respect me so much, *David.*"

He chuckled and pulled her to him, holding her tight. "Yes, I do, *Emma.*"

She sighed. "Okay. Thank you. I think...maybe I need to go jump in the cold lake. It's awfully hot."

David laughed. "Me, too."

He stood and offered her his hand, surprised she hadn't pulled away when he mentioned marriage.

"David?"

"Yes?"

"Kiss me?"

Wrapping his arms around her, he brought his lips to hers. Their tongues tangled as she gripped his hair and his back. He felt the heat emanating from her body, and desire coursed through his veins. He'd never wanted a woman more than he wanted this one. The night sounds became distant and dulled by their heavy breathing. He wanted to devour every inch of her, and it took supreme effort to pull away.

"Emma," he choked out as her body slid down his back to the ground. He held her at arm's length. "Dear God, we have to stop, honey."

"Do we? I mean, I'm ready to try this. It's the twenty-first century. We can be friends with benefits. I've been tested. I can't get pregnant," she replied in a voice husky with need.

Her warm, fragrant skin called to him in a primal way. Frazzled, he silently began naming the states in alphabetical order — backward, no less — to pull his mind away from tearing off her clothes.

Wyoming, Wisconsin, West Virginia, Washington...

When he could formulate a halfway complete sentence, he gasped, "Not until we're m-married."

Rising on her tiptoes, she kissed the sensitive spot behind his ear. His resolve wavered, fading fast.

Virginia, Vermont, Utah…

It started as a soft giggle at first, which soon turned into a laugh, and she collapsed in his arms, wiping her eyes as she held her side. "Is-isn't waiting until we get married s-supposed to be my line?"

David laughed and tweaked her nose. "Don't be sexist." He pretended to howl with pain when she playfully hit him, and he pulled her back to the blanket. She laughed so hard, she got the hiccups. David tried to teach her how to scientifically raise her diaphragm to release them, causing them both to laugh even harder. They lay together, side by side, silent for a few minutes, their fingers intertwined.

"I love you. Marry me."

"David. That's a little drastic. It's only been six weeks…"

"But technically, we've known each other for years."

She didn't answer, but she squeezed his hand. Her thumb rubbed in slow circles, and he picked up the list of states again. He made it to *Alabama* and reluctantly stood. He helped her up before grabbing the blanket and flashlight. "I guess I better get you home before I forget myself and act like one of my students," he grumbled.

"Well, it's your fault. You're the one who brought me here where you said kids come for hanky-panky time."

"Emma! Did you just make another joke?" Mildly shocked, it pleased him to see her so relaxed. At the same time, his sexual frustration made it hard to see straight.

"I believe I did, or maybe I wasn't joking." She giggled.

"So, Ms. Devine, since this date went so well, will you go out with me again? Or better yet, marry me?" He opened her car door.

"I'll think about it."

David paused before getting in the driver's seat to give a victory arm pump out of Emma's sight. She was joking around, and she hadn't run off screaming when he mentioned marriage. She was even considering it — this was progress.

"You can come in, if you'd like." Her breathless voice sounded foreign to her ears after their heated good-night kiss. If he did, she'd keep the lights off and then, maybe, get the courage to tell him the worst thing Scott had done to her…

"I don't think that would be a good idea. Tempting as the offer is."

"I think it's a great idea. No one would know." She pressed her body into his, feeling his need for her.

"I would know, and I have to live with myself. I promise to make love to you every night until I'm in my grave, *after* we're married."

"Every night until you're in your grave? What if you live to be, oh, one hundred and nine?" Emma teased, but nerves made her tremble. Her courage waned. *Will he still want to marry me after he sees what Scott did?*

"Why not? I hear they make this recreational wonder drug called Viagra." He chuckled and ruffled her hair, seeming unaware of her inner turmoil.

"Don't you think marriage is rushing things? We've only been on one date."

"Probably, but you're the mother of my daughter, and I love you."

Emma looked at the ground and stalled, wanting to tell him *everything* and move forward in their relationship. But she was scared. Fear kept her mouth shut.

"You know the day after tomorrow is the Fourth. We could do something as a family, and there's a fireworks show that night. Kenzie can't wait to see them." He smiled. "I remember another girl who loved fireworks."

"Yes, I'd like that." Maybe saying good night now was for the best. She should talk to her therapist about how to tell David about her permanent tie to her old life.

"Good night, Em. Sweet dreams."

David's hands cupped her face and his mouth covered hers in a kiss that quite literally took her breath away. After a moment he moved his hands down her neck and shoulders to her upper arms, putting some distance between them.

"You're a sadistic woman, putting an all-you-can-eat buffet before a starving man." He gave her a final kiss on her forehead and headed down the steps. "I love you," he called as he walked back to his car.

"I, uh, thank you," she whispered in return, still amazed that this wonderful man said he loved her.

After he drove off, Emma sat on the front steps, trying to peer up at the sky through the tall pines. *Marriage.* It scared the hell out of her, yet gave her a tingle of pleasure and excitement. Could she imagine her life without Kenzie and David? *No.*

David made her feel safe. And her therapist had told her repeatedly she couldn't live in constant fear. She needed to be brave and honest.

I love him.

Emma held her breath as she tried to grasp the concept of marrying David. Could she possibly imagine her life as the wife of a schoolteacher, or a preacher?

No.

Maybe.

Yes.

Yes? Was she insane? How could she marry David? She'd never been a wife before. In spirit, she'd felt married to Ken. It had been a desperate, crazy kind of love, born of loneliness and raging hormones, and torn apart too soon by his tragic death. Her relationship with Richard had been platonic, but he'd been a dear friend and confidante, and he'd taught her a great deal about dedication and loyalty. She'd been honored to care for him in his final days.

She'd loved Ken and Richard, but with David, all the fragmented pieces of her story fell into place. Marrying him would give her a happily ever after. But it would be far from the end. It would be the beginning of a story she'd never dared dream was possible, a future full of hope and joy.

She suddenly wanted to know everything about him: his feelings, his thoughts, what made him smile, what made him sad, and more importantly, how she could complete *him.* Enlightened by her love, the concept of two becoming one became crystal clear. It wasn't just sex, it was so much more—something on a totally different plane. Something she'd never experienced before.

Her love for this man and her daughter infused every cell of her body. It was the blood coursing through her veins.

They were her life.

And her life was full of love.

Patient and kind, David had filled the emptiness in her heart. Could she give him what he needed and deserved? Could she make him happy? She rubbed her damp palms on her jeans. Would he truly be able to look beyond her past—and the visual reminder of it?

A need to see him and tell him what he meant to her overtook all rational thinking. She had to speak before she lost her courage. For the first time in her life, she believed in divine intervention. They were meant to be together.

She dashed inside and grabbed a flashlight and barreled through the woods. As she raced toward the man she loved, her body felt light as air. Surely, if she opened her arms, she'd fly. With David's love, she could soar above any problem or difficulty life threw her way. It was the most liberating feeling in the world.

But her lingering doubt inched in as she ran—the way fear does—insidiously wrapping its tentacles around her happiness. The ugliness in her past came to the forefront of her thoughts, taunting her. Why would someone as good as David want a woman like her? She was damaged goods, worthless. She was someone else's property. All used up...

No, no, no, her heart screamed in retaliation. *He loves me!*

Emma no longer knew if she was running to be saved or running from her fears. Despite the cramp in her side, she sprinted through the woods toward the man offering her everything. Things she had only imagined from the time she was a small girl—love, acceptance, security, laughter...

A sign, she needed a sign.

If David was still up and the light was on, she would know it was meant to be. She would tell him she wanted a future with him and Kenzie. That she wanted to be more than his friend, more than the mother of his child. She wanted to be his wife and lover.

I'll tell him I'm in love with him.

When she reached the edge of the woods, she stopped, gasping for breath, and her heart sank. The house stood shrouded in shadows. The only light piercing the darkness came from the dusk-to-dawn light on the dock.

He was already in bed.

A dose of reality edged in, and she realized how silly she'd been. Divine intervention? Seriously? For her? Maybe he'd just been caught up in the sexually charged moment. Would a man like David really wed a former prostitute? *No way in hell.* How foolish could she be? She needed to think things through by the light of the day, not by the magic of a star-filled night hyped up on sexual frustration and ridiculous dreams.

Emma sank to the ground, clutching her flashlight, overcome by disappointment. As her heart shattered, the pain suffocated her. She lay still for a moment, allowing grief to consume her, so overwhelmed she couldn't move. The scars of her past burned.

This is what it feels like to die of a broken heart.

Taking a shallow, tortured breath, she eased to a sitting position. It was time to admit defeat and go home. With the last of her overwrought energy, she summoned the fortitude to stand. Out of the corner of her eye, she detected movement from the dock and caught her breath. The roaring in her ears drowned out the night sounds. Trembling, she rose to her feet.

Am I hallucinating?

David walked toward her with his hands in his pockets, looking at the ground. He kicked a pebble, and his shoulders sagged.

Look at me, look at me! Please God, let him look at me...

He raised his head. Although it was dim under the dusk-to-dawn light, his eyes locked on hers, widening with surprise, and a smile spread across his face. Motionless, they stared at each other for a few seconds. When he started running toward her, she met him and jumped into his arms, wrapping her legs around his waist. David caught her and staggered to regain his balance, holding her tight.

"Are you okay? What's wrong, honey?"

She giggled, feeling delirious. "Call me crazy, but I love you! David Michael Patterson, will you marry me?" She held on to him as if her life depended on it.

If he said no she would die. No doubt about it. His hands wrapped around her and cradled her butt, and he spun her around, kissing her, his lips promising a lifetime of love and joy. Tears of happiness streaked down her face as she showered his lips, his cheeks, and his neck with kisses.

"Well? Aren't you going to answer me?" she asked.

"Okay, crazy. I thought you'd never ask. Yes, I'll marry you." He chuckled and pulled away, his forehead touching hers. "Hey, wait a minute—wasn't that my question?"

"Don't be sexist, David," she answered with a grin, kissing him thoroughly.

Chapter
Nineteen

Emma unwrapped herself from David's arms. It was now or never. The subdued lighting helped bolster her courage. "Wait. There's more."

"More?"

"I have to tell you something. But I'm scared…"

"I'm the snake slayer. I'll keep you safe," he murmured, hugging her to his chest.

She pushed him away. "I'm being serious."

He tipped her chin up. "So am I. You can tell me anything. Be brave, Emma."

"There's a reason I don't own a swimsuit." She rubbed sweaty palms on her jeans. "Scott…He did something."

"Do you want to go inside and sit down?" David asked quietly.

She shook her head, staring at the ground. Blowing out a deep breath, she looked up, making herself stand tall and look him in the eye. She could do this.

"He marked me. It's permanent."

"So?" David shrugged.

Emma blinked. "I-It won't come *off*."

"It doesn't matter. I love *you*. All of you."

Her mouth dropped. "D-Do you want to see it before you say that for sure?"

"Where is it?"

"My inner thigh."

He chuckled and kissed her forehead. "I better not. I only have so much control. I may be a snake slayer, but I'm totally human."

"You really don't care? Am I dreaming?"

He pinched her butt. "Nope. Now come here and kiss me."

Laughing, and feeling truly carefree for the first time she could remember, she jumped back into his arms and kissed her future husband.

"Em?"

"Yes?" She pulled away and stopped nibbling on his neck, stopped whispering how much she loved him and needed him. She took in his frown and wiggled her way out of his arms. Her lower lip quivered as she shoved her hair out of her eyes and behind her ear. "W-What?"

"You're about to push me over the edge of reason; we have to stop." Panting, he held her by the shoulders, an arm's length away.

Emma relaxed and began to giggle. "Why don't we make a bet?"

"A bet? What kind of bet?" The look on his face made her love him even more.

"I bet you a dollar if we make love right now, God won't strike us dead."

He laughed. "Sorry, I won't take that bet. I don't want to put Kenzie at risk of being an orphan," he teased. "Plus, I don't gamble."

Emma clenched her fists and stomped her foot. "Dammit, David. This was a big step for me, and now I want you—all of you."

"I know, honey, me too. But I've vowed to treat you with respect and honor you."

"You're so stubborn. It isn't like we'd be hurting anyone."

"I take it you don't want a long engagement?" He smiled.

"If you don't marry me tomorrow, I'm pretty sure we'll both combust from sexual frustration."

He laughed. "You're probably right."

"So let's do it tomorrow."

"Tomorrow? Don't you want a real wedding? I want to take vows with you, in church, with Kenzie there." The longing in his voice told her he meant it.

Her heart soared. *He loves me!* "Are you willing to compromise?"

"Only if it results in us getting married." He held her close, his heart beating steadily, in perfect synchronicity with her own.

It was meant be, it was meant to be…

As his hand stroked her hair, she wanted to crawl inside him, purr like a kitten, and melt into a puddle at his feet—all at the same time. She couldn't get enough of him.

"Marry me tomorrow at the courthouse, and then we'll have a church wedding when your family can be here in a few weeks." She chuckled. "This will give your mom time to come to terms with it, but not be able to prevent our marriage."

"Sounds like a plan to me." He kissed the top of her head.

"Really? So, since we're getting married tomorrow, will you make love to me tonight?"

"Nope."

"Bastard."

He laughed. "Just think about how wonderful tomorrow will be."

She squirmed to look at his watch. "Technically, it already is tomorrow…" She walked her fingers up his arm and grinned.

"Nope. Not until you're officially Emmanuelle Summer Devine Patterson." He rubbed the backs of his fingers along her jaw and gave her a quick kiss.

She sighed and curled her fingers around his biceps. "Okay, but I'm scared to go home. Please don't make me." She trembled, the adrenaline suddenly fading.

"Scared? Why, honey?" David held her close.

"I'm scared I'm going to wake up and this will all have been a dream. Please?" She looked back up at David. "We don't have to do anything, just let me stay."

"It isn't a dream; I'm marrying you tomorrow—today." He smiled down at her and took her hand in his. "Of course you can stay tonight. You can sleep in my room. I'll sleep on the couch."

"Thank you." Relief nearly buckled her legs, and David picked her up and carried her.

"Does this count as carrying you over the threshold?" he teased as he put her down and turned on the lamp.

She nodded sleepily, now feeling foolish. "I'm sorry; this is silly. I can go home."

"No. Wait here."

He left, and Emma heard the water running in the bathtub. When he came back, he handed her a pale blue T-shirt and a pair of pajama pants.

"Here, you can take a quick bath to relax and sleep in these. Your toothbrush from the last time you were here is in the cabinet over the sink. But don't sleep in too late. The courthouse opens at nine, and we have to pick up Kenzie and get rings." He smiled and gave her a quick kiss. "I don't know if we'll be able to get the license and have the judge do it the same day, but I hope so."

"They have to!" Emma wailed.

"And speaking of rings, I'll buy you any ring you want, but for now, this was my grandmother's." He took her left hand and slipped a small solitaire diamond on her finger.

"Oh." The ring made everything seem real and permanent. She felt her stomach unclench. "It's beautiful. Thank you. Are you sure?"

"Of course. Are you?" He kissed the finger with the loose engagement ring on it. The depth of love in his eyes made her heart sing.

She nodded through tears, but a huge smile spread across her face. "I'm terrified, but yes."

"I'm the pro at handling scared, remember?"

Emma nodded and hugged him tight before slipping into the bathroom. Placing the ring on the counter, she brushed her teeth and smiled at her reflection.

"Yes, I'm checking, you crazy dog…"

She could hear David talking to Molly in the kitchen, assuring the dog he was okay before he took her outside. She'd read that some dogs could be trained to help diabetics, and Molly already seemed to have a knack…She'd look into that after the wedding.

She paused, overcome by emotion. She was going to take care of David. And Kenzie. And even that silly puppy. She belonged here, with her family.

Look at you, Emma Devine.

Mother. Bride. Wife. Lover.

A blush crept across her cheeks. Spitting out the toothpaste, she rinsed her mouth, stripped off her clothes, and sank into the warm bath, studiously ignoring *his* mark. *It doesn't even matter*, she told herself. She was grateful David had understood her need to stay here tonight. She smiled and shook her head. David understood her better than anyone, including herself.

Married. I'm getting married later today.

Emma couldn't contain the glee any longer and sank below the water to scream her excitement.

A few minutes later, when she was done and drying off, she trembled as she passed the towel over the reminder of her ugly past. *He said it didn't matter, but he hasn't seen it yet.* Would he be repulsed by the permanent mark?

Nervously, she padded down the hall. David's door remained cracked open, and the soft light from his bedside lamp lit a path into the darkness, beckoning her like a lighthouse on a stormy night. *He's in his room. Wait, he told me to sleep here…*

Timidly, she peeked in, and her mouth went dry, her heart hammering in her chest. Sitting on his bed, wearing navy pajama pants, David turned the pages of his Bible. She gazed at his defined abs, the brown curls at the nape of his neck, the cut of his biceps, and desire coursed through her body. Even his glasses were hot.

Good God, I'm a pervert. The man is reading his Bible, for heaven's sake.

David looked up and smiled.

"I, uh, thought you told me to sleep in here…I don't mind taking the couch, though. I'll just say good night." She offered a small wave, feeling guilty.

"To be precise, it would be good morning," he replied, his voice husky. He pulled off his glasses. "Come here, Emma."

Nervously, she turned back to face him, but smiled with surprise when he pulled the cover down beside him, patting the bed. He frowned when Molly stood on her hind legs, wagging her tail.

"Not tonight, and not any night," he grumbled.

Emma giggled. "Me or Molly?"

"I want you here every night." He crooked his finger, motioning her toward him.

As if in a trance, she moved to his bed. "But you said…"

"Like you, I'm afraid this is a dream, and when I wake up, you'll be gone. I figure if I hold you, you can't escape."

She crawled into bed, and he turned out the light. He remained on top of the covers and rolled onto his side, drawing her close. "This is the twenty-first-century version of bundling." He gave her a kiss. "I love you."

Emma smiled as she closed her eyes, feeling secure, safe, and loved. "I love you, too." She yawned and snuggled in closer. "Leave it to the history teacher to find a way to compromise. Tonight, after we're married, no covers between us."

"Damn straight. I want you naked."

Emma murmured sleepily, "Did you just say damn?" She yawned.

"Good night, Em, love you."

"Good night, David. Love you more."

Chapter
Twenty

"You're what?" Jennifer's mouth dropped and her eyes widened. She shifted Rory to her other hip as she flipped a pancake, shut the refrigerator door with her foot, and gave Angela and Kenzie a mom look of warning.

David decided it must be a specific gene that allowed women to multitask with such ease. He certainly couldn't do it. Apparently Dylan couldn't either. His fork hung suspended midair, syrup dripping from the bite of pancake. His smirk faded when Jennifer glared at him, too.

"You heard me. I'm marrying Emma. Today. I called in a favor with the judge; he goes to church with me. We want you and Dylan there as witnesses, if you're available. Bring the kids; Kenzie'll be there." David leaned against the kitchen counter, sipping his coffee.

"Are you out of your mind? Married? She's been back in your life all of one hot minute, and you're getting married?" Jennifer hissed, keeping her voice low so the kids couldn't hear. "I mean, I'm really starting to like her, but this is too fast."

"I don't remember you and Dylan having a long courtship," he pointed out.

"That was different."

"Uh-huh." David snorted.

He glanced at Dylan for backup, but he shook his head with a no-way-in-hell-I'm-getting-involved look. *Chicken.* David glared at him.

"Dylan…" Jennifer turned to him for help as well.

"Yes, dear?" He looked at his watch. "Ah, geez, look at the time. If we're going to a wedding today, I better get some work done. Just tell Jen the time and place, deacon. We'll be there."

Dylan gave all three kids and Jennifer a kiss goodbye, adding a slap to Jennifer's butt before beating a hasty retreat.

The girls screamed with laughter and Rory started crying.

"Children, settle down." Jennifer sighed and turned her attention back to him. "Fine. It's your life. What time and where?"

"The courthouse. I'll call you, but I guestimate around three. We still have to get the rings, and Emma wants to shop for new dresses." He glanced over to where Kenzie was giggling with Angela and making a mess, unaware of the upcoming changes in her life. "Shopping, my least favorite activity." He shuddered. "Kenz will be ecstatic."

Jennifer patted his cheek and gave him a worried smile. "You'll survive. If you're sure about this, of course we'll be there." She hugged him, causing Rory to squirm between them. "You know I want you to be happy. And Kenzie, too."

"I know. Thanks. I am." Turning to Kenzie, he picked up her overnight bag. "C'mon, Kenzie McFrenzie. We have a lot to do, and I have some big news for you."

Nervous didn't begin to describe Emma's feelings. Something was off, and she couldn't put her finger on it. It was like a sense of doom had thickened the air, making her jumpy and irritable. She glanced over her shoulder. She had that unsettled feeling like she was being watched again. Irritated by her ridiculous, overactive imagination, she blew out a deep breath and squared her shoulders.

This was just pre-wedding jitters. David had the marriage license in his pocket. They'd bought simple gold wedding bands at a jewelry store in the mall. The kind jeweler was even resizing her engagement ring and promised to have it done by the time they finished their shopping.

David gave her a quick kiss on the cheek. "I'll take these packages to the car. Meet you at you-know-where."

Emma smiled weakly and nodded. She still found it hard to believe that in a few hours she would be Emma Patterson. Somehow, David had finagled an appointment at the courthouse for them to marry at four.

Kenzie chattered incessantly about princesses and brides, adding to her nerves. Emma smiled distractedly at Kenzie's happy babbling. She was going to be uncontrollable when she found out David's last surprise. He planned to take her to get her ears pierced. She'd asked daily since Angela's were pierced a few weeks ago. They meandered toward the store, looking in windows.

Where the hell is he? Something caught her attention out of the corner of her eye, and she spun around, but she didn't see anything out of the ordinary. Relief swept over her as she spotted David sauntering toward them, looking handsome in his jeans and pale blue button-down shirt. He'd wanted to get his hair cut before the wedding, but Emma had begged him not to. She liked running her fingers through the unruly waves at the back of his neck.

"Hey, you. What's the matter?" he asked, scanning her face.

"Nothing." She squirmed. "Okay, I was afraid you'd changed your mind and run."

"Ha! Think you're going to get out of this that easy? No way." Chuckling, he gave her a kiss on the cheek and pulled Kenzie's pigtail. "Ready?"

Already feeling nauseous, Emma couldn't stomach the thought of seeing Kenzie crying in pain. "Um, care if I skip this part? I think it would be nice for you two to have some time alone. Besides, I have a special something I need to buy." She nodded toward the toy store, and David grinned.

"Su-ure." Giving the word two syllables, he followed it with squawking noises.

"Busted," she muttered, making him laugh.

"Go. We'll meet at the food court in thirty minutes."

Emma didn't hesitate and scurried away. She hadn't been lying; she wanted David and Kenzie to have a little time alone. Although their daughter had been enthusiastic about the wedding plans, Emma knew Kenzie would need time to adjust once things settled into a daily routine.

Once again, the creepy feeling of being watched slid over her shoulders. She stopped and looked in a store window, using the reflection to assess her surroundings, but found nothing unusual. Mentally, she chastised herself and wandered into the toy store to buy bride and groom dolls for Kenzie. Avoiding small talk with the clerk, she hurried out with her purchases just in time to hear Kenzie's shriek echo down the length of the mall.

Already on edge, Emma headed toward the bathroom, feeling sick. Trembling, she threw open the door and hurried to the sink. David must have nerves of steel. No way she could have handled that today.

The cold water she splashed on her face helped, and she gripped the sink, keeping her eyes closed until the nausea abated. Then the door behind her opened and closed. Opening her eyes, she looked up into the mirror and froze.

Her past stared back at her.

Cold, stark fear solidified inside her chest, and a dull roar filled her ears.

Scott stood with his back against the bathroom door. When he turned to lock it behind him, Emma broke out in a cold sweat. Her knees knocked together as she trembled. Feeling lightheaded, she forced air into her lungs.

I'm in deep trouble.

"Miss me?" His soft voice made her skin crawl. "I've gone to a lot of trouble to find you. I'm particular about my property."

Emma attempted to swallow, but her mouth tasted like sawdust. This man haunted her nightmares. He was heavier than she remembered, and his hair was shorn short, but his dark eyes remained cold and soulless. Her eyes dropped to his huge hands and the gold ring with his initials. She rubbed her thigh, feeling the burn…

Dear God, why now?

He cracked his knuckles, and the image of his fists pounding her almost senseless washed over her. She wanted to vomit. Her conditioned reaction was to drop her gaze and cower. But she wasn't the same whipped girl. She now had reason to get out of this—and get out alive Squaring her shoulders, she looked him in the eye. Maybe she could fake him out with a show of strength.

"Get out of my way, asshole."

"Still got that smart mouth, don't you? I got better uses for that mouth." His evil eyes raked her from head to toe. "Nobody leaves the family unless I tell them they can. You're mine, Fourteen."

She flinched at being called by her number.

"Get out of my way, or I'm going to scream for the cops." Glaring at him, she held the package with Kenzie's dolls like a shield. She had to figure out how to get past him to the door. But trying to think clearly was like navigating through a thick fog.

He shook his head. "You don't belong here. You know it, and I know it. Eighteen told me how you abandoned your kid and left that poor shmuck to raise her. Now I ask you, what kind of woman would leave her baby? Shit, a fuckin' dog is a better mother than someone like you."

She swallowed, but refused to look away. To get out alive, it was imperative that she remain calm.

"I own you, and I don't like having my shit stolen," he continued. "I've bided my time, waiting until you had something to lose. And despite being a shit mother, I think you've started to care. Why else would you stick around this crappy little town? So now, if you don't cooperate, I'll make sure *you* know what it feels like to lose something valuable."

His eyes seemed to undress her as his tongue snaked across his loose mouth. "Look at you, you fuckin' whore. I bet you think you're respectable with your teacher boyfriend." He shook his head as he approached her.

Her eyes bugged. How long had he been watching her? How did he know so much? *I need to be brave. He thrives on fear...*

"Once a whore, always a whore, no matter how nice you dress. I wonder, will your kid follow in your footsteps? Is being a fuckin' piece of meat in your genetics? I mean, look at your mother. The apple didn't fall far from that tree. You're a selfish bitch, not showing up for your poor mama's funeral. Did you even know she was gone? She died choking on her own puke, strung out on China White. It was disgusting."

"You were there?" she gasped, trying to keep him talking.

"She's no loss. I'm sure you'd agree, I did the world a favor." Pure evil stretched across his face. "Anyway, you're mine, Fourteen. You bear my mark, remember? I own you, and I'm going to make damn sure you remember this time."

Bile surged in her mouth, and she forced herself to swallow it back down. With a sob, she choked, "No!" The sack with the dolls made loud crackling sounds, and her heart pounded in her ears. She couldn't stop shaking. But she'd die before she'd submit to him again.

"Cooperate," he said. "And I'll go easy on you. If you don't, I'll kill you." He snapped open a wicked-looking knife as he approached her. "Better yet, I'll send some friends for your boyfriend and kid. They can watch you do what you do best, and then I'll kill him and bring your daughter into the family. That way you won't have any reason to leave me."

Paralyzed by fear, Emma watched him stalk toward her.

"P-Please, no. I'll do whatever you want. Leave them alone." Tears sprang to her eyes, and blackness threatened to overwhelm her. Shaking, she dropped the package. *I was wrong. I'm not brave.*

"That's a girl. Come with me nice and quiet." He reached for her, and she darted to the left, but he caught her by the hair, shoving her roughly to her knees, holding the knife to her throat. "That was a mistake, Fourteen."

Kensington.

David.

Her family.

Her reason for living.

Emma's self-preservation kicked into high gear. She grabbed his wrist and twisted with all her might. She screamed at the burning sensation in her scalp as he pulled her hair out by the root, but it didn't matter. Her goal was to get away. She head-butted him in the groin, seeing stars from the impact. His furious yelp echoed in the enclosed space, and his grip loosened just enough for her to scramble to her feet. Kicking him where it counted, she screamed for help. The knife fell to the floor, and she dove for it, but he managed to boot it out of the way. He followed with a swift kick to her back, and she stumbled to the cement floor. He continued to kick her, making it nearly impossible to move.

Frantic, she tripped him and crawled, attempting to reach the door, but he grabbed her by the ankle, yanking her back. Snarling like an enraged bull, he backhanded her across the face.

"Bitch!" His ring split her lip, and her vision blurred from the impact. As she fought, her clothing ripped, and he clawed at her bra.

Screaming, she struggled, refusing to go down without a fight. Red fury washed over her. She wasn't fighting for just herself. She fought for her daughter. She fought for every girl who had ever been forced to do something she didn't want to do. She fought for those, like herself, who had done unspeakable things simply to survive. Feral, she used everything in her arsenal — scratching, biting, hitting, and kicking. Shouting obscenities, she continued her ruthless assault. Blood spurted from his nose.

She heard pounding on the door just as it splintered open. It took three men to pull her off.

When her vision cleared, she stared at her shredded clothing, covered in blood. She had no idea if it was hers or his. The adrenaline surging through her body dropped, and the room spun. Someone moved her toward the door.

Emma clung to whoever escorted her to the mall office. No matter how hard she tried, she couldn't stop shaking.

She sank into a chair and whimpered, "I'm going to be sick."

Someone handed her a garbage can. She retched until dry heaves wracked her body. A security guard handed her some paper towels, and someone wrapped a blanket around her.

"Th-Thank you." Emma stared at the floor, numb. Was she going to be arrested? David! What was David going to think? Her vile attacker's words looped through her brain, and she covered her ears, rocking to soothe herself. "No, no, no," she muttered.

The police arrived and began their questions, which she answered in a flat, monotone voice. Why wouldn't they leave her alone? All she wanted to do was crawl under that desk and hide.

"Emma!"

She raised her head, recognizing panic and fear in David's voice. Her chest hurt so badly she wondered if she was having a heart attack. She couldn't seem to breathe. She held the blanket tight.

"I'm looking for Emma! Please, where is she?" David burst through the doorway. His wild eyes locked on hers as he panted for breath, one hand holding Kenzie's, the other gripping the doorframe.

"Oh my God." He stood frozen, his face contorted into a mask of red rage.

"Mama?" Kenzie started crying and clung to David's leg.

The look of distress on her daughter's face pushed her over the edge. Covering her head with her hands, Emma whispered, "For God's sake, please, David. Take Kenzie home." She turned away, not wanting them to see her like this.

David picked up Kenzie, turning her so she couldn't see Emma.

"What's wrong, Daddy?" She squirmed, trying to look. He moved just outside the door, rocking her gently, comforting her.

He'd been in the jewelry store picking up Emma's engagement ring when the storeowner told him something had happened in the women's restroom. When Emma didn't meet him at the food court, a knot of fear had formed in his stomach. Rushing to the mall office, he hadn't been prepared for the sight of her. Even more terrifying than her split lip and torn, bloody clothes was the hopelessness in her eyes.

"What happened to Mama?" Kenzie cried, clinging to his neck, trying to find her mother.

"Shh, Mama's fine. Everything's going to be okay. She just, uh, had an accident," David explained, walking her farther away from the situation.

He dug his phone out of his pocket and sent a text asking Jennifer to come get Kenzie as soon as possible. He was too angry to think coherently.

He felt lost even as he offered reassurance to his daughter.

A female officer stepped out of the office holding a package. "Are you Kenzie?"

Kenzie peered at her suspiciously.

"Your mama wanted me to give this to you. Why don't you come with me to open it in this office over here and let your daddy check on your mother, okay?"

Kenzie hesitated, but the lure of the package drew her to the officer. David handed her over with a whispered, "Thank you."

He rushed back into the room where the police were questioning Emma. The mall security officer gave him a pat on the back and murmured, "She's okay. She fought him off. That's more his blood than hers."

David nodded and went to Emma, placing a hand on her shoulder. She jumped and pulled away, hunching down in the chair into a near-fetal position. Her reaction devastated him.

"It's me, Emma." Sick with anger, his vision momentarily went black, but he reined it in for her sake. The jerk who did this to her would rot in prison for the rest of his miserable life, no matter what it took, or how long.

Emma glanced up and turned away, her face flushing. Her arms crossed over her chest, and she curled tighter, as if to make herself as small as possible. Her hair curtained her face from him, and he felt shut out, powerless to help her. Unbuttoning his shirt, he shrugged out of it and offered it to her. When she nodded, he moved the blanket and helped her into it.

"Thank you, Ms. Devine. We'd like to send you to the hospital to be checked." The young officer looked at Emma and then David.

"I want to go home." Speaking in a flat monotone, it was as if Emma had distanced herself from the situation. She stared at the floor. "Please, David…"

He leaned closer to hear her choked voice.

"Please take Kenzie home. The lady officer said she'd take me wherever they want me to go."

Squatting in front of her, he gently buttoned his shirt. "Honey, I don't want to leave you. Jennifer's on her way to get Kenz. I'll take you."

"Just go, David! Leave me the hell alone!" She covered her face with her hands, and her shoulders shook.

David closed his eyes. He hurt for Emma. Her pain made him want to hit a wall, hit anything. Rage consumed him unlike anything he'd ever felt before. Not wanting to add to her suffering, he kept silent and still. But he stayed, despite her objection. He would not leave her. He blinked back his tears and stood when Jennifer walked into the room.

"Emma, Jennifer's here to get Kenzie. I'll take you to the hospital," he urged softly. He wanted to take her in his arms and hold her, but he restricted himself to stroking her hair. She still cringed, and he pulled his hand away.

"Emma," he whispered brokenly.

She refused to look at him. "Go away."

"I'll take care of Emma; you go be with Kenzie." Jennifer spoke in her soft-but-firm nurse voice.

He hesitated, torn. They both needed him. Again he reached out to Emma, wanting to hold her, make her feel safe. Again she shrugged away.

For her sake, he pushed his own insecurities and needs aside. "Em, will you let Jennifer take you?"

She gave a barely perceptible nod, still sitting hunched over, rocking herself.

David leaned in and kissed her forehead. "I love you. Kenzie and I will be over to see you after you get cleaned up, okay? She needs to see you. I need to see you and hold you, honey. Please?"

A tear leaked from her closed eyes, and she nodded with a re-signed sigh.

David kissed the top of her head as he left to find his daughter.

As he entered the office across the hall, Kenzie looked up with a smile from playing with the bride and groom dolls with the female officer. "Where are your clothes, Daddy? Is it time for the wedding?"

He picked her up and held her close, burying his face in her neck so she wouldn't see his tears.

"Not today, Kenz. Mama isn't feeling well." Surreptitiously, he wiped his eyes and plastered on a smile for her sake. "But soon, okay?"

Emma gazed at her folded hands, grateful for Jennifer's silence on the drive home from the hospital. Aside from some deep tissue bruising and her busted lip, she was physically okay—though every bone in her body ached. Mentally, she felt numb, dead even. How could this have happened? The years she'd spent away from Scott had been erased. She was right back where she'd always been.

She looked at the steps to her apartment and sighed. They seemed as insurmountable as Mt. Everest. Thankfully, Jennifer allowed her to take her time. Once inside, they headed straight for the bathroom, and in a capable, no-nonsense manner, Jennifer helped her step out of David's shirt and her torn, bloody clothes. Emma covered her thigh and kept her eyes downcast, refusing to look in the mirror. She couldn't bear to see the dirty girl reflected there.

"It wasn't your fault. You know that, right?" Jennifer said. "And I'm so proud of how you fought. You did the right thing, Emma. Something a little similar once happened to me, and it's a horrible feeling, to feel powerless, trapped. But you fought, Emma. You fought him off. He will go to jail and not be able to hurt anyone else."

Emma moved to step into the shower, and Jennifer gasped.

Eyes wide, she stared at Emma's thigh and covered her mouth. "Oh my God. Emma."

Emma placed her hand over the *14* seared into her skin, but nothing could cover her humiliation.

Regaining her composure, Jennifer silently helped her wash and get into her pajamas.

She was sitting on the closed toilet while Jennifer combed through her hair when Emma heard the front door open. Immediately, she mentally checked out, unable to face David. Not like this. Sinking into a state where there was no pain, no degradation, no feelings, she distantly heard Jennifer speaking, yet couldn't make out the words. Instead the old refrain played over and over in her tortured brain.

Whore, bitch, terrible mother...

Chapter
Twenty-One

Without looking up, Emma felt his presence. Heat suffused her body. She couldn't face him right now. Tightening her arms around her body, she folded into herself, trying to disappear. The shame and humiliation were unbearable. Dirty and damaged, she didn't feel deserving of the man in the doorway.

"Where's Kenzie?" Jennifer asked.

"Thank you," Emma whispered, staring at her feet. She took the pain pill Jennifer offered, eager to slip into unconsciousness.

"I left her at your house. Dylan's playing fairy princesses with the girls. I wish I'd snapped a picture for blackmail," David replied with a forced laugh. "I'll take over from here, if it's okay with Emma."

"It's up to you, Emma. I can stay if you need me," Jennifer said.

She shrugged, too weary to answer.

Leaning in close, Jennifer hugged her. "I'm leaving you in good hands," she whispered. She gave David a hug on her way out.

David stepped forward and kissed her forehead.

"I love you, my darling, brave girl."

Emma turned her face from him and closed her eyes. "Just go home. I need to be alone."

"I'm not leaving." He guided her to her bedroom and turned down her covers. Like a zombie, she crawled into bed.

David sat on the bed beside her. He spoke about her bravery, how much he loved her. Ignoring him, she closed her eyes, covered her ears and slipped into narcotic-induced oblivion.

Six hours later, she awoke with a start and instantly regretted moving so quickly. Pain shot through every nerve in her body. One of Mrs. Jordan's roses sat in a cup by her bedside. David was gone. Struggling out of bed, she managed to get herself to the bathroom. Staring at her reflection was like going back in time. She took another pain pill and made her way to the kitchen to eat something. Vomiting wasn't an option as her stomach was tender from being kicked.

An odd combination of relief and annoyance swept over her when she found David asleep on her couch.

He woke up under her gaze and sprang to his feet. "Hey! Let me help you. What do you need? How are you feeling?"

"I'm fine."

He frowned, opened his mouth to say something, and shut it again. He rubbed his hands against his eyes and stretched, yawning. "It's only four in the morning. But I could cook you some breakfast or something."

"I told you, I'm fine. Go home."

"I don't think you should be alone…"

Ignoring him, Emma popped two pieces of bread in the toaster.

"What can I do to help you?"

"How many times do I have to tell you I'm okay?" she snapped.

David got the butter and jelly out of the refrigerator and started a pot of coffee. "Last night, I phoned the after-hours number for your therapist. Today's a holiday, but she's going to work you in tomorrow. I'll take you. While we're there, I think it would be a good idea to set up some family counseling."

"I didn't ask you to do that." Smoke billowed from the toaster and she popped it. "Dammit!" She threw the toast on the counter. "Just go! I can take care of myself! And I'm not sure we're still getting married."

He flinched, which pissed her off even more. She didn't want or need his help. His very presence a reminder that she didn't belong in his world.

"I'm not the enemy, Em. I love you, and I'm worried about you."

"Stop it." She couldn't deal with this. Not now. She felt out of control, as if she were on a train and not able to get off.

David scraped the toast, his face grim, his motions jerky. "What about Kenzie?"

Guilt washed over her like a tsunami. She hadn't even thought about her daughter…

"Get out," she hissed.

"Dammit!" He threw the knife down and stormed out of the house.

Emma sank into the chair, covered her face and rocked, sobbing and screaming.

Yet no sound escaped her mouth.

David slammed the door and collapsed on the top step. The despair he'd been holding in check since the incident at the mall broke loose. Covering his face, he wept. Anger and rage tore his soul apart, leaving him raw. Hate consumed him and terrified him. He'd never felt this way before. He wanted to kill that sonofabitch. His despondency soon led to an outright rant against God. He railed and questioned everything he'd ever believed in, feeling bereft and alone.

It wasn't the first time he'd questioned his faith. He'd struggled before, being no different than most. He knew some questions were just unanswerable. But this was different. The powerlessness he'd felt seeing Emma bloodied and bruised was the lowest point of his life. He should have been there for her. It was his responsibility to keep her safe from that despicable, miserable excuse of a human being.

But the flat look in her eyes scared him most; was she breaking mentally? She'd said she might not want to get married. Was she going to run again? He couldn't imagine his life without her. He needed her. Kenzie needed her.

He forced himself to get up and start walking home. *Tell me! Tell me why this happened. Please, tell me what to do… Tell me she'll be okay…*

Opening the door to his screened in porch, he collapsed on the glider, exhausted. He needed a glimmer of hope. His phone vibrated in his pocket, and he dug it out. It was a text from Emma.

What time is the appt?

He typed a response:

Tomorrow @ 9

Relief swept through him, and he said a quick prayer of thanks. There was hope. Surely they'd get through this.

"Kenzie enjoyed the fireworks last night. I'm sorry you missed them." David tried once again to make casual conversation. "It was a job keeping her contained. Jennifer and Dylan and the kids were there. Rory almost took a tumble into the lake. Dylan was freaked out. He said he's going to build a seven-foot fence up and down the dock."

Emma didn't respond. Yesterday, he'd told Kenzie her mother wasn't feeling well after she'd refused to join them for a quiet Fourth of July celebration. The only smile he'd seen on her face since the incident was when she looked at the get-well card Kenzie had made her. But after looking at the card, she'd thanked him and closed the door in his face. She hadn't even taken the plate of food he'd brought her.

But she'd been ready this morning when he'd picked her up for her appointment. Her lip looked better, and the bruising on her face was an array of purples, blues, and greens. Her icy demeanor remained.

He took his eyes from the road to glance over at Emma as he drove her home from the therapy session. Arms crossed, she stared out the window. The therapist had spoken with him for a few minutes after her session, offering tips on what he should do—patience, reminders that it wasn't her fault, and understanding being key.

"Would you like to stop by and see Kenz?"

"No!" Emma's eyes widened and panic laced her voice. "Not like this. Not yet."

"Okay, okay." He spoke soothingly and reached out to hold her hand. She jumped as if burned. He sighed. "I think that journaling stuff your therapist mentioned sounds like a good idea."

She didn't say another word.

At her place, he cut the engine. Emma bolted from the car, but she was slow going up the steps, and he easily caught up to her.

"Let me help you."

"I've got it," she ground out, huffing with the effort.

He meant more than up the steps. His frustration mounted as she continued to push him away. She unlocked her door, but he blocked her from closing it on him. "Don't shut me out. You're here but you're not here, honey. Don't leave me…"

Emma stared at her feet. She'd made very little eye contact with him since the attack. "I need time, David."

"Okay." He nodded and left. What else could he do?

A week later, Emma's phone rang with a familiar number. She muted the mindless television show she hadn't really been watching. It was on just to cover the growing, bubble of silence around her.

"Hey."

"Fuck, Emma. What can I do? Are you okay? I'm sorry—I ran out of minutes. I just got your message."

Hearing Angel's voice made her smile, something she hadn't done much of for the past week. "You always run out of minutes. I'm okay."

"Liar. Tell me that sonofabitch is going away for life this time."

"The cops seem to think so. I'm healing. I kinda look like a tie-dyed shirt. Where are you?"

He chuckled. "Groovy. I'm back in Boston. So how's Kensington? Things going okay there? You still working?"

"I've taken some time off to heal, but I guess I'll go back soon. Boston? Have you been in touch with Damien?"

"Is that code for am I clean? Yeah. I'd give you the exact number of days, but you know numbers aren't my thing. Tell me about your kid. You still seein' a head doc?"

"Yes. Kenzie's beautiful and has Ken's mop of curls. I wish you could meet her."

"Someday. And this David sounds like a good guy. You deserve someone who will take care of you. Hold on to that happiness, *amiga*. Look, I gotta go. You need me to come down there? You know I'm codependent as shit and would do anything for you. I'm just short on cash right now."

Emma giggled. "Listen to you, talking that twelve-step talk. I'd love to see you, but I'm good. I have my family…" She took a deep breath and repeated softly, "I have my family." Tears sprang to her eyes. *Hopefully.*

"Okay, Mrs. Cleaver. I'm out. Talk to you soon." He hung up.

Emma sat back, thinking long and hard about her life. Angel's advice struck a chord. She'd pushed away the man who'd committed himself to being there for her. But her heart now urged her to take a chance. *Be brave.*

After her third bath of the day, she sent David a text asking him to come over.

Chapter
Twenty-Two

David knocked on Emma's door and swatted at a mosquito. *Answer the door!* He'd prayed all the way up the path this was a good sign, but he didn't know. What if she was leaving?

Emma opened the door in her robe. Her hair was wet and exhaustion circled her eyes, adding to the colorful bruising. Her eyes and nose were red, as if she'd been crying. He wanted to kiss her, but she'd rebuffed any contact with him for over a week. So he waited.

"Thank you for coming." She motioned him in and shut the door behind her. She looked fragile, ready to break. "Is Kenzie okay?"

"She's fine. I took her to Jennifer's. Did you want to see her? She misses you. I can go get her."

"No. Yes." Emma shrugged. "I don't know."

He smiled. "I love you."

She looked at the floor. "Don't."

"Don't what, honey?"

"Don't love me. I'm not—I mean, I want you to, but...You can't..." Her voice broke on a sob.

"My love doesn't have a switch to turn on and off. It's constant and true, and it's yours. You need to accept that. Do you love me?"

She looked up at him through her tears. "Yes, but I don't think I'm very easy to love. I know it'll be hard work—"

He shook his head. "My dad once told me nothing worth having is easy. I'm up for the job. Don't you see? *You* make me a better man. We're meant to be together. Think about how we met. What are the chances unless it was by design? I need you, your daughter needs you, and I think you need us, too, Emma."

"I'm not Emma."

Gingerly, he cupped her cheek and raised her face, but she squeezed her eyes shut. Half afraid of the answer, he asked, "Who are you, honey?"

"I'm Fourteen, a nobody."

"Fourteen? I don't know what you mean. But I know this for certain: you're *my* somebody." He brushed away her tears. "Look at me, please."

She took a deep breath but did as he asked.

"I'm Fourteen, just a number in Scott's stable—"

She never got to complete the sentence. Something in David shifted. He was no longer willing to treat her as something fragile. It was time to fight for her. He covered her mouth with his, kissing her deeply.

"Stop it. That is not who you are. Do you hear me?" He took her by the hand and dragged her to the bathroom turning her to face the mirror, her back to his chest. He wrapped his arm around her, holding her close.

She whimpered and turned her head, unwilling to look at herself.

"Open your damn eyes and look in the mirror, Emma." His voice boomed in the small bathroom.

This jarred her into compliance, and her gaze met his in the mirror. She wanted to turn away, but she couldn't with his firm hold on her chin.

"No, please...Don't look at me," she begged.

"I want you to see what I see." His voice softened, and his hold on her chin became a caress as he stroked his fingers across her split lip. "These soft, beautiful lips smile at me, kiss me, and make my world spin. I've spent countless hours fantasizing about them. They kiss my daughter good night and make her feel secure.

"Your lovely eyes haunt me. They always have. Did you know they change color? When you're mad, they're like topaz. When you're aroused, they're green. These eyes have witnessed more of the disgusting, atrocious side of this world than I can imagine, and yet they still reflect goodness and compassion. They still light up when they see those they love. In your eyes, I see your beautiful, untarnished soul."

She trembled as his hands moved lower. Her robe opened, and he cupped her breasts reverently. She sagged against him, accepting his strength to hold her up.

"These breasts drive me to distraction. Do you know how I have longed to kiss them, to feel their weight in my hands? They're beautiful and perfect."

He chuckled. "Remember the leaking incident after Kenzie was born? You were so upset and adorable. It's one of the first times I remember you really laughing after your got over your embarrassment." His hands roamed lower to her stomach. With one finger, he traced the faint scar from her C-section, and her skin tingled.

"You carried Kenzie in this beautiful body and gave birth to her. You gave me the most precious gift I've ever received. I want to cherish and love your body with mine. You're an integral part of me. We're one in spirit, and someday we'll be one in body, Emma."

She held her breath as he gently took off her robe. Holding her hands in his, he spread her arms wide as he continued to look at her in the mirror. He kissed her shoulder and worked his way down her arm to her left hand. From his jeans pocket he pulled her engagement ring, which had been resized. He slipped it on her ring finger, kissing her bruised hand.

"These hands hold me, hold our daughter, and make us feel loved and cared for. Have I ever told you how much I love it when you massage the back of my neck? It isn't a conscious thing you do, but you seem to know when I'm tense, and it feels so good. And how I love to see your hands covered in flour, with dough under your nails, because you're teaching Kenzie how to cook.

"I know you're scared. But don't fear love. Grab it, Emma. Grab it, embrace it, and fight for it. Don't hide from it. Don't throw it away."

Tears streamed down her face and her knees buckled.

He caught her.

He always did.

"Quit living in the past, honey. That man will never hurt you again. He's up on so many charges he'll never see the light of day. I'll do everything in my power to make sure of it. We're in the present and looking to the future—a beautiful future together as a husband and wife, as parents to Kenzie. Will it always be joyful and pain-free? Of course not. Life isn't like that. But together, we'll get through the bad times. I'm going to take my vows seriously—for better or worse, in sickness and in health. *Forever,* Em."

She shrugged out of his grasp. "But I'm marked, David! I've been his property since I was twelve. I'm a number, no better than livestock. I don't know how to—"

His mouth closed over hers, shutting her up. It was a kiss of possession, of need tempered by love. Pulling away, he examined the brand on her inner thigh and shook his head. She reached for her robe.

"I hate that," he said through gritted teeth.

She hung her head, but again he forced her to look at him. "I hate it because of the way it's hurt you. I don't care about a mark on your body. Don't you understand? It doesn't affect how I feel about you! It doesn't affect who you are. You are *not* your past. You are not some mark on your body. Would I love you less if it was a scar from an accident or an illness?"

She closed her eyes.

"Answer me!"

"N-No," she choked out through tears.

Kneeling, he covered another man's hatred with a tender, loving kiss. Dotting kisses up her body, he stood and held her face in his hands.

"I love everything about you. I love your laugh, and I wish you laughed more often. I love how you always fold the bath towels precisely in thirds, yet throw the plastic containers in the cabinet without their matching lids. I love that you burn toast, but make the best macaroni and cheese I've ever eaten. However, just so you know, I'll never tell my mother yours is better than hers. I'm a coward at heart.

"I love the fact you're reading that silly *Parenting for Dummies* book and that you snore when you're really tired. I love how you watch my carb and sugar intake because I'm not disciplined enough to stay away from sweets.

"Are you perfect? No. But you're perfect for me. You're a good person, a compassionate woman, a mother, and soon to be my wife and lover. You can do this. *Trust me.* You are the love of my life and my Emma divine." He folded her in his arms again and held her gaze in the mirror.

"How can you forgive me, much less love me with everything I've put you through?" she croaked, gripping his arms, afraid to let go.

He shook his head. "I can't explain love. I don't think anyone can. All I can do is show it."

He shrugged. "This is meant to be. I love you. Plain and simple. You're more than this body, more than your past. You're my future. And Kenzie's. Please, truly look at yourself and see what I see."

Naked, both physically and emotionally, she gazed at their reflection. He saw all her ugliness, her shame, her guilt, and yet he still loved her, believed she could be more. A tear rolled down her cheek, and he leaned in and kissed it away. She turned around and clung to his neck. David pulled her closer, holding her tight. Never before had she felt this loved, protected, and cherished.

I'm safe, and David loves me…And I love him.

A burden fell from her shoulders. She hardly knew who she was anymore, but she wanted to be the person David loved.

"Don't leave me," she whispered. "I do love you. You are a gift, and I promise I'll treasure you always."

"Never. You're stuck with me. In sickness and in health, through good times and bad." He kissed her closed eyes, her lips, her forehead.

"Even if I burn your toast?"

He smiled. "I love burnt toast."

She tightened her hold, melding her body as close as she could get. David nourished her battered soul, giving her the strength to love and be loved. "I shouldn't have shut you out. I feel like I've been living in a fog. I was so scared that day. He threatened to hurt you and Kenzie. I knew I couldn't let him get to my family. Even now, I can still feel his touch, smell him, and hear his horrible threats…I still feel dirty."

She didn't quite make it to the toilet. David held her hair as her body heaved. "I'm sorry," she sobbed as she cleaned up the mess on the floor.

"You did the same for me, remember?" He ran bathwater as she brushed her teeth, her body shaking. Then he helped her into the tub.

Emma closed her eyes as he bathed her. "We're not married," she murmured as he washed.

"Nope. Hop out of the water, lightning might strike me dead," he teased.

"David?"

"Yes?"

"I need help."

"Did I miss a spot, Emma divine?"

"Are you really making a pun on my name? Emma divine?"

He chuckled. "Uh, no. Technically I think it was homophonic heterograph."

"Smartass." She opened her eyes and stroked his cheek. "I mean I'm a mess, in my head. What if I never get better?"

"You don't give yourself enough credit. Trust me, we can overcome this. Together."

Looking down at her bruised body, she began to scrub with rough desperation.

"Not so rough. You're not dirty; you're just taking a bath."

Emma stopped, knowing what he meant. It wasn't possible to scrub her past away; she simply had to put it behind her. She closed her eyes and relaxed, letting David resume his work. His gentle touch soothed her, and she hummed with pleasure.

"Thank you. David?"

"Yes?"

"I don't want you to leave. I need you."

"I don't want to go, either."

She smiled. "I have an idea…"

"This takes bundling to a whole new level," David whispered.

"Shh, Daddy."

"You shh, Kenzie. And don't think this is going to be an every-night occurrence—just on special occasions." David teetered at the edge of the bed, lying on his side.

Emma giggled. "We should have done this at your house. Your bed is bigger."

Kenzie elbowed her in the stomach. Emma yelped.

"You okay, honey?"

"I'm perfect."

"I rather thought you'd be in the middle, Em." He spit Kenzie's hair out of his mouth and barely dodged her kick.

"I can't get to sleep. Daddy keeps talking," Kenzie grumbled with a big yawn.

Emma laughed, and he smiled. As uncomfortable as this was, he wouldn't change a thing. Well, maybe their positions—Kenzie once again kicked too close for comfort.

"Okay, let's get organized. Everyone needs to turn on their right side," David instructed. Kenzie turned to her left, and so did Emma. He chuckled. "I can understand Kenzie not knowing her left from her right, but c'mon, Emma."

"I never want to turn away from you again," she whispered, stroking his cheek with the back of her fingers. Kenzie settled with a sigh into her mother's arm and fell sound asleep.

David smiled. "Works for me." He stretched his arm out to hold the most important people in his life.

Emma would be okay.

They would be okay.

Together they would work through hell and back to find their slice of heaven.

Chapter
Twenty-Three

David dressed after his shower but decided to skip shaving. He still hated cutting grass, but since Emma had agreed to come stay with Kenzie bright and early this morning, he was done before breakfast.

The weeks had flown by, and he was back to school next week, with students coming the week after that. Emma was better, both physically and mentally. They'd even begun couples counseling.

Soft laughter drifted from the kitchen. He brushed his teeth, checked his glucose, and made his way out. Emma quickly hung up her phone and shifted her eyes.

"What's going on?" he asked.

"Nothing," she and Kenzie replied in unison.

They shared a knowing look, and he realized they were up to something. But it didn't seem to be anything to worry about…yet. Dressed in shorts and a pink T-shirt, Emma appeared at ease. Kenzie sat in a kitchen chair, kicking her feet and looking smug in her purple nightgown and princess crown. Molly, ever hopeful for a table scrap, waited at her side.

"Nothing's going on, huh?" he asked with a smile as he leaned in and gave Kenzie a kiss on the cheek.

"Owww, Daddy. Biskers!" She rubbed where his beard stubble had scuffed her face.

He chuckled. He turned to Emma and cupped her cheek. Her eyes were clear and dark green as she turned her face into his hand and kissed his palm.

"Morning," he whispered, kissing her.

"Oww, David. Biskers," she teased. "Did you check your glucose?"

"Yes, dear," he replied with an exaggerated sigh, pinching her upturned little nose. "What are your plans for the day?"

"Oh, nothing special." She shot a look at Kenzie and frowned, shaking her head.

David had the distinct feeling he was out of the loop.

"Oh, but Jennifer sent a text, and Dylan could really use your help today. He needs to pick up some equipment or something at his brother's house. He had it sent there, and his brother wants it out of the house. You know Dylan; it's probably been there for months."

"He wants to go get it today? I only have three more days off before school." David grumbled.

Kenzie giggled, and he narrowed his eyes.

"Maybe he wants to see his family." Emma shrugged and stirred the oatmeal. "He's been good to you; I didn't think it would be a big deal. Kenzie and I will stay here and make some cookies or something."

David placed his hands on her hips and nuzzled her neck. "I don't want to leave you…"

Emma moved the oatmeal off the hot stove and turned in his arms. She looked directly into his eyes and smiled. "You don't have to babysit me. I start back to work next week, too. I need this—a nice day with my daughter, doing mundane things like cooking."

"You're sure?" He searched her face for any lingering fear or doubts; he didn't find any.

"I'm positive. Now eat. Dylan will be here in a few minutes."

"Yeah, eat, Daddy. You have to *leave*," Kenzie insisted.

Emma shot her a warning look. Kenzie's hazel eyes, so like Emma's, twinkled with devilment as she tried to contain her giggles.

David pursed his lips. Obviously Emma wasn't going to tell him what was up. He'd get it out of Kenzie. With feigned innocence, he took his bowl of oatmeal and sat next to her.

"What are you going to do today, Kenz?"

Emma stepped behind Kenzie, placing a gentle hand over her mouth. "David, just eat and go. We *do* have a surprise, and I'm not going to let you trick it out of Kenzie."

Kenzie laughed behind the hand over her mouth and struggled free.

"I'm not telling! Go away, Daddy!"

David looked sharply at Emma. She still seemed relaxed, and her smile brightened the room.

"Okay, you two. Just don't get in to trouble while I'm gone." David shook his head and began to eat. He quite liked being out of the loop, if it meant Emma was all right.

"You're sure David's family will be here?" Emma asked, hammering a nail to hold the strand of white Christmas lights on the dock. Her sweat-drenched T-shirt clung to her body, and damp tendrils had escaped her ponytail.

Jennifer mopped her brow with her shirttail. Similarly dressed, she looked just as hot and sweaty. "Positive. That's where they've gone—to get them at the airport. Dylan flew them up on a private plane. He's supposed to tell David it's so they can be here for his last weekend before school. However, knowing my husband, he'll probably spill what's going on—just be warned." She held up the other end of the light strand.

"Oh goodness, I knew I'd get tripped up on lies starting with the equipment excuse. David's already suspicious, so I'm sure he'll worm it out of Dylan. It might be for the best. That way he'll at least be in a suit and not his World's Best Dad T-shirt and jeans."

Jennifer nodded as she plugged in the lights to test them.

"And your bodyguard can really marry us?" Emma asked, pleased when the lights worked.

"Yes, Tyrone is more than happy to do it; he's a preacher, too. He just looks big and forbidding. On the inside, he's a big ol' softy and a fine man. Once I caught him with a crown on his head pretending to drink tea with Angela."

Emma smiled as she paused, looking out over the lake at all the boats filled with happy people celebrating the last few days of summer vacation. Being in the sunshine and hearing people laugh helped lessen the anxiety she still experienced from time to time. The incident with Scott almost seemed like a lifetime ago, thanks to David and his love.

And tonight, I'll be married!

She turned her attention back to Jennifer. "I want to thank you for everything. You're important to David, and I'm happy you're willing to be my matron of honor. I know we didn't have a good start to our friendship—"

Jennifer held up a hand, interrupting her. "David's my best friend, and we care about each other. I'm sorry I gave you such a hard time. If it makes you feel any better, when I started dating Dylan, David gave him a hard time, too!" Mopping her wet brow, she laughed. "It's surprising how well David and Dylan get along now. They've both mellowed over the years. Do I think things have moved too fast for you two? Possibly. But as David pointed out, who am I to talk? Dylan and I didn't exactly have a conventional romance, either. What I'm trying to say—in a roundabout way—is I'm happy to be your matron of honor. And I do like you, a lot."

Emma smiled and hugged her. "Good God, I'm becoming one of those sappy brides!" She giggled. "I've never been a touchy-feely girl."

Jennifer smiled. "I won't tell anyone. Look, we need to get busy. We have a wedding to pull off in a few hours, and I'm pretty sure the kids are running circles around Mrs. Jordan."

Nodding, Emma unwrapped another string of lights, her smile growing wider as she worked.

Chapter
Twenty-Four

Other than the usual pleasantries, which ran dry after about five minutes, Dylan hadn't spoken a word since leaving Pine Bluff. Instead, he sang along with the radio for almost two hours, beating out the rhythm on the steering wheel.

David bit his tongue to keep from screaming. He toyed with the idea of jumping out of the car or running into traffic when they stopped, just to get away. Dylan had a great voice, but the in-car performance wasn't helping David's mood. This wasn't now how he'd envisioned spending the day.

"You're brooding. And I don't like people encroaching on my territory," Dylan observed. "I'm the angst-filled, creative, handsome musician—I should be the brooder, not you. You're the teacher and wannabe preacher. Shouldn't you be all goodness and light and shit?" He glanced in the rearview mirror and ran a hand through his hair.

David glared at him. "Humility has never been your strong point. I'm not stupid. Emma's up to something, you're in on it, and this is not the way to your brother's house."

Dylan shot him a look and laughed. "How dumb do I look? Don't answer that. Do you really think I'm gonna risk the wrath of my wife and your fiancée by telling you what the hell is actually going down?"

"In honor of the brotherhood of men, yes."

"Hell, I didn't even like you the first year I knew you," he protested.

"The feeling was quite mutual, I assure you," David muttered.

With an exasperated sigh, he turned to stare out the window. This was a mistake; he should have stayed with his family. He'd intended to ask Emma to marry him again. He was sick and tired of stupid cold showers.

Dylan interrupted his pity party. "You can talk to me. I'm a captive audience."

David took a moment to collect his thoughts. He hadn't really opened up to anyone after Emma's attack except the therapist. "I don't know what to do. I want to marry Em, but I don't know when the right time is to bring it up again. I mean, things are better, but she still seems distant at times. I've never felt so helpless and useless in my life. It's my job to protect her and take care of her." He punched the dash. "Ow." He shook his aching hand.

"Hey, man, don't be bashin' the Benz, and it's okay to cuss, 'cause that had to hurt like fuckin' hell," Dylan joked.

David sighed.

Dylan glanced over and switched off the music. "Hey, I know what you're going through—the helpless part—and it sucks. Emma's tough, though. She's already made a lot of progress, and I really think she'll be okay. Thank God she was able to fight that guy off, and I swear, whatever it takes to keep that sick bastard locked away, I'll help do it."

"Thanks." Leaning against his hand, he closed his eyes.

"Look, you're gonna love the surprise. It'll prove to you that everything's going to be all right. Just sit back and enjoy."

David nodded, and soon the lulling motion of the car eased him to sleep.

"We're here," Dylan announced sometime later.

David opened his eyes. *Why are we at the airport?*

"There are some folks here eager to see you. I'll see you back in Pine Bluff. Don't take too long, or Jen and Emma will crucify both of us."

"What's going on?" David asked, feeling bleary.

Dylan slapped him on the shoulder and grinned. "You, my man, are joining the rest of us poor pussy-whipped bastards. You're getting married this evening! Now, you can go collect your family, or run like hell. Your choice."

"Married? Collect my family?" Stunned, he looked to where Dylan pointed.

"My folks are here?" His mouth dropped open.

"Yep, they just flew in, and there's a rental van ready to go if you'd get your ass outta my car and go get them."

"I'm getting married?" David's grin widened. "I'm getting married!" He laughed and launched himself from the car. "Thank you!" He slammed the door shut and found himself attacked by his two nephews.

"Your mother isn't happy." Michael Patterson straightened the knot in his tie and looked at David in the mirror.

"I know, Dad. But it isn't her life to lead." David tried for the third time to get the knot right in his own pale blue tie.

"True enough." His father smiled and reached over to help him. "As long as you're sure about your decision — not just marrying Emma because of Kenzie — I'm behind you. You know your mother's concerned because she loves you."

"I know. And yes, I'm positive Emma is the one for me. Once you get to know her, you and Mom will love her. I'm still floored that you're all here on such short notice. It's funny, I didn't realize how lucky I was until I met Emma. Growing up, I had the all-American childhood, complete with two loving parents, a bratty sister, and a dog. Emma had the opposite, and yet she's still capable of love. We're nothing alike, but…I can't explain it. Crap, I'm not making any sense."

"Love never makes sense." His father chuckled.

Then he rubbed the back of his neck, a sure sign he was uncomfortable with what he wanted to say. David braced himself.

"She isn't pregnant, is she? I mean, this is all kind of rushed."

David had to choke back a laugh. His dad looked as embarrassed as he had years ago when they'd had "the talk."

"No. She's definitely not pregnant."

His father's shoulders relaxed. "We don't need to discuss anything, do we?"

This time he did laugh. "No, Dad. We did that when I was in middle school. Everything's fine." He glanced in the mirror, ran a finger around the collar of his white shirt, and straightened the lapel of his gray suit. "It's really hot, and I'm already sweating. We're inside with the A/C. I kind of dread going out on that boat dock."

"Pre-wedding jitters, totally normal. I married your mother in February and sweated like a pig at a barbeque. It was snowing at the time."

David chuckled, feeling a little better as he glanced at his watch. He shook his arm. Time was standing still. He looked up when his brother-in-law, Jared, came in.

"Countdown time. You can still back out," Jared teased.

"Back out? I don't want to back out. Did you want to back out of marrying Carole?"

Jared shook his head. "Can I plead the fifth since I'm in here alone with her father and brother?"

David and his father laughed. Jared had been crazy about Carole since they were in grade school.

"Your mother, your future wife, your best friend, and I think even that dog have all told me to remind you to check your glucose."

David rolled his eyes. "I did, I did. Has anyone checked on Emma?"

"Not to worry, from the *oohs* and *aahs* heard coming from her room, she and Kenzie must look spectacular. You wouldn't believe the cackling and whispers. I'm telling you, women have dirtier minds than men. And don't worry, Carole has managed to keep your mother away from Emma. Just relax. Only a few more minutes to enjoy your freedom." Jared gave him an affectionate slap on the back.

David took a deep breath and started pacing.

"Beautiful!" Jennifer exclaimed as David's sister, Carole, finished doing Emma's hair. She had rolled it up on the sides with antique combs that had belonged to David's grandmother.

"Your something old and borrowed," Carole said with a pat as she looked at Emma in the mirror. Carole had the same dark brown eyes as her brother and father. Her short, light brown hair framed her gamine face, and her pale yellow dress accented her willowy figure. Emma had liked David's sister immediately.

Dressed in a lavender-colored sundress, Jennifer handed Emma a blue garter. "This is your something blue. Mrs. Jordan made it for you."

"Thank you. That was really sweet of her. Thank you, everyone, for everything. Has anyone checked on David? Is his glucose okay?"

"He's fine and, according to Jared, impatient as all get out," Carole reported.

"His glucose is fine. I bet he's more anxious about the wedding night," Jennifer teased.

"Ugh! TMI, Jennifer. He's my *brother*. Yuck." Carole covered her ears.

Emma bit her lip, not needing the blush Carole applied to her cheeks.

Kenzie and Angela flew into the room, giggling and chattering.

"Girls, you cannot wear the fairy wings during the wedding," Jennifer admonished.

"Why not?" they cried in unison.

Emma laughed. "I don't mind the wings. They can wear them."

"And our crowns?" Kenzie asked.

Emma wrapped one of Kenzie's curls around her finger. "Definitely. All princess fairies need crowns." The girls squealed and jumped up and down, holding hands.

Someone knocked, and Emma called out over the noise, "Come in."

"Wait, what if it's David?" Jennifer yelled.

"It's me." Vivian Patterson opened the door and smiled at Kenzie and Angela. "My, my, don't you girls look pretty. Like little butterflies."

"No, Nana, we're fairy *princesses*," Kenzie protested. She danced around in her pale blue dress, making her gossamer blue fairy wings flap. A rhinestone tiara bobbled precariously on her brown curls.

"Silly me, of course," Vivian replied with a smile. "May I have a moment alone with Emma?"

"Mom…" Carole frowned, placing a hand on Emma's shoulder.

"I'd like that," Emma replied, her voice clear and unwavering. She turned around in the chair to face her future mother-in-law.

Carole and Jennifer gave her worried looks but rounded up the two little girls and left, shutting the door behind them.

"You look lovely, Emma." Vivian ran a trembling hand down her silver pantsuit.

"Thank you."

"I'm very thankful you're okay. That was a terrible thing to go through—all of it." Vivian sat on the bed, facing Emma. She looked down at her clasped hands. "I'm sorry we got off on the wrong foot. I was…concerned. David was so lost after you left him with Kenzie. But he's my only son, and I won't lose him. I raised him to be a good man with sound judgment. So I have to trust him—"

"You love him. I understand," Emma interrupted, placing her hand on top of Vivian's. "I love him, too."

Vivian considered Emma for a long, heart-stopping moment. Then she smiled and squeezed her hand. "Yes, I believe you do." She stood and leaned over to kiss Emma's cheek. "Be good to my boy, and take care of him. Watch his sugar; he gets careless."

Emma smiled. "I will."

Vivian nodded. "Thank you." She slipped out the door.

Emma turned and stared at her reflection. In her simple white dress, she felt pretty. She applied lip gloss and patted her hair one more time. A smile inched across her face. The dirty, scared little girl was gone. Staring back at her was a young woman in love and full of hope. Feeling whimsical, Emma leaned in and kissed her reflection. Winking at herself, she took a deep breath and left the room, ready to embrace her future.

David waited impatiently on the covered boat dock. The white Christmas lights had transformed it into a magical gazebo. The sun had just set, and a soft breeze whispered across the water, making the heat bearable.

He grinned at his family and Mrs. Jordan, who held Rory in her arms, dabbing at her eyes with her handkerchief. Tyrone, the McAthies' bodyguard, held a Bible in his large brown hands, smiling at everyone. David had always liked Tyrone and was happy he'd agreed to perform the ceremony.

Everyone's attention shifted to the end of the dock as Dylan started strumming his guitar. With his father by his side, David watched Jennifer approach. Angela walked with her mother, throwing rose petals—probably from Mrs. Jordan's garden—along the dock. Her pale green fairy wings flapped with the wind, and she bit her lip to keep from giggling. She blew a kiss to Dylan, who winked in return, and everyone chuckled.

David caught his breath when Emma stepped onto the dock. She glided toward him with a quiet confidence and bright smile. The white dress clung to her curves as the wind caught it. Instead of a bouquet, she held their daughter's hand.

Kenzie's blue wings flapped, and she held the beloved Teddy as she walked with her mother down the dock. Looking every bit like the fairy princess she proclaimed to be, her excitement was contagious as she pulled her mother's hand, urging in a loud whisper, "Hurry, Mama. Daddy's waiting."

Unable to contain her excitement, Kenzie broke free and ran the last ten feet to David, squealing when he lifted her into his arms. He shifted her to his hip and grasped Emma's hand with his free one. Breaking tradition, he gave Emma a quick kiss before turning to face Tyrone.

"Ew, stop, Daddy."

"Whoa, now, hoss. We haven't got to that point yet," Tyrone added.

David felt the heat rise in the back of his neck. Emma squeezed his hand and gave him a quick kiss back.

"I think we need to get going. These two seem anxious to get to the good part," Tyrone said with a broad grin.

With no time to write their own vows, they repeated the ones Tyrone read. Once that was done, David turned to Emma and softly quoted, "'Love is patient, love is kind. It does not envy, it does not boast, it is not proud. It does not dishonor others, it is not self-seeking, it is not easily angered, it keeps no record of wrongs. Love does not delight in evil but rejoices with the truth. It always protects, always trusts, always hopes, always perseveres.'" He paused and emphasized. "'*Love never fails*,' Emma."

Emma wiped the tears from her eyes and nodded. "I love you, David," she whispered. "I promise to never leave, to always be brave and never shut you out again—"

David hushed her with a kiss and whispered against her lips, "You won't."

Clearing his throat, Tyrone announced, "I now pronounce you husband and wife. *Now* you can kiss your bride, *again*."

David pulled Emma close and kissed her with everything he had.

Kenzie wrinkled her nose. "They're kissing again? Stop!"

He kissed Kenzie on the cheek, as did Emma, and everyone broke out in applause.

After they greeted their guests, his mother insisted he and Emma have a wedding dance, so Dylan sang and played "Can't Help Falling in Love." David caught hold of his wife and swayed with her in the limited space. When Kenzie complained loudly about them kissing again, he grabbed her hand and danced with both his girls.

The song ended and fireworks appeared overhead, adding to the magic of the moment. David laughed, delighted by this last touch to a perfect evening. He pulled Emma close as he held Kenzie, watching their faces light up as the lights exploded in the sky above them.

Emma wrapped her arms around his waist. "I'll always associate fireworks with you and happiness."

He kissed her forehead. "Me too. I think I started to fall in love with you that night. This is the perfect ending to a perfect day."

"This better not be the end," she warned with a laugh.

Chapter
Twenty-Five

"Alone at last, Mr. Patterson," Emma said breathlessly.

"I thought they'd never leave, Mrs. Patterson," he replied with a slow, seductive grin. He took her hand and paused. "Your place or mine?"

Emma laughed. "Definitely yours. You have the bigger bed. Besides, Jennifer's already moved most of my stuff over there."

"Good choice. Molly and Kenzie are at the McAthies' for the night. Less steps to carry you up, too." He swept her into his arms.

"Absolutely. I wouldn't want you throwing your back out on our wedding night. I've waited too long for this," she murmured.

She tangled her fingers in his hair, and he growled in response. He wanted her. Now.

"Ha! Not nearly as long as I have. My God, if I had to take one more cold shower…" He carried her into his house, devouring her mouth.

Emma smiled against his lips. "You always taste of peppermint."

"They're sugar-free, promise."

"I know. I made sure of it. I promised your mother I'd take care of you."

Peppering kisses across her jaw, he whispered, "I'm counting on it."

She looked up at him with a wicked little grin, and her eyes darkened with desire. He loved her eyes.

"I don't think she meant it the way you're thinking," she said, sighing softly as he hit that spot behind her ear.

"I'm thinking you're probably right. But I'm also thinking I don't care what my mother meant." He placed her gently on the bed. Leaning in to kiss her slowly, he savored her taste. "I love you," he whispered as he took the antique combs from her hair and placed them on the bedside table. He tangled his hands in her hair, drawing her closer and sucking on her lower lip, teasing her mouth with his tongue.

Nibbling down her neck, he inhaled her scent. "I want you naked. Oh, hell, I don't care. Naked, dressed—I just want you." He tore off his jacket and threw it on the floor.

She giggled and, using his necktie, pulled him down and rolled him onto his back. "Did you just say *hell?*" She kissed behind his ear and nibbled his neck.

Insane with need for his beautiful wife, his hands moved over her body.

"I'm a bad influence on you," she teased, licking and blowing in his ear.

"I don't know. Did I say that? I can't think..." He brushed her hair out of her face and fumbled with her dress. God, he felt inept. "Help me, please?" he begged as he kissed her, ready to tear the dress off, if need be.

She giggled. "Impatient, are we?"

Standing up, she unzipped the dress and let it fall to the floor, standing before him in a white strapless bra and a wisp of white lace panty. She blushed a pretty shade of pink as he stared. He couldn't help it; she was breathtakingly beautiful. He'd seen her naked twice. But this was different. She was now his wife, and no longer off limits. He wanted to shout a rebel yell and beat his chest like Tarzan. Except he was so awestruck, he couldn't speak for a moment.

Somehow he managed to croak, "You're perfect. But I want you to know, if you're not up to this, I understand." He wanted to be sure she was ready.

"You're not getting out of this, mister. I'm just moving a little slowly."

"Be gentle with me," he teased.

"Ditto. Isn't that supposed to be my line?" She giggled.

She carefully climbed back on the bed and straddled him, untying his tie. He managed to figure out the front clasp of her bra and snapped it off as she undid the buttons on his shirt. She trailed her lips behind each button, and he stirred, set on fire by the heat of her kisses.

When she finished unbuttoning his shirt, she helped him out of it. Taking his hands in hers, she held them above his head as she kissed him. Her hand brushed the book he'd accidentally left tucked under his pillow, and it fell to the floor with a loud *kathunk*. David groaned as she leaned over to pick it up, whether from embarrassment or the fact that her beautiful breasts brushed his face, he wasn't sure. Probably both.

"Just leave it, honey." He grabbed her waist, pulling her back to him, but she managed to pick up the book.

She straddled him and looked at the cover. Her eyebrows shot up and her eyes widened. A surprised grin spread across her face. He threw an arm over his eyes, totally mortified. But embarrassed or not, he had no intention of stopping.

"*The Idiot's Guide to the Kama Sutra?*"

He peeked at her. She was biting her lip, trying hard not to laugh. She didn't succeed. She opened the book and looked at a page, turned it, and looked at it again with a frown. "How in the world..." She showed it to him and pointed. "I don't think I can bend like that!"

"Would you believe me if I said it was for a comparative religion course?" he whispered, pinching her hardened nipples.

"Is that your story?" she asked, tossing the book to the side and sliding down his body, kissing her way down his neck to his chest, biting his nipples in the process.

"Can I plead the fifth? And I truly think you *could* bend like that. Just sayin'..."

She looked up at him, her smile full of promises. "I'm going to have you pleading, no doubt about it. Let's start with the basics and work *toward* that, 'kay?" She licked his chest and nipped his neck.

He swallowed nervously and grinned back at her. "Okay, and I'm already begging. I'm going to embarrass myself soon if you don't quit teasing." He flipped her over on her back and smiled down at her. "I love you." He somehow managed to kick off his shoes and socks.

"I love you too." She helped him unbuckle his belt and yanked the rest of his clothes off in one fluid motion. He nearly came undone when she stroked him, her gaze never leaving his.

"Em." He pulled her panties off and buried his face in her breasts. Breathing in the scent of her warm skin, he held her for a moment, trying to regain some control. He wondered if she had an inkling of how terrified he was of disappointing her.

"Yes?" Her soft, whispery voice swept across his hair.

"I don't want to…I mean, I'm afraid I don't know…I've never done this before," he confessed.

"It's been a very long time for me, too. Be brave," she teased with a smile.

"Brave. Got it…" He lost his train of thought as he began kissing, licking, and nipping her breasts, enjoying her gasps of pleasure. Slowly, he worked his way down her body, memorizing every detail of her skin with his eyes, his lips, and his hands. Cupping her bottom, he raised her hips and tasted her with his tongue, wanting more, wondering if he'd ever get enough of her.

He followed his instincts, noting her nonverbal and verbal cues, loving the purring sounds she made as he explored her body. He circled her clitoris with his tongue and caressed inside her with his fingers.

"Who's teasing now?" she gasped, moaning.

He smiled and kissed her burned thigh, holding her legs apart when she tried to close them.

"Stop. I want to love all of you. Let me try to erase that memory and replace it with one of love."

She reached toward him, and he entwined her fingers with his. Slowly, deliberately he rained kisses upon her soft flesh. She was panting with need, not fear, when he once again flicked the spot that made her whimper for more. He continued with renewed vigor until she grasped his hair, screaming his name with her release. A faint sheen of sweat covered her body.

He blew on her warm skin as he kissed his way back up to her neck, his hands caressing her softness. He wanted to devour every inch of her like a sugar-laden dessert, knowing he could indulge freely—she wouldn't throw him into a diabetic coma.

She grasped his face in her hands and kissed him as he plunged into her, the sensation nearly undoing him before he even got started.

He paused for a moment, using every bit of self-restraint he possessed to gain control.

"Emma."

"David," she breathed as her legs wrapped around his waist and her inner muscles clenched. Thrusting deep inside, he threw his head back. The feeling intensified, making him hyperaware of them as one. He ground against her, rubbing her clitoris as he drove inside, her hips meeting his thrusts. Her name slipped from his lips with a primal yell before he collapsed on top of her, out of breath and sweating. She held him tightly, running her hands through his hair, softly cooing words of love.

"You okay?" he choked.

"Better than okay."

"Dear God, that felt good," he gasped when he could get the words out.

She laughed and kissed his forehead. "Yes, it did."

He chuckled but turned serious. "Honey, if I did anything wrong—I mean, I want it to be good for you. I want you to feel loved, special." He searched her eyes.

"You were perfect, promise." She stretched and purred like a sleepy cat.

David rolled to his side and pulled Emma to his chest, kissing her forehead. "Love you."

"Love you more."

"Not possible," he replied with a happy sigh.

Sultry hazel eyes stared up at him and a smile curved her beautiful mouth. She rolled him to his back and her lips trailed across his chest. Moving on top of him, she reached for the book.

With a wicked laugh she said, "Now, where to begin your comparative religions studies?"

David laughed, grabbed the book, and threw it across the room. "I never was one for studying. I'm a hands-on kind of guy."

The End

The series will continue with Angel Sinclair's story in
The Rehabilitation of Angel Sinclair

Author's Note

Everyone has the potential to discover a human trafficking situation. While the victims may sometimes be kept behind locked doors, they are often hidden right in front of us at, for example, construction sites, restaurants, elder care centers, nail salons, agricultural fields, and hotels. Traffickers' use of coercion — such as threats of deportation and harm to the victim or their family members — is so powerful that even if you reach out to victims, they may be too fearful to accept your help. Knowing indicators of human trafficking and some follow-up questions will help you act on your gut feeling that something is wrong and report it.

Human Trafficking Indicators

While not an exhaustive list, these are some key red flags that could alert you to a potential trafficking situation that should be reported:

- Living with employer
- Poor living conditions
- Multiple people in cramped space
- Inability to speak to individual alone
- Answers appear to be scripted and rehearsed
- Employer is holding identity documents
- Signs of physical abuse
- Submissive or fearful
- Unpaid or paid very little
- Under 18 and in prostitution

Where to Get Help

If you believe you have identified someone still in the trafficking situation, alert law enforcement immediately at the numbers provided below. It may be unsafe to attempt to rescue a trafficking victim. You have no way of knowing how the trafficker may react and retaliate against the victim and you. If, however, you identify a victim who has escaped the trafficking situation, there are a number of organizations to whom the victim could be referred for help with shelter, medical care, legal assistance, and other critical services. In this case, call the National Human Trafficking Resource Center described below.

9-1-1 Emergency

For urgent situations, notify local law enforcement immediately by calling 9-1-1. You may also want to alert the National Human Trafficking Resource Center described below so that they can ensure response by law enforcement officials knowledgeable about human trafficking.

1-888-3737-888
National Human Trafficking Resource Center

Call the National Human Trafficking Resource Center, a national 24-hour, toll-free, multilingual anti-trafficking hotline. Call 1-888-3737-888 to report a tip; connect with anti-trafficking services in your area; or request training and technical assistance, general information, or specific anti-trafficking resources. The Center is equipped to handle calls from all regions of the United States from a wide range of callers including, but not limited to: potential trafficking victims, community members, law enforcement, medical professionals, legal professionals, service providers, researchers, students, and policymakers.

Information provided by: U.S. Department of State:
www.state.gov/j/tip/id/index.htm

Acknowledgments

It takes a village to write a book. Or in my case, a city the size of NYC. Thank you to Jessica Royer Ocken for holding my hand and putting up with my comma splices and inability to spell T-shirt. The lessons in puppy care were appreciated for this cat lover. You always push me to do better and working with you is a joy.

Thank you to Shannon Lumetta for the beautiful cover design. It's perfection. And heartfelt thanks to Chantell Reid and Taylor Kendal for the stunning cover photograph. All of you took my idea and made it come to life. It is sheer perfection.

Coreen Montagna, thank you for the beautiful formatting. You always make it so pretty on the inside. And for the careful line edits!

Jennifer Locklear and Fiona Tulle, thank you for the information from a personal POV on dealing with diabetes and allowing me to pick your brains. And to sweet Molly, be glad you aren't my dog, I'd never remember to take you outside. Ha! Jennifer Lane thank you for sharing your insight into dealing with trauma victims.

To my fellow SLOBS, we will figure this out. Thank you for sharing your experiences, your love and putting up with my rants.

My Cain Raisers, you make me smile, we have fun together and we are truly a family. Michele, Tanya, Gabriella, Denise, Brenda, Vickie, Eunice, Jo, Marla, Edie, Joyce, Beverly, Marie, Rhiannon, Lis, Robin, Jean, Riva, Cara, Jennifer, Karen, M.J. Edie, Angelica and so many others…thank you for your love and support.

To my fantastic agent, Stephanie Phillips and all my SBR Media Authors, thank you for always being my cheerleaders!

To the Alabama Maniacs, book friends truly are best friends. Especially when margaritas are involved.

Many thanks to Carrie, Jill, Carla and Vickie for beta reading and suffering through the terrible first draft.

And to Debra Anastasia, who encourages me to be brave and to not be afraid of all the "feels."

And to my family, without your support and love, I wouldn't be doing this. I'd also be cooking a hot meal every now and then…

About the Author

During the day, Nancee works as a counselor/nurse in the field of addiction to support her coffee and reading habit. Nights are spent writing paranormal and contemporary romances with a serrated edge. Authors are her rock stars, and she's been known to stalk a few for an autograph, but not in a scary, Stephen King way. Her husband swears her To-Be-Read list on her e-reader qualifies her as a certifiable book hoarder. Always looking to try something new, she dreams of being an extra in a Bollywood film, or a tattoo artist. (Her lack of rhythm and artistic ability may put a damper on both of these dreams.)

Website: nanceecain.com
Blog: nanceecain.com/blog
Goodreads: goodreads.com/Nancee_Cain
Facebook: facebook.com/NanceeCainAuthor
Reader's Group (Cain Raisers): facebook.com/groups/Cain.Raisers
Twitter: twitter.com/Nancee_Cain
Pinterest: pinterest.com/nanceecain
Instagram: instagram.com/nanceecain
BookBub: bookbub.com/authors/nancee-cain
Newsletter: eepurl.com/bhFMtX
YouTube Channel: bit.ly/2xsU6Ad
Spotify Playlists: open.spotify.com/user/12184539074

Books by Nancee Cain:

Paranormal Romance (Angels)
Saving Evangeline
Tempting Jo
Loving Lili (novella)

Contemporary Romance (Pine Bluff Novels)
The Resurrection of Dylan McAthie
The Redemption of Emma Devine
The Rehabilitation of Angel Sinclair
The Redirection of Damien Sinclair
The Reinvention of Jinx Howell
The Reintroduction of Sammie Morgan
The Realization of Grayson Deschanelle

Contemporary Romances

Although each of the titles in this series can be read as standalone stories, this is the preferred reading order:

The Resurrection of Dylan McAthie
A Pine Bluff Novel

Maybe You Can Go Home Again

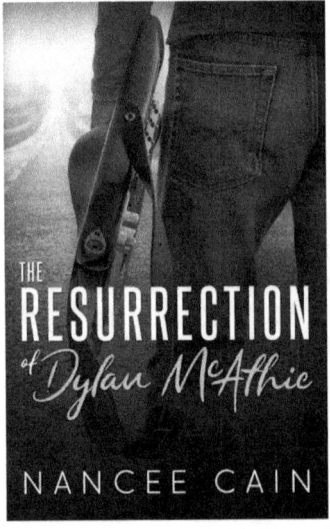

Hounded by paparazzi, Dylan McAthie—the former lead guitarist for Crucified, Dead and Buried—craves quiet anonymity to regroup and sort out his life. An accident leaves him dependent on the family he once ran from, with no choice but to return to the small town of Pine Bluff, Alabama.

Hired by Dylan's estranged brother, private-duty nurse Jennifer Adams remembers the charming boy Dylan was before fame and misfortune. And she notices he's developed a knack for blaming everyone else for his problems, rather than bothering with introspection. She's not having it.

Despite their clashes, as her patient heals, the chemistry between them grows undeniable—until scandal finds Dylan again, threatening to destroy the progress he's made and the couple's growing respect and affection. Can Dylan fix what fame has so easily broken? Or will his public resurrection mean the death of any relationship with Jennifer?

The Redemption of Emma Devine
A Pine Bluff Novel

A Little Shake-Up in Life Can Be Devine

Emma Devine is on the run and fighting to survive. Her tortured past makes trust difficult, especially where men are concerned. But she has no choice other than accepting the help of the man who catches her shoplifting on Christmas Eve.

When not stopping shoplifters, David Patterson leads a quiet life in Pine Bluff, Alabama, working as a high school teacher. His random act of Christmas kindness brings unexpected joy to his life, as he finds himself drawn to the mysterious Emma. When she leaves, his world is turned upside down, and his dreams are changed forever.

Four years later, Emma returns in search of long-overdue redemption. But despite an undeniable attraction between the two, trust is an even greater issue now—for both of them. Can they find their way to a place of understanding? Or have yesterday's mistakes destroyed their chance for a future together?

The Rehabilitation of Angel Sinclair
A Pine Bluff Novel

Love — the Hardest Addiction to Kick

Angel Sinclair arrives in Pine Bluff, Alabama, determined to make amends for his past and move on. But that changes after a chance encounter with a beautiful inn owner, and instead he finds himself pursuing two things that haven't been in his life for years: love and trust.

Still reeling from a bitter divorce, Maggie Robertson wants to focus on making her business a success. Getting involved with anyone in this gossipy little town is the farthest thing from her mind...until she finds herself tempted by a younger man.

Neither Angel nor Maggie can ignore the sizzling heat between them. But Angel's secretive nature soon fills Maggie with doubts about the man she's allowed into her heart.

Was she wrong to believe love could conquer all? Is their age difference an obstacle they can't overcome?

The Redirection of Damien Sinclair
A Pine Bluff Novel

Sometimes You Get What You Need

Acclaimed divorce attorney Damien Sinclair has witnessed more than his share of love's ugly aftermath. He keeps things black and white, preventing anyone from getting too close. But his illusion of control fades when an attempt on his life leaves him struggling with PTSD.

Enter Damien's childhood friend, the free-spirited Harley Taylor. Shrugging off the awkwardness of their teenaged fling and her broken heart, she appoints herself his caregiver. The man needs to learn not to take himself so seriously, and she's hellbent on snapping him out of his brooding funk.

After a decade apart, Harley and Damien find their attraction is stronger than ever. Could Harley's sunny disposition be the bright spot Damien needs in his life? Or will their differences overshadow any hopes of a future together?

The Reinvention of Jinx Howell
A Pine Bluff Novel

Can Love Unmask Their True Selves?

Hiding behind her wigs and heavy makeup, Jinx Howell masks her insecurities — which even she doesn't understand — with bravado, slashing through life with reckless abandon. Lonely, but unwilling to get close to anyone, she finds the ideal solution: a hook-up with the campus's most notorious heartbreaker.

In similar fashion, Mark "Two-Time" MacGregor protects his heart and keeps himself unencumbered through a string of one-night stands. A chance meeting with the edgy Jinx in a dark alley seems like destiny. She claims to want sex with no ties, making her perfect. *Like attracts like.* But this girl with a switchblade has more hang-ups than he does, which is a hell of a lot.

When tragedy strikes, Mark's hit-and-run lifestyle takes a backseat to his need to protect the broken girl whose secrets are unraveling. Along the way, both of them will find their truths unmasked. Can they forge a real relationship, or will they give up on their romance as jinxed?

The Reintroduction of Sammie Morgan
A Pine Bluff Novel

Can Life Get Any Crazier?

Still reeling from the tragic deaths of his wife and daughter, Matt Tyler trudges through life, caring for his young son, managing his cantankerous father, and working as much as he can. Despite his best efforts, bills are piling up and his vindictive in-laws seem determined to take Luke away from him.

Things change when he stumbles upon Sammie Morgan — with a car that won't run and her mother's ashes in the backseat. Best friends growing up, Matt and Sammie have spent years apart following very different paths. Now they've both run out of options. Without a dime in her pocket, Sammie has nowhere to go. And Matt lacks the stable home life he needs to fight his former in-laws.

Their hasty solution? A marriage of convenience.

But how convenient will this reintroduction be if it means Matt and Sammie have to relive the most painful parts of their past?

The Realization of Grayson Deschanelle
A Pine Bluff Novel

Sex, No Strings Attached

Despite a high-profile clientele, fashion photographer Grayson Deschanelle prefers being behind the lens, away from public scrutiny. After his movie star girlfriend dumps him, he flees to his stepbrother's remote cabin to hide from the paparazzi.

Caught by surprise, Grayson finds Lissy much different than the girl he's known for years. She's no longer a child—though her teenaged crush is still very much intact. Snowed in with her, he tries to fight his growing attraction. But being with Lissy brings what his life is lacking into sharp focus.

The ice melts, and they return home. When their families discover their secret, Grayson must decide what kind of life he truly wants—and whether he'll fight to keep Lissy by his side.

Paranormal Angel Romances

Although each of the titles in this series can be read as standalone stories, this is the preferred reading order:

Saving Evangeline

Tempting Jo

Loving Lili (novella)

Saving Evangeline

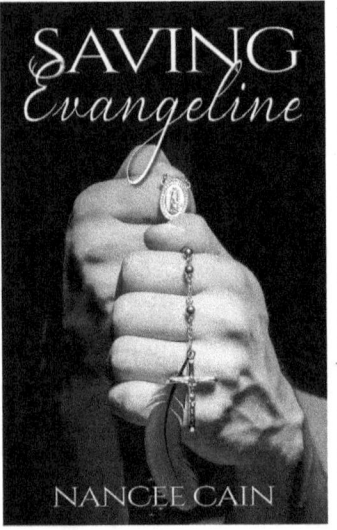

Evangeline is the town pariah. Everyone knows she's crazy and was responsible for the death of her last boyfriend. Even her mother left her and moved cross-country. Lonely and desperate, Evie decides to end her life.

Rogue angel Remiel longs to return to Earth, but there's just one problem. He tends to invite trouble and hasn't been allowed back since Woodstock. The Boss sends him to save Evangeline, but there's a catch: he can't reveal his angelic nature, and he must complete the task as *Father* Remiel Blackson.

Forced together on a cross-country trip, a forbidden romance ignites and love unfolds. A host of heavenly messengers tries to intervene, but Remiel and Evangeline are headed on a collision course to disaster. Will his love save her, or will they both be lost forever?

Tempting Jo

Forbidden love is hell…

Confident and quirky, Jo Sanford thinks her boss is God's gift to women — and she couldn't be further from the truth. Devilishly handsome, Luc DeVille will stop at nothing to lure his administrative assistant right into his arms — and bed.

Over Rafe Goodman's dead body…

Rafe, Jo's best friend, refuses to sit by and watch as Luc tries to win the heart of the woman he's always protected. After all, Rafe is her guardian angel. Suddenly, Jo's caught in the middle of a battle between good and evil. But the closer she gets to the fire, the hotter it burns. Now, Jo's going to learn that when love battles lust, Heaven and Hell collide.

Loving Lili (novella)

Their lovemaking is hot and dirty. Their break ups are nasty and epic.

Tired of taking the blame for every wicked thing that happens on Earth, fallen angel Luc DeVille decides to write a tell-all-book exposing The Boss.

Sharing a long and passionate history, Luc is shocked when Lili Nix arrives to interview for the job as editor. Immediately the verbal sparring begins, but the sexual chemistry remains combustible. Fascinated by this heavenly creature, Luc changes his game plan. After all, she's the only angel who has ever held his attention and understood his intentions.

Being in this world, but not of this world, is a lonely business. Can two lost angels connect and make it last this time?